The
Deepening
Stream

ZONDERVAN HEARTH BOOKS

Available from your Christian Bookseller

Book Number

Hearth Romances

1	*The Doctor's Return*	Ken Anderson
2	*The Deepening Stream*	Francena Arnold
3	*Fruit for Tomorrow*	Francena Arnold
4	*Light in My Window*	Francena Arnold
5	*The Barrier*	Sallie Lee Bell
6	*By Strange Paths*	Sallie Lee Bell
7	*The Last Surrender*	Sallie Lee Bell
9	*Romance Along the Bayou*	Sallie Lee Bell
10	*The Scar*	Sallie Lee Bell
11	*The Substitute*	Sallie Lee Bell
12	*Through Golden Meadows*	Sallie Lee Bell
13	*Until the Day Break*	Sallie Lee Bell
15	*Love Is Like an Acorn*	Matsu Crawford
16	*This Side of Tomorrow*	Ruth Livingston Hill
17	*Give Me Thy Vineyard*	Guy Howard
19	*Judith*	N. I. Saloff-Astakhoff
20	*Trumpets in the Morning*	Lon Woodrum
21	*Light From the Hill*	Sallie Lee Bell
22	*The Bond Slave*	Sallie Lee Bell

Hearth Mysteries

8	*The Long Search*	Sallie Lee Bell
14	*Candle of the Wicked*	Elizabeth Brown
18	*The Mystery of Mar Saba*	James H. Hunter

Sebastian Thrillers

23	*Code Name Sebastian*	James L. Johnson
24	*The Nine Lives of Alphonse*	James L. Johnson
25	*A Handful of Dominoes*	James L. Johnson
26	*A Piece of the Moon is Missing*	James L. Johnson

A HEARTH ROMANCE

The Deepening Stream

Francena Arnold

Author of *Not My Will*

ZONDERVAN
PUBLISHING HOUSE

OF THE ZONDERVAN CORPORATION | GRAND RAPIDS, MICHIGAN 49506

THE DEEPENING STREAM
Copyright 1963 by Zondervan Publishing House
Grand Rapids, Michigan

Fifteenth printing   1979

ISBN 0-310-20212-4

Library of Congress Catalog Card Number 63-15745

Printed in the United States of America

1

THE GROUP AROUND the fireplace in the church parlor sat in silence until the sound of the starting car outside told them that the pastor had gone with the guest speaker. Then Sara Rossiter broke the silence. A confusion of voices followed.

"Now, honestly — "

"That's what *I* say!"

"Could anybody, but *anybody,* believe all that stuff?"

"How gullible can you get?"

"Aren't we supposed to have *any* wills of our own? Do we just sit like bumps until the Spirit comes along and leads us by the hand?"

Norm Nelson, the group leader, rose to his feet and pounded on the table with a teacup.

"Let's have a little order here! The girls can carry off the plates and cups while the fellows straighten the chairs and pick up the napkins. Then we can sit down and have a real discussion if that's what you want. All in favor get busy!"

By the time they had finished their tasks, some of their first reaction to the speaker's words had worn off and the young people were willing to engage in an orderly discussion of the things that had disturbed them.

"Now, let's get to it," said Norm, after the group had filled the circle of chairs around him. "Two things we can agree on about the fellow who spoke to us. He didn't put anyone to sleep, and he certainly brought us a stirring message. Suppose some of you tell us what riled you. Just when did the speaker step on your toes, Sara?"

Sara faced the group. "Norm thinks I'm a featherbrain and can't give a logical reason for my remarks. Well, he's *so* right! I can't be logical, but just the same I can have an opinion. And I don't believe that everything that happens to us is for our good. There are lots of things *nobody* could ever find any good in. Like measles. What good are they?" As usual Sara got a laugh, for everyone knew that only three weeks before she had missed the Labor Day Group Retreat because of measles.

When the laughter stopped, Neil Abbott said gravely, "I think Sara is right in general. I don't think we're expected to go through life like dumb animals, just piously taking what's handed out to us and being thankful for it. That doesn't make sense. But take that matter of the measles: there was real good to someone in that. Old Ben Franklin here couldn't go to the retreat because he had to work that weekend, and it was *so* nice for him to entertain the convalescent. There's just no telling where the good effects of those evenings will end."

That brought another burst of laughter as the young people observed the red faces of the two who were sitting together.

"You're way off the subject, Neil," said Sara disgustedly. "Anybody knows that big things have a purpose for good. But that man this evening implied, if he didn't actually say it, that the commonest things of every day, the things that frustrate and annoy us, even things like an accident on the street or a house burning down — *all* things happen for our good, he said. I just can't buy that."

Sara's intensity was increasing, but her opponents were not yet silenced.

"None of us is silly enough to think God means us to

accept everything we meet,'' said Bruce Franklin who was usually called B. or Ben. ''The speaker probably thought that we should weigh things to find out if they were sent to direct us or to test us. Even if they seem wrong, if we can't change them we can accept them as God's signposts, sort of.''

''You sort of don't know what you mean,'' retorted Sara.

The comments and discussion continued another half hour until Norm brought the meeting to a close.

''We're talking too much and thinking too little without the use of our authority. Let's lay this question on the table until next meeting. In the meantime try to find out what Scripture says. Fred, will you pray?''

After the prayer Neil waited for B. Franklin. They shared both an apartment and a car. If B. intended to take Sara home, and if Sara did not have her own car, it would mean that Neil must catch a bus. He wondered idly if being unable to buy a car by himself was one of the things that would be working for his good. Franklin came then and his face showed embarrassment.

''Listen, fellow, Sara's dad isn't letting her use the car now. Don't you think we should take those two girls home?''

''*Two* girls? What do you mean? Sara's only one girl. You take her. I'll — ''

''No, oh, no! I need you. Didn't you see that Sara has a guest? We should take them home.''

''Oh, we should? Well, we *must* do what we should. You go and get them while I bring the car around. I presume I get to ride with the guest while you and Sara whisper in the back seat.''

His presumption was correct, and he soon found himself trying to think what a fellow could possibly find to talk about with a completely strange girl whose face he couldn't see too well and whose name he hadn't heard in the hurried transfer, in the cold fall rain, from the church to the car. He could hear Sara and Ben chattering away in the back seat, and he knew he should say something. Perhaps the girl liked this arrangement as little as he did. He certainly didn't want her to think

7

he was ungracious. But what *should* he say? While he was pondering this, a laughing voice spoke in the darkness.

"You aren't too pleased by this arrangement, are you? I'm sorry, but you know how Sara is! Let's try to think of something to say, so those lovebirds in the back seat won't think we're eavesdropping."

He drew a long breath of relief. Maybe it wouldn't be so bad, after all. "I'm not really resentful, just bashful."

"So am I. But surely we can talk about something."

"I suppose we can. Shall we try the subject of the evening? Do you have any ideas that haven't been discussed?"

"Yes, I do. I'd have spoken if I had been at home in my own crowd. Sara and I have been friends ever since we were children and learned to swim at the same beach, but we've always met in *my* atmosphere since her folks have a lodge a few miles from us. They spend most of the summer there, and sometimes they go up in the winter for skiing. This is the first time I've ever been in her city home and it's — different, especially for a small town girl."

"Do you like the city?"

"I've liked this visit. But I'll be glad to get home again. I think the most interesting thing I've seen is the *Ledger* plant. We spent a whole wonderful day there. Did you ever go through the plant of a big newspaper?"

"No, not through it. I just got *in*, and I'm having to work my way out."

"Oh! You're on the *Ledger*. That's really thrilling. I think it would be the most interesting job in the world."

"I agree. But just now I'd rather hear what you think about this business of all things being for our good. Or of us waiting for action until we've found what we interpret as God's leading. Do you think that's the way we're supposed to live?"

"Well, I think that's how we *ought* to think. But there are a lot of times that I just can't. I can't accept it at all. Take for instance a man's career. I'll admit that God gives him his talents and abilities. But it's up to him to use them and carve out the career he feels is best. If something comes along that has to be overcome before he can achieve his goal, I don't think he should let it divert him. He should lick the problem."

"I see what you mean, and in a way I agree with you. But what if it won't be overcome? And how does one know when to fight and when to accept? My first impulse is to fight. I guess I rather like to fight. But I *know* I shouldn't be determined to win my own way. After all, I'm not all-wise, and maybe God does have a purpose in everything He sends to us. I haven't thought much about that verse. I've just read it and accepted it. But there is room for a lot of thinking. My heart really wants to do right, but my head and will want to do just what *I want* to do!"

"Do you suppose it depends on the interpretation, as one of the girls suggested tonight?"

"I don't think so. Why should a simple verse like that need interpretation? It must say exactly what it means. There isn't any other thing it *could* mean but just what it says, that all things happen for our good if we love God. Sounds simple."

"But it must have a different shade of meaning. It's so obvious that even to those who love God, things happen that aren't for any understandable good."

"Couldn't that be the secret? 'Understandable good,' you said. It could be that those people the things happened to just didn't understand. Later, they might recognize that something they thought was a hindrance or a real handicap was a turning point in life, and good."

"Well, what would you do if one of these hindrances or handicaps came along that seemed entirely wrong to you, and yet you couldn't do anything about it? Or what would you do if the only thing you could do seemed absolutely wrong? I don't mean morally wrong, but just so unwise that it seemed wrong to follow it. Would you consider *that* God's will?"

She was hesitant about answering, but finally said, "I know of a case like that. It's the one thing that bothers me

9

about this 'will of God' thought. A terrible thing happened to a woman I know. It has made her life tragic, but it wasn't her fault and apparently she couldn't do anything about it. She has accepted it as God's will and I — I think she's wonderful. But I still don't think it was for any good that she should be hurt so cruelly. It's that kind of thing that I can't understand."

"Maybe she knows more about it than you do. Can't you ask her about it?"

"I wouldn't dare. She doesn't dream that I know it."

"Well, I know what I'd do in a case like that. I'd fight. And I'd keep on fighting. I have my career planned and I'm going to make my goals."

"What are your goals?"

"I intend to be a big newspaper man someday, and I intend to marry — "

"Whatever is going on up there in the front seat?" Sara's voice interrupted. "For people who met less than an hour ago you've reached the arguing stage quickly."

"Nothing serious, Sara," B. Franklin assured her. "I've been listening to them with one ear and to you with the other. They're still trying to settle the question of the evening, and have reached an absolute stalemate. I'll take Neil home and give him a tranquilizer."

At the door of the Rossiter home, Sara's guest turned to Neil. "Thank you for coming with us. I'd have felt fifth-wheelish without you."

"The pleasure was mine. I haven't talked to such an interesting person in a long time. You haven't convinced me, but you've made me think."

Nothing more was said as the boys drove on to their apartment, but when they were preparing for bed Neil burst out again.

"Let's apply it personally, Ben."

"What are you talking about? What are you going to apply personally? Rheumatism troubling you?"

"This business of all things being for our good. Let's get it settled."

"Let's do. You make your closing argument, and I'll agree. Then we can go to sleep."

Neil realized he was getting nowhere, so he muttered, "Oh, just skip it. But let me tell you one thing." His voice rose. "I'm going to make my own things happen for good. I'm going to be a big man on the *Ledger*, and I'm going to marry Jane Barr as soon as she'll have me! Then it will all be for good. Now you can go to sleep, B. Franklin."

2

ONE EVENING IN late October Neil met his chum at the elevator on the fifth floor of the County Building. As they squeezed themselves into the already overcrowded space, he asked, "Headed for home or for the salt mines?"

"To the saltiest mine," answered B. Franklin with mock sadness. "I have to make the deadline on the Garrity case. The boss told me I'd better, or else."

"Hope you make it. It's already too late for the *Star* to get it, but the morning papers will have it. If you let them scoop us, it'll be just too, too bad for your romance with the big boss's daughter. Even the intervention of the *Saturday Evening Post* couldn't save you then."

"I'm afraid you're right. Coming along?"

"Nope. Anything I got this afternoon isn't worthy of being in the same edition with your malodorous news. No one would read my small items. You'd better hurry. I'll see you at supper. I'll peel the potatoes tonight!"

He turned a corner to see a bus loading, and broke into a run. He slid through the door, barely in time to save his coattails. The apartment Neil shared with Franklin was in an outlying district, and the time consumed in travel was often irksome. Today he did not mind it, for he had much to occupy his thoughts. There would be a letter from Jane when he reached home, he was sure. One of the nice things about Jane — and there were so many nice things that he could not name them all — was her dependability. She never kept a fellow wondering why she didn't write. Her letters came regularly every Tuesday, and she certainly wouldn't keep him waiting for this most important letter.

As the bus rumbled on, his thoughts were not of the traffic roaring about them, or of the changing character of the neighborhoods through which they traveled. He thought, instead, of how he would soon be going home, not to B.'s or his own uninspired cooking, but to the kind of meal he was sure Jane could prepare; not to a disordered room such as he had left that morning, but to a beautifully furnished home which would be well-ordered and efficiently managed.

By the time the bus came to a full stop he was swinging off, and before he reached the apartment house he was almost running in his eagerness to get the letter he knew would be in the box. When he had it he was tempted to sit down on the step and read it at once, but with the feeling of virtue that self-restraint brings, he made himself walk decorously up the three flights, hang up his hat and coat, then go back to the kitchen, scrub two big potatoes, wrap them in foil and put them into the oven before he let himself sink into a big chair and open his letter.

An hour later when Franklin reached home the potatoes were done and on the prepared table. He looked critically at the canned stew that was being dished up and the unadorned chunks of lettuce that comprised the salad.

"Thought we planned pork chops for tonight. I bought some yesterday. You served stew last night. Twice in a row is illegal. Potatoes in the stew and potatoes in little silver jackets. What's eatin' you fellow? I'm going to get me a wife that can cook."

"In which project I wish you luck."

"Why the heavy sarcasm? Has the milk curdled in your little bottle? Didn't you get your regular letter today?"

"I got a letter. I'm sorry about the chops. I forgot, and stew was all I could find on the shelf. I'll take you out for supper tomorrow by way of atonement."

"Don't be so meek. It doesn't fit your personality. I was kidding about the meal. I've served too many sad flops to fuss about this one. Something *is* the matter with you. You were feeling on top of the world when I left you two hours ago. What happened?"

"I'll tell you after supper. I need to talk to someone, and maybe you can make more sense out of my case than I can."

When they had settled themselves in the living room, Ben on the davenport and Neil in the one big chair, Neil began slowly, "I don't know just how to start, or to say what I want. I guess I'd better get your idea on a general question first. How do you think about Christianity? Just what is it? Am I a Christian, or am I just a good moral fellow? What's the difference?"

"Hmm. Has your Jane been calling you a heathen?"

"Not quite that. But you didn't answer my question. What *is* a Christian? What would you answer if a real heathen did ask you?"

"Having been raised in a liturgical church, I could repeat pages of catechism to you, but I guess that's not what you want. You want to know just what Christianity means to me. To my best understanding a Christian is a person who believes that Jesus Christ, the Son of God, came to earth as a Baby, was born to a virgin mother chosen by the Holy Spirit, that He died on the cross to atone for the sins of the world, that He rose from the dead for our justification, that He is now reigning in Heaven with God the Father, and that He will eventually come again for those who believe in Him, and after that He will reign forever. Does that satisfy?"

"Yes, I'm sure it does. And by that standard I've believed for many years that I was a Christian. Now I'm beginning to have doubts."

"Does Miss Jane doubt you?"

"She didn't say so. But she has some radical ideas. Someone's been monkeying with my gal's religion. In your book are there various kinds of Christians?''

"Of course. Methodists, Presbyterians, Baptists — ''

"That isn't what I mean at all. Is there better *quality* in some Christians? And I'm not speaking of habits of living. I mean a sort of — well, an inner something that makes a fellow different, like — well, like maybe the thing the gang was talking about the other night at church. Are there some people who are so submissive to God's will that they've lost their own identity and follow what seems to them God's way, specially designed and fitted to them? Do you think an omniscient and omnipotent God could have much fellowship with such childish souls? They would seem like robots. No challenge in life at all for them.''

"What's all that got to do with you?''

"Possibly a great deal. What do you think? Don't we have anything at all to say about our destiny? Do we give up all power to shape our life when we become what Jane calls 'yielded'?''

"I don't know. Sara and her dad and I were talking about the subject Sunday night after church. He seems to agree with what the speaker said that night. He says we are too immature as Christians to be able to appreciate an idea like this, that we've had too much milk and too little meat in our diet. That we'll have to grow up before we can get the meaning of the deeper truths of the Spirit's teaching.''

"That all sounds nice and pat. But believing this idea means that we think God has a hand in every detail of our lives. I can't quite buy that. If God didn't mean for us to use our brains and our will power, why did He give them to us? If we are so immature as that, there can be no 'meeting of minds' between us and God. We are like babies then. A person can love a baby and care for it, but he can't fellowship on his own level with it.''

"Why come to me with your arguments? What are you driving at, anyway? What does all this have to do with Jane? She wasn't at that meeting the other night.''

"Of course I know she wasn't. But she comes into the plot, anyway. We had been writing regularly and I thought

15

she knew how I felt and was, well, at least receptive to it. I couldn't have been more mistaken. She not only is surprised to find I'm thinking of marriage, but she acts as if it were a matter in which she is unprepared to come to an opinion at all. In short, she doesn't know what is God's will in the matter. *That* from Jane!''

''Don't you want His will in such a matter?''

''Of course I do! But the mutual attraction, the similarity of tastes, the years of friendship, are all evidences of His will for us, I think. Jane doesn't deny them. She admits that she has never had a friend who meant as much to her. Yet with all that she can't tell if it's God's will for us to marry.''

''As one buddy to another, did she say she loves you?''

''No-o. I gather she's waiting on God about that, also. You ought to hear the crazy scheme she has cooked up. She doesn't say 'no.' She just puts me on probation. She suggests that for a few months we don't see each other or even write, but concentrate on praying for God's will to be revealed to us. The first week in January she's coming through here with some friends. They're going down to Mexico for several weeks. She'll let me know just when she'll come, and says she'd like to meet me and talk. I have a feeling she wants to give me a spiritual I.Q. test.''

''Is she so spiritually minded?''

''Never was when we were in college. But just now she seems terribly concerned about things she never thought of before. She gave me a lot of Scripture to study while we're not writing. And she wants me to be seeking 'leading.' *Why* can't she decide for herself whether she loves me or not? I don't need any leading. I already know.''

''Why don't you forget her and get a girl with more of your kind of sense?''

Neil looked at his friend in astonishment, and his face flushed.

''I couldn't do that,'' he said. ''Jane is the only girl there is for me. There never will be anyone else. But she's not going to be telling me what to do in my relations with God. If I ever jumped through *that* hoop for her, all my self-respect would get scraped off on the sides. My religious life *has* to be my own.''

''What are you going to do about Jane's letter? Just let it go unanswered?''

''I'll write and agree to her silly little plan. I won't criticize it; I'll neither praise nor condemn. I'll sit tight for the next ten weeks or so, and she'll be eaten by curiosity as to how I'm bearing up under her absence. I've dealt with that gal before, and the way to handle her is to beat her at her own game. I'm not worried. I'm just disgusted. I still say it's a raw deal!''

When Thanksgiving was past he felt that the worst was over, and began to look forward to the coming meeting. He counted off the days as he used to do when he was a child and Christmas was near. He went home with B. for one day at Christmas time, and on their return to the city said happily, ''Just a little over two weeks, Bennie!''

''You won't be any happier than I am,'' answered B. ''I feel like a mother who sees the quarantine sign go down after a siege with whopping cough. Now we can plan on living again.''

3

"Do you have to work New Year's weekend?" asked B. next evening as the friends were cleaning the kitchen.

"No. I have several days coming to me because of the time I put in during the strike at the mills. Any suggestions? Are you asking me to work for you?"

"Not at all. This is something special. Sara just called and wants us both to go up to their lodge for three days. Reports are that skiing and tobogganing are tops, and the Rossiters want to take a dozen of their kids' friends up for a breath of good country air in our city-polluted lungs. Reports are that Terry was with a gang that got more than a little high last year, and the boss wants to show him that he can have a good time without the aid of such hoopla. So the whole dozen of us are invited to Hemlock Lodge."

"Hemlock Lodge! Sounds woodsy. I hope it doesn't prove to be a circle of tepees. Are they equipped for cold weather?"

"Wait till you see it! I was there last summer. Remember? I guess it was while you were on vacation. It's as big as the whole tenth floor of the *Ledger* building — well, almost. And you don't need to fear for your comfort. It's plush, all plush, seventy-two inches wide and plush on both sides. Will you go?''

"Sure. They'll need someone to take care of Terry while the rest of you play. I gather that none of his college crowd is to be there.''

"Right you are. Mr. Rossiter wanted to invite some kids of his own age from the church, but Terry wouldn't agree to that. He'll probably spend the time sulking in his tent. You'll earn the family's everlasting gratitude if you can get him out of his shell. Just now he's the family problem.''

"Sounds intriguing. I've never known him well. He looks like a sharp fellow though. I like boys, even spoiled ones.''

The two-car train with its inadequate but determined engine chugged its way through the snow-covered landscape. Mrs. Rossiter had refused to consider bus travel over the snowy hills so some of the young people were enjoying their first trip by steam locomotive. This one short line owned the only remaining steam-powered engine in the entire midwest, and a ride on it was something to boast about. Sometimes they passed through open country where small farms were interspersed with second growth timberland. The big dairy farms had been left far behind on the other side of the little city where they had changed from the streamlined through train to this "dinky" which would take them into the heart of the north woods. Already they sensed a feeling of isolation when they passed through a tract of huge trees. Then again they would sweep out into the open where they could see for miles across the white hills.

Neil was alone in a seat at the rear of the train and he found it restful to sit and watch the winter landscape glide past. In the rush of the city it became all too easy to forget that there was a world outside that was clean and undisturbed. In all his life Neil had never been in such a country, and its impression on him was awesome. He had vacationed in camps or at resorts; he had skied on man-made slides near the city; he had tobogganed on manufactured snow. Always there had been crowds, with laughter and talking and the sounds of traffic. Here, outside the window was only snow and blue, incredibly blue, sky, and the tall trees where there were occasional glimpses of squirrels playing on the branches, or birds startled from their feeding by the train.

The surroundings were full of a peace that he had never known. It was difficult to remember that just last night he had lain awake and fretted at the hours in the ten days that must pass before he would see Jane. Now he could not focus his thoughts on even such an important thing as that. The city with its problems had slipped away as the train plowed northward. And he was glad. For a few hours at least, he was going to let go of every matter of concern and rest in the goodness of a God who had made such a world as this one.

The sun, in a blaze of orange and gray that spread completely around the horizon, had dropped out of sight. In an unbelievably short time the stars were out and the shape of a crescent moon showed over the hills. In the front of the car, where Sara and her friends had been gathered in a noisy group, there was increased activity. Terry Rossiter, who, like Neil, had been sitting alone, now rose and beckoned.

"Here's where we get off, Abbott. Everyone else seems attached. Want to come along with me?"

"Good. Where are we?"

"Welcome to the greatest little village in the world, Appleboro. Population, negligible. Its claim to distinction, the Rossiter gang will sleep here! Our bus is outside ready to carry all dozen of us. Chartered from the local school board for the weekend. Nothing lacking but the sleigh bells."

As they moved through the twisting road into the hills the trees hung so low over them that often they heard the scratching of the twigs on the bus top. This was no well-traveled road, but a way into the hills and the secluded lodge. Terry, who had seated himself by Neil, drew a long breath of satisfaction.

"I love this place. If I had my way, I'd never go back to the city even to get my clothes. I'd buy another pair of socks and stay here. Isn't it wonderful?"

Neil watched in interest as the boy gazed in complete absorption from the window. He had never known Terry as well as he had Sara, who was one of the group in which most of his social activities centered. Terry, younger by several years, had shown interest in another kind of social life, one that caused his parents deep concern. He seemed petulant, rebellious against authority, and disinterested in the career his father was planning for him. His present mood showed a side of his personality that Neil had not suspected. As they passed through the stretch of woods so dense that no moonbeams found their way in and the only thing to lighten the darkness was the piled snow, Terry whispered softly,

> The woods are lovely, dark and deep,
> But I have promises to keep,
> And miles to go before I sleep!

Neil said nothing. He was enjoying the revelation of character in this apparently misunderstood boy. He hoped there would be further disclosures but they would have to come freely. If he could cultivate this acquaintance a bit, the trip could prove more interesting than he had expected.

Winter in the country! Winter in the hills! To Neil, city-born and bred, the experience was a new one and he thrilled to the wonder of it. The early rising while it was still dark, the breakfast at the big table that was stretched across the living room in front of the huge fireplace, the gathering of logs for the fire, hauling them in with the stout little pony, going with Terry to see the barn where the pony and three cows munched in their stalls — these were all unique experiences to Neil and he would never forget them. After breakfast Mr. Rossiter insisted that they gather for Scripture reading and prayer.

"If you once get outside with those skates and sleds and skis you'll forget everything else. So let's start the day right by thanking the Lord and asking His care for the day."

Then there was the dash out into the tangy cold air, the race for ski or toboggan slide, the long flights that gave one the feeling of flying, the ride back up by way of a lift powered again by the pony, then once more the release and the flight. It was exhilarating, and Neil, for the time, forgot his impatience at Jane's dictum and his eagerness for the days to pass.

Terry, who had apparently brought none of his friends, attached himself to Neil with puppy-like devotion. As there seemed an uneven distribution of fellows and girls anyway, that arrangement suited Neil. He was finding it a pleasant experience to be accepted as friend by one who was supposedly unfriendly.

On Sunday morning Mr. Rossiter told the group that the skates and skis must be laid aside until they had all been to church. The town where they had left the train was three miles away, the roads were clear, and their pastor back home would be expecting a report on the sermon. The bus from town would be out at ten-thirty, and anyone who wanted dinner afterward had better be ready at that time. Neil had thought once of pre-empting Sara's society, to tease Bruce, but when Terry appeared beside him looking wistful, he changed his mind. After all he was sure to get more good out of the sermon with Terry as seatmate rather than Sara. He hoped the sermon would be one in keeping with the setting.

For five years he heard no other preacher than his own pastor, Dr. Harlan, except for an occasional TV speaker. He loved and admired his pastor, had found him a friendly counselor, an inspiring preacher, and a stimulating proponent of the views that Neil himself held, that the Christian life was a life of *doing* and serving, of living cleanly and going forth to achieve. He hoped this pastor would have as stimulating a message. The mimeographed bulletin gave the sermon title as "The Royal Road to Service," and Neil settled himself contentedly against the back of the seat. Even in an out-of-the-way place like this, Christianity was the same.

4

THE TUESDAY MORNING train stood at the station surrounded by the group from the lodge. Some of them clambered inside at once, but kept coming to the door to call to the ones outside or in the tiny station. Neil had been on and off several times and was preparing to settle down to save a seat for Terry who was saying good-by to some local friend, when he missed his camera. He knew at once where he had left it. He and another fellow had jumped off the bus as they passed through the village and had bought candy and magazines for the return trip. He had left his camera on the counter of the small shop.

A quick glance at his watch told him there were ten minutes before leaving time. Not waiting to tell anyone where he had gone, he sprinted down the street. The distance was greater than he had thought, and as he grabbed the camera he glanced at the clock on the wall.

"Is that clock right?"

"Sure is. I set it from the University station not a half hour ago."

His last words were lost in the slam of the door as Neil rushed out and down the street thinking furiously, *Ben said I should throw this watch away. I will when I can stop long enough.*

He raced along with his anxious eyes fixed on the lazy puffs of smoke coming from the engine beyond the station. Just as he began to feel assurance that he would make it, the increased frequency in the puffs of the smoke told him that the train was starting. He put forth his best speed, but when he reached the platform the train was disappearing down the track. He stood with his hands on his hips looking at it in disgust.

"Not a single soul on the platform to see me and stop the thing! Well, it looks like a few more hours of vacation for me. And what fun it will be all alone in this burg! I could go back to the lodge, I guess, but the caretakers were going away for a week. I heard them tell Mr. Rossiter that some kid would come to look after things."

"Whatsa matter, mister?" said a voice behind him. The station master was peering from the door. "Get left? I thought I saw you get on."

"You probably did, but I didn't know enough to stay on. Now what do I do?"

The old man chuckled. "You either chase it till you catch it, or wait till this time tomorrow. And it's gettin' farther off every minute. You'd better start if you're thinkin' of chasin'."

"Do you mean there're no more trains today?"

"One a day. That's all. Take it or leave it."

"It left me. How about a bus?"

"Nope. Not in winter. We run lots of buses in the summer, but just the train in winter."

"That's great! Just great! Do I spend the night on this soft bench here? Or is there a hotel in the place?"

"None that could be properly called such. Mrs. Klaffee, down the street, has a room or two she rents out to travelin' men when they're here overnight. Want I should take your baggage over? I'm goin' home for some coffee now."

Neil looked at him in dismay.

"My baggage! It's on the train."

"Is it checked? I checked a lot for the girls."

"It was only one bag. I put it in the rack."

"You'd better send word ahead for somebody to take it off for you."

"I guess I should. I'd better send a message to Mr. Rossiter, too. I hope I have a job when I get back. Will you wire for me?"

"Telephone for yourself. Only cost you one-sixty and you can tell 'em what you want."

"I'll tell them to explain that I'm stuck here on a big story. Nobody will believe it, but it sounds better than to say I got on the train and then jumped off and watched it pull out without me. That will be the big story I'm working on. I want to write it myself."

By the time he came out of Mrs. Klaffee's house after arranging for a room for the night, snow was falling and the temperature that had been pleasantly moderate yesterday, was now dropping rapidly. As he felt the sharp wind from the northwest Neil reflected that he wouldn't care to be flying on skis in the face of it.

"Brr! This could get to be unpleasant. Wouldn't Jane get a wallop out of it? She always did think I was the world's worst bungler. Which makes me wonder, would she consider my being left behind by a dinky one-track train a 'leading of the Lord'? I wonder what it could possibly lead to. I'll ask her when I see her. What a place to be marooned. But if I try hard enough I may be able to kill an hour looking over this fair city. Even in a snowstorm it's pretty."

It was not large enough to be dignified by the name of city. It was definitely only a village, but an unusually lovely one that nestled among the surrounding hills as if to seek shelter from them. Its streets were bordered by large trees, mostly hard maples and oaks. Almost every lawn had its evergreens, not the dwarf, ornamental trees that were seen in the suburbs around the city, but great pines with tall masts reaching the sky, or twisted cedars with thick foliage that hid winter birds and squirrels. These were trees that had been planted by nature, and the lack of planned grouping made them doubly attractive to the city-bred young man.

In the center of the village was the town square with the town high school in the middle. Around it were the stores that comprised the shopping district — drug and hardware stores, the small shop where Neil had left his camera, several food shops, a five-and-ten, and a general store that seemed to sell everything from a spool of thread to automatic washers and dryers. One side was almost completely taken up with a dairy and an adjoining store that sold dairy supplies. The church they had attended Sunday stood on one corner, and a doctor's and a dentist's office on another. Tucked in between a barber-shop on one side and a small meatmarket on the other, Neil saw something that gave promise of an interesting hour or two to help speed this wasted day. The sign on the window proclaimed it to be the office of *The Appleboro Advocate*, and peering through the glass, Neil could make out a young man bent over a desk.

"Probably the managing editor — and the city editor, sports editor, and the whole reportorial staff," he said with a chuckle which certainly could not have been heard inside. Nevertheless he felt a sense of shame at having said it, for at that minute the young man looked up and saw the loiterer.

"Caught! Now there's nothing I can do except go in and extend fraternal greetings."

The young man came forward with a smile. "Anything I can do for you?"

"No, except to let me look about a bit. I'm a newspaper man myself. I have a little time to kill so I thought I'd drop in and see how it's done in this town."

"Quite different from your town I'm sure. You're from *The Ledger*, aren't you?"

"Yes. How did you know?" asked Neil with a moment of apprehension. Had the story of his folly been broadcast over town already?

"I saw you in church with Terry on Sunday. I have the Rossiter houseparty all written up for the paper which will go to press soon. Or rather, our society editor got it. She'll be in later."

"I *was* with the Rossiter party and I wish I were now. I'm embarrassed to say that I missed the train. So I'm a guest of your city for the next twenty-four hours."

"That's good. Want to watch how it was done in the dawn of the century? That's our era."

"I surely do. Mind if I loaf around this morning? Killing a whole day promises to be dull business."

"I have a deep abhorrence against anyone loafing — anyone except myself. How about trying your hand at an editorial? Our editor-owner is on the sick list. I'm only the printer, and I can't think of a thing to write about. Which makes no difference. If I had a hundred ideas I couldn't put them down. Come on. Help a brother in distress."

Neil laughed at the thought. "I usually have plenty of ideas, but I can't think of anything just at this minute except the folly of going back after a cheap camera, thus missing a train."

"That's it! The folly of the lost opportunity. Go to it!"

Neil protested with embarrassment and laughter, but the other man was persistent and the idea began to make its appeal. It would be a break in the monotony and would be an amusing incident to relate when he reached his own office again. A copy of the paper submitted to Mr. Rossiter might be accepted as the big story he was supposed to be trailing. He hung his coat and hat on the rack in the corner.

The introduction, written by the printer and signed "Marv Stebbins," was terse and to the point.

> Due to the illness of Mr. Richardson, Mr. Neil Abbott, a well-known newsman from the *Capitol Ledger,* will write a guest editorial today. Welcome, and thanks, Mr. Abbott.

"That lacks the human interest that Uncle Dick could give it, but it contains the facts and that's what I want. You will supply the other elements."

While Neil was writing, Marv and a young girl were busy in the back room, and soon the noise of the press told him that the outer pages of the paper were being run. It all seemed like a business venture by small boys. He determined, however, to make the editorial a good one, and when he had finished he wished he could show it to Ben and the other fellows who were always joking about his editorial ambitions. When he handed it to Marv he felt inordinately pleased at the enthusiasm it evoked.

"This is great! Uncle Dick will be happy to read it. I'll have Lissa tell him when she goes home for lunch. She's getting ready now. Lissa, this is Mr. Abbott, our guest for today. Tell Uncle Dick he has taken care of the editorial for us in fine style. Mr. Abbott, this is Lissa Harding. We could never run this place without her, and sometimes we wonder how we can run it *with* her. She's mighty hard to get along with, but impossible to get along without. She's our man Friday."

"And Saturday, Sunday, Monday, Tuesday, Wednesday, Thursday, and the next Friday." The girl extended a grimy hand as she spoke. "Please excuse the ink. I'm never quite rid of it. And excuse Marv also. He thinks he's funny, and we all laugh to please him. We have to keep him in a good humor since he's the only printer we have, and the only person in the county who can make this press work. Without him we'd be sunk. And we can't run any risks with the *Advocate*. We'd all rather miss two meals a day than to miss our *Advocate*. Thanks for your help. Good-by now! See you at one o'clock." She was out of the door before her last words reached them.

Marv laughed. "She's a grand kid. Has a sort of tough time, I think, though I don't know why. But nothing seems to get her down. We really couldn't get along without her. Now we're going to my house for dinner. We close shop at noon for an hour. All the business places do. That's one of the joys of a small place. No, don't object. I telephoned my wife awhile ago and an extra plate is already on the table."

As they came out into the street after lunch Marv observed that the wind had become violent, and the snow was much thicker.

"Looks as if we're in for a real storm."

"Any chance that I can't get out tomorrow morning?"

"Oh, no. We're just as proud of our train service as we are of our newspaper. The 8:20 goes at 8:20 every morning. There's only one track, less than fifty miles long. But it goes! And you'd better be on time tomorrow."

All afternoon Neil worked with Marv and Lissa. To one who knew only the routine of the work of a big city newspaper, it was an interesting and amazing thing to see these people work. He had never stopped to wonder how an issue of *The Ledger* went through the process of folding. There were great machines, of course, to assemble the many pages. Here, the folding and assembling was done by hand, and both he and Lissa worked at it. At two o'clock, when enough papers had been folded to make a great pile, Lissa took them and went in to the long table in the office.

"I have to get the mailing ready tonight because the train and rural carriers go before we could do it in the morning," she explained. Neil wondered how large the mailing list was as he saw her come again and again for a new supply. Surely this whole valley didn't have so many people in it, and who else would want this queer little sheet?

At four o'clock two boys whom Lissa introduced as her brothers came in from high school asking if the papers were ready for delivery.

"It's awful out," one said breathlessly, shaking the snow from his cap. "There's about ten inches now, and it's coming down in a solid mass. I hope we make it!"

Marv looked from the window. All afternoon they had been too busy to note the increased intensity of the storm. Now the high school only a few rods away could hardly be seen, and the few people on the street were struggling through deep drifts, fighting their way against the wind. Marv turned from the window.

"Listen. I don't want either of you boys out alone in this. Stay together and do the town stuff. I'll take the Hollow. I'll go on snowshoes. That's the only way anyone could get through."

"You aren't going alone, are you?" Lissa asked as the boys went out with their loads. "I'll go with you. I'm as good on snowshoes as you are."

"You will *not!* This is no little girl's job. You stay here until the boys report in. Then all of you head for home. I'll check on you when I get back. I'll want to tell Uncle Dick that we made it."

Lissa protested, but Neil interrupted. "I'll go with him. We can finish in much less time if we work together."

"He's right, Lissa. Call Carol and tell her we'll be there for a late supper, but don't tell her where we're going. She can't worry about what she doesn't know."

The Hollow seemed to be another village. It lay over a mile from the edge of the town proper. Reaching it against the wind was a task that ruled out any attempt at conversation. Every few steps they had to turn their backs for a breathing spell. The snow was blinding, and before they had been out ten minutes Neil felt that they were hopelessly lost. But Marv forged resolutely ahead and all he could do was to follow. Certainly he would never be able to find his way back alone. He was not an expert on snowshoes and often Marv had to wait for him as they fought their way up the long slope, then down into the depression that gave the settlement its name.

Even when they reached the houses Neil could not see well enough to tell whether they were log cabins or modern ranch houses. The lights from the windows were lost in the swirling whiteness at a few feet. Neil handed the papers to Marv who knew where to leave them.

"I don't dare throw them. They'd never find them. I'll lay them at the doors and give a loud knock. That ought to do it. This storm is really a honey!"

"Have you ever had it as bad before?"

"I think so. But never on *Advocate* day. The storm makes no difference, however. *The Advocate* must go out."

When their load was almost gone Marv knocked on a door and waited until it opened.

"Good evening, Mrs. Brown. Here's your *Advocate*."

"Marv Stebbins! What are you doing out in this storm?"

"Delivering your paper and hoping you have a pot of coffee on the stove. We need a bit of rest before we go back."

"You needed a bit of sense before you started out. We could have gone without the paper for once."

"That's what you say. But haven't you been worrying for an hour over the boys and wondering if they would make it? And if we hadn't come you would have worried all night. Now, wouldn't you?"

"I guess you're right. And I've not only got coffee that I can heat, but I baked bread today and there's some apple butter open. You sit down and rest while I get it ready."

The rest was most welcome to Neil, for the battle with the wind was more strenuous than any exercise he had taken for years. The coffee, with its accompanying bread and apple butter, did its reviving work, however, and in half an hour they were on their way back. It was easier without the heavy load of papers, but there was no doubt that the storm was increasing in violence. Neil was heartily glad when Marv led the way into the bungalow where his wife and children waited for them.

Marv talked to Lissa and reported that all was well and she should tell Uncle Dick so. Later, in Mrs. Klaffee's front bedroom Neil thought over the day with a sleepy wonder. Who could have dreamed such a situation? He dug deep under the blankets. This was just the night for sleep. And several miles through the drifts could really make a fellow appreciate a good bed.

5

It was still dark when Mrs. Klaffee called him, but it was the darkness of a black day rather than that of night. The clouds hanging low above shut out any chance for normal daylight. The snow was still falling, coming down with a vengeance as if it meant never to stop. He was tempted at first to pull up the covers and go back to sleep. This was the kind of day that was meant for sleeping. But the clock on the dresser said five after seven, and he reluctantly got out of bed.

As he plowed his way to the station through the drifts, Neil thought that it was fortunate that trains had snowplows to help them, for even a big engine would have a hard time with the drifts that were bound to be in the cut where the train came through the hills. Last night he had wished for his luggage. Now he was glad he had only his small camera to carry. The streets seemed strangely silent. Surely someone should be out by eight o'clock. There were a few footprints, but they had been quickly covered with snow.

As he turned the corner he could see a group of men gathered on the station platform, and Marv came to meet him.

"You're not going home this morning, friend," he stated.

"Isn't the train going?" asked Neil in dismay.

"Worse than that. It hasn't come yet. Didn't get in last night. Drifts fifteen feet deep in the cut, then a rock slide to complicate matters. And more snow on top of that. The conductor telephoned from The Falls last night."

"When do they expect to have it open?"

"No expectations yet, as far as we know. During the night there were probably other slides, either of rock or snow. Uncle Dick has been preaching for several years that the cut was unsafe. Guess we'd better be thankful no one was there when it hit."

"And no train! I may as well go back and tell Mrs. Klaffee she'll have a guest again tonight."

"Better engage the room by the week."

"I wouldn't think of doing that. I have to get back to the city, and if there's no other way I'll start walking as soon as this snow stops."

"Don't count on that very soon. Radio reports this morning say another storm is due to hit and mix with this one this afternoon. You'd better sit tight and start to write the story you're going to send in. This might prove to be the tall tale you promised Mr. Rossiter. If that other storm hits, this could become a disaster area."

"But I *have* to get out. I have to be back at work."

"If it's work you're wanting, there'll be plenty of it when this snow stops long enough for us to find our snow shovels."

"I'll start walking. I could do that."

"In which direction are you planning to walk? Even in good weather the Gap is the only way in. Both the railroad and the highway use it. Both are cut off now, and may be for several days."

"With snowshoes I could go over the hills."

"You might in clear weather and if you knew the woods and if you were a great deal better on shoes than you were last night. Get some sense, fellow."

"Okay, okay. So I'll go back to that little warm room and read *Hostetter's Almanac* for 1929 and twiddle my big thumbs and be thankful. Good-by, pal. See you when the roses bloom."

He started off resentfully, but Marv called, "Not so fast. Why don't you try to find the profit in the situation? Uncle Dick says it's always there."

"Profit he says. I'll be losing my job."

"I don't believe Mr. Rossiter will fire you for what you can't help. Paste a smile on your face and come back to the office with me. We'll make ourselves a Community Morale Committee. It's going to shock folks no end when they find we don't have train service. We're dependent on that train."

Back in the office Neil thought of calling the *Ledger* but Marv was at the desk calling someone about a meeting, and Lissa asked him if he would stay by the radio on Uncle Dick's desk and catch any news that might be helpful to the situation or useful for the next issue of the *Advocate*. Whenever there was no news he typed the items he had taken, for his shorthand was such that no one else could read it. Marv kept busy at the telephone. The lines through the cut had been broken by the slide, but a line led over the hills toward Mendon, the county seat, and this was still open. It was protected by the tall cliffs between it and the storm and was not in danger, the office in Mendon reported.

Neil learned as he listened that Marv was indeed a Morale Committee. This little office was the nerve center of the community. Not only was its staff supposed to know why the train didn't come last night, but when it *would* arrive. When would the snow stop? Would the roads be clear so that the children could go to school tomorrow? How would the milk trucks from the dairy get out to the farms? How would things be brought in from outside if the Gap were closed? Patiently Marv answered them all, telling an encouraging truth if he could, quieting and reassuring by his own calm acceptance of the situation. Neil wondered at the patience and kindness of the young man. Why didn't he tell these folks off as he had done *him* that morning? Was this his way of keeping up the community morale in a trying situation? All afternoon it went on, and as reports came in that crews had been heard working on the other side of the slide, Neil began to hope that the train might get in. If it did he could leave here tomorrow morning and be back at his desk by evening. What a price he was paying for one small mistake. The sooner the episode ended the better he would like it.

For some time the radio had been giving the news. Now it switched again to the weather and the report was not promising. The storm from the west was proving a bitter one, and in its path electric and telephone lines were down and highways closed. Marv called the newspaper at The Falls and learned that the workers at the Gap had been called off because of another and larger rock slide. The situation was too dangerous for any work. Until the weather cleared and engineers could appraise the situation no one was allowed in the area.

"It's getting too big for me," said Marv as he turned from the phone. "I'm calling Buckman. As village president he has the first responsibility."

Mr. Buckman, however, could not discharge that responsibility. His wife reported that he had endeavored to shovel the front walk so that he could get out and survey the situation, and had been stricken with a heart attack.

"Well, Neil, looks as if it's up to us to get mobilized," Marv said after he explained to Neil. "Let's do some heavy thinking."

"Who wants that kind of thinking?" asked a breathless voice from the door. Lissa had been out making the rounds of the stores for news, and her snow-covered clothing and red cheeks told of a tussle with the storm. The laughter in her voice, and her sparkling eyes proclaimed that she had enjoyed it.

"You shouldn't be out in this," scolded Marv. "But we can use you anyway. You hold things here for the next hour. Neil and I are going out. We may have to round up the old Civilian Defense gang. We're going to need all the brain and brawn we can muster in this crisis."

"What crisis?" demanded Lissa. "I think this is fun!"

"Fun, she says," snorted Marv. "There's been another slide, and the Gap is closed indefinitely. Nothing, and I mean *nothing*, can get in from the outside, and we can't get out. Stop and think where that leads us, little lady. And when the big blow hits here this afternoon the phone and lights will go. No food shipped in, either. Do you call that fun?"

"I'm sorry. I didn't know about all that. What will we do?"

"That's what we have to figure out. Neil and I are going out and contact every store in town and warn them to conserve all supplies, sell nothing until we can get organized. Neil, you take the east and south sides of the square. Tell them there's a meeting at the church as soon as they can get there. Tell the boss himself to come even if he has to shut up shop for an hour. Tell them to *come!*"

That meeting, in the same church which he had attended with his friends a few days ago, was an experience Neil never forgot. In the time that he and Marv were busy making their rounds, telephone service had gone, and as they entered the church the lights went out, an evidence that some place up in the mountains the power lines were down.

The men who had gathered realized with sober conviction that upon them rested the welfare of the community. They seemed to take for granted that, in the absence of the president, Marv should be chairman, and the minister was drafted as secretary. They were here for one purpose and they met the issue with decision. Committees were named to plan for food conservation, for its distribution, for transporting supplies to those unable to get out on snowshoes, for carrying medical supplies wherever the doctor requested, and for any other emergency that might arise. Neil found himself, as one of the younger men, on "the snowshoe gang" committed to the transportation of supplies wherever the chairman might choose to send him.

On the way back to the office he realized that he had not had a chance to telephone the *Ledger*. Now it was too late. There was no use to spend time worrying about what it might mean. He had a task, one that promised to take all his time and strength. By the time they got to the office Lissa had begun to comprehend the scope of the needs and had compiled a list of all the babies who would need milk. With her aid six of the young men drew up route sheets and prepared to make their first tour of duty to distribute canned milk and try to allay the fear of frightened mothers.

Neil was sent out with Ernie Hunter, the druggist's son, and their route lay to the Hollow and a few straggling houses on the return road. At house after house they stopped, bringing relief into worried faces as they gave assurance that tomorrow more milk would be delivered.

All the teams got back eventually, one of them bringing in three hunters whom they had discovered lost in the snow.

"If you'll go with Neil over to the diner you can get a good warm meal," Marv told them. "You must need it. When you get back we will have found a place for you to stay."

"Is there a place where I can get a few articles of clothing?" Neil asked before they left. "I don't even have a spare handkerchief with me."

"Try Porters. Two doors beyond the diner. If you don't have plenty of money, tell them I'll stand for you."

"I have plenty, for awhile at least. We'll surely get out of here by the first of the month."

When they came back, after eating and buying the supplies they needed, they found Lissa in charge.

"Marv went home for supper. Neil, you're to take these men to Mrs. Klaffee's house. She can make room for three."

"Fine. And what becomes of me? I saw her first."

"You're going home with me. We have a small room that's empty, and Uncle Dick wants to see you."

"So he's *your* uncle too?"

"He's everyone's uncle. We've always called him that. But he really is kin to me, distantly. He's my grandmother's cousin. Since he doesn't have a family, he boards with us. Right now he's in bed with flu, and since his heart hasn't been good for years, the doctor says he has to stay in bed several weeks. He says he just *has* to see you."

As they battled their way through the drifts Neil found that his small but sturdy companion set a pace that called for his best. She was evidently at home on snowshoes and, undaunted by wind and snow, she soon left him behind. She knew her way so well that there was no hesitation as she sped along.

"Can you wait a minute?" he panted finally. "I'm not used to this kind of exercise, and I've been out all afternoon. Can we take it a bit slower?"

"I'm sorry. I get so much fun out of this that I forget the other fellow. I love the snow. I'll try to remember that it's a new experience for you."

As soon as their steps sounded on the back porch the door was opened and a boyish voice called out, "Are we glad to see *you!* Mom's half crazy about you and doesn't dare show it because Uncle Dick is already threatening to get up and go after you. I'll go tell them you're here."

He sped away, and Lissa ushered Neil into a warm kitchen lighted now by a kerosene lamp on the table. Clustered in a doorway on the other side of the room were several other children, whom Lissa introduced as her three sisters, Ruth, René and June. The boy came running down again, accompanied by another, and Neil recognized them as the two delivery boys whom Marv had sent home last night.

"Liss, Mom says you're to feed yourself and the man, and then he's to come upstairs. It's time Uncle Dick was settled for the night, and he won't be still until he's got something off his chest. There's soup on the stove and some sandwich stuff in the old icebox in the pantry. We put things in it when the refrigerator went dead. Pug and I whacked some ice off the pond to put in it. It works fine but Mom says we mustn't put any in water or eat it."

After he had gone, Lissa turned to Neil. "Put your wraps in the hall. I'll have the soup warm in a few minutes."

"I don't want to eat, really. We had a good meal at the diner. If I can go to my room I'd like to get into some dry clean clothes before I go to see Mr. —— What *is* his name?

I'm a stranger and I can't just burst in and call him Uncle Dick.''

"He'd be delighted if you did. but he does have a name. It's Richardson, Mr. Richard Richardson, if you please. By tomorrow night you'll be calling him Uncle Dick. Everyone does.''

She led him upstairs to a small room at the end of the hall. "I'm sorry it's so tiny. And if it smells antiseptic that's because it *is*. It's our hospital room. I've spent many a measley and mumpy day here. That cupboard holds all sorts of things to amuse a sick child. Help yourself. Uncle Dick's room is next to yours, and the bathroom at the other end of the hall. When you're ready just go in and introduce yourself to Uncle Dick. I heard Mother go down the back stairs as we came up the front.''

"Thanks for being so kind to a wayfarer.''

"Oh, it wasn't my idea. It's just the way my mother does. Anyone in need of help of any kind finds an open door here. But I don't think you should be talking of kindnesses after all you've done for the *Advocate* and the town in the last two days.''

When Neil tapped gently at the neighboring door a weak voice called for him to come in. The frail looking man sitting up against the pillows reached out a hand in welcome.

"So this is the kind stranger who has so adequately filled my shoes at the office. I'm glad and proud to meet you. I'm grateful for the fine service you rendered yesterday, and especially appreciative of the way you've given of your strength and energy today. I'm lonesome in my room up here, and Marv Stebbins hasn't had time to visit me. So Grace and I decided it would be nice to have you under our roof. In that way we can keep informed officially about conditions. It's hard to get along without a telephone. Won't you tell me about your day?''

There was nothing to do but to tell the old man the full story and the predictions that had been made about the duration of their isolation. When he heard of the greater slide and the increased violence of the storm that had cut off all communication with the outside world, he shook his head in distress. But when the story was told of the way the town had rallied to meet the emergency his eyes shone with pride.

"That's my town, my brave little town! We've had troubles before and we've met them and come out on top. We'll do the same this time. What's the news from outside? Do they realize how we are situated?"

"I don't know. Lissa may be able to tell you. She's been in the office all day while I've been out. If anyone has battery radios we can get word from outside, but we can't send any out. All the electric and telephone lines are out."

"That's bad. But God is still with us. Don't doubt that, my boy, even though it must seem quite a hardship for you to be held here against your plans. But God also has plans. He sent you here for just this time."

"He sent me? I haven't been able to see it that way. I was careless and foolish and was left behind. And I can't believe that I'm going to be worth much here. Lissa is much better at getting about and gathering news than I am."

"But she doesn't know how to run the paper. She can't write the editorials and you can. That one yesterday was fine even if it did poke a bit of sarcastic fun at yourself. Most important, I believe you can write the articles for the schools. I have notes prepared far ahead, and I'm sure you can do it. I may soon be able to do it myself, but I'm so weak that Grace and the doctor say I mustn't write a line. You can do it, and by doing it save the reputation of the *Advocate* all over the nation."

"What do you mean?"

"I mean that the *Advocate* must come out every time right on time. The telephone may fail and the train be held up by a snowslide, but the *Advocate* goes out!" His voice was rising in excitement, and Neil feared that Mrs. Harding would be appearing to quiet both of them.

"I'll do anything I can, sir, but Marv does much better than I. This — this is quite different from being just a reporter on the *Ledger,* you know."

"I'm sure it is," Uncle Dick said, laughing. "But you

can swing it. Marv will have all he can do to clean up that old hand press in the basement and get it into working order. They've all been laughing at me because I kept it, but I knew I might need it sometime!''

"When do we have to get the next paper out?"

"Let's see. This is Wednesday. It comes out Friday afternoon. Now let's decide how it's to be done. Get that folder off my desk and I'll give you the article in there. I always keep the school page prepared a bit in advance, so you won't have any trouble there this time."

For over an hour they talked until Mrs. Harding came in and insisted on ending the interview.

As Neil lay in bed waiting for sleep he thought of his conversation with the old man and of the article he had read before retiring. "The article for the school," Uncle Dick had called it. It had proved to be a historical piece about the early days in Arkansas, one that was based upon authenticated history and yet told with such an appeal of human interest that it had proved fascinating reading. Did the schools of the community, he wondered, use material that Uncle Dick prepared for their classrooms? Quite a unique idea and certainly should make the study of history more real and alive.

Then he thought of his situation. Would God really let him do such a foolish thing as miss his train and endanger his job and hold him here just to get out a small-town newspaper? These people seemed to think so, but to him it seemed a petty way for God to work. What would the fellow who had talked to the group at church that night, say about it? Or what would Jane say? He hadn't thought of Jane all day. How very far the old familiar world of last week seemed for him now.

"I'd never even heard of Appleboro until B. Franklin invited me into this mess. Now it seems I'm one of the leading citizens. What a rut I've lived in all these years! It was a nice rut, however, and if I could wake up in the apartment with B. tomorrow morning I'd be glad to blot out this whole experience. The idea of getting out a small town newspaper appeals to me not at all."

41

6

Two MORNINGS AFTER his conversation with Uncle Dick, Neil wakened in a room even colder than usual. Mrs. Harding had explained the night before that they had given up the effort to keep the furnace going, so Neil knew it would do no good to wait for heat. His clothes were as cold as if they had been outdoors all night in the continuing snow, and he put them on quickly.

He tiptoed down the hall, but his precaution proved futile. A shaky voice from Mr. Richardson's room hailed him and he had to heed it. The old man was propped up on his pillows with his breakfast tray before him. The room seemed delightfully warm after the frigidity of the hall, and Neil was glad to see an oil stove in the corner.

"I'm snug as toast in here while the rest of you shiver. Grace would have it that way. I have the only stove in the house besides the wood range in the kitchen. There's a register over it that heats the bathroom. I suppose the family is living in the kitchen."

"You wanted me, sir?"

"Yes. Tell me how things are going. Marv said he got the old press to work. Are you going to go to press on time?"

"Yes. I plan on six pages. That will contain all the local stuff and leave one page each for the Arkansas article and the news of the storm."

"Did you get plenty of news about how folks are getting along in the snow? That's what they like, news of their friends."

"We still have more than we can use. I'll use stories like that to fill in every place there's a spare inch. I'll leave out a lot of the ads if you don't mind. I'm sure the merchants will understand."

"That's right. Get in every story you can crowd in. Put your account of the storm on the same page with the Arkansas story. That's the one that is read outside, the one that goes to schools. Put in the names of the folks who are helping, no matter how small the job."

"We will try to follow orders in every way, sir. Now I have to go. Mrs. Harding said we weren't to talk."

"If that's her order it must be obeyed. But she can't object if I lie here and thank the Lord for you."

When Neil and Lissa stepped out into the brightness of the morning they gave simultaneous exclamations of wonder. The clouds of the previous day had gone and the sun shone upon a world that seemed strange. Not a fence was in sight. The trees were buried to their branches. In places the drifts were so high that they shut off the view of the surrounding fields.

On the village square they could now survey the damage. Windows had been blown in, storm shutters ripped off. Several trees from the high school lawn had fallen. Limbs were torn from others and lay buried in the snow that had smoothed the debris into knobs and mounds. Men were beginning to shovel and were already dismayed at the problem of disposal. Where could they put so much snow? At the office Marv was waiting for them and opened the door to help them clamber over the drift that hindered.

"Everything's ready for work, you laggards! The press will operate if handled carefully, but it will be slow. One of you will have to help. My strong arms will be busy and someone else will have to feed the animal. If we get ten copies between breakdowns we'll be doing fine. Ever run one of these things, Neil?"

"No, but I can learn."

"It's just a case of brains and brawn."

The old machine did better than Marv's predictions. There were several times of difficulty, but he seemed to know where to expect trouble and was ready for it. Hour by hour the press clanked away slowly. The sheets came out one at a time instead of in the smooth stream in which the electric press ejected them. Upstairs Lissa greeted the callers who came down the narrow lanes of white to inquire about their tasks for the day or to bring in bits of news.

Neil was upstairs with her, taking a much needed rest, when the door opened to admit a figure that, to Neil's astonished eyes, looked like the Abominable Snowman. Wrappings were peeled off layer after layer, and eventually there stood revealed a lanky youth whose labored breath and red cheeks told of a struggle through the drifts.

"Can I help you?" Lissa inquired. "You're Bill Banning, aren't you?"

"Yes. From the Hollow. Who's runnin' this show?"

"I — I guess we all are. Do you want something?"

"Well — it's about the milk. Our kids need more of it. Some of them won't take that powered stuff the teams have been delivering."

"I'm sorry. We're doing the best we can."

"That's why I came. Nobody asked us to help. Us boys in the Hollow can get real milk for the kids."

"Why — how?"

"I'll betcha the farmers are pourin' out milk they can't sell. Let us go out and get it."

"How do you plan to do it if the farmers can't get in?" asked Neil, breaking into the conversation.

"We can do it, all right. We can do things the farmers never thought of. Give us a try. I'm goin' now to get milk for my little sister, and if you'll count us in regular, we'll haul in enough milk for all the babies and sick folks."

The minister had come in and heard the boy's proposal. "Let them try," he advised. "How are you going to do it, Bill?"

"We got ways," Bill said with a grin. "No snowplows can get in until the cut is opened, and no trucks can make it through the drifts between here and the farms. You better let us try."

"Go ahead. Take it to the dairy and they'll get it ready for the distributors. When can you bring in a load?"

"We'll make one by four this afternoon. We'll have to get something to eat and some rest before we start back, but we'll guarantee you can deliver milk tomorrow morning. There's twelve of us guys, and we'll bring in at least twelve cans of milk!"

He went whistling out of the door, and Neil shook his head in bewilderment. "Did he come out of a cave in the woods?"

"No. He heads up the group of boys who live in the Hollow and come in to high school. They're all shy of the townfolk, and sometimes they're almost antagonistic. The other people from the Hollow are friendly, but those boys won't mix with us at all. I've been afraid of trouble from that direction — gang trouble."

As the hours passed, others came and went, bringing stories of hardship and need.

Dr. Anderson came in for a few minutes of rest in Uncle Dick's old rocker. His eyes were bloodshot, and the dark lines under them told of too much exertion and far too little sleep. Lissa scolded him with the freedom of old acquaintance.

"You've *got* to take some rest and quit worrying. There isn't a thing anyone can do about that medicine you need. If you get sick the whole town will go to pieces. We need your morale as well as your medicine. Don't we, Eddie?" she asked of a young man who had just come in. "And how in the world did you get here? I thought you were at the lodge."

"Just walked and crawled and slid," he grinned. "How I'll get back is yet to be seen. It's uphill all the way. To your

45

other question I'll say that I don't know what you're talking about, but if you think so, I do too."

She laughed triumphantly at the doctor, then turned to Ed. "Isn't it crazy?" she asked. "If we could just get to the other side of the Gap we would have the world at our disposal. It's only five miles. But it's five hundred years as far as we're concerned. We're back in the dark ages, this side of that slide. Can't even get any news in. The last battery radio is dead!"

"I think there's a battery radio of some sort up at the cabin. It's one of those you can talk two ways on, but I don't know how it works, or if it works at all."

Neil sat up with a jerk. "A short wave?" he asked excitedly. "Where is your cabin?"

"It's the Rossiter Lodge," explained Lissa. "Excuse me for not introducing you. This is Ed Walsh, the man who is taking care of the Rossiter place just now. Ed, Neil Abbott is one of Mr. Rossiter's friends."

Neil spoke hurriedly, with little attention to the amenities. "Is there really a workable short-wave set up there?"

"I can't say whether it works or not. Pierre calls it that 'ham thing,' and he says Terry sometimes sits at it all night."

"Does anyone in this town know how to operate it? Is there a science teacher here? Could you take us up there? Maybe we can get word out by it."

Without waiting for an answer to his question Neil was getting into his jacket and reaching for his snowshoes.

"George Perry is the science teacher. Ed knows where he lives." Lissa had no time to add more before the young men were gone. She turned back to the doctor.

"A fine publisher *he* is! What do you think's eating him now? He's left Marv to finish the run-off alone, and the papers have to be folded and put where we won't get them mixed with tomorrow's run. And he leaves at a time like this!"

Stop the first strong chap that comes along and get him to help Marv. Abbott may be out arranging the salvation of this little burg." The doctor, who had apparently forgotten about being tired, shrugged into his coat. "I'll try to catch them at Perry's place and let you know what's up."

"What *is* up?" asked Marv coming up from the basement. "Where's Neil? If we're to get the paper out tomorrow someone else has to run that junkpile awhile. I'm bushed!"

"Sit down and rest. I'm just going out and I'll send someone to help you. I have to catch Abbott and tell him what to order!"

Out in the street Neil and Ed were hurrying down the ghostly aisles that were the streets. All day men, boys and girls had been laboring, and narrow lanes had been opened to most of the houses. It was down one of these paths that Ed led the way, to find the teacher laboring with his two sons to open up the street. When told that there might be a useable short wave radio at Rossiter's, he was enthusiastic.

"Sure I can make it work if the batteries are all right. I'll be mighty glad if the doctor can get the medicine in. My little girl is one of the children he's worried about. Dave and Jack, go in and tell your mother where I've gone. Don't know when I'll be back, but I'll be all right. It may take me all night to catch someone to help us. Tell her we may be able to get the medicine for Patty."

At the corner they met the doctor. "I couldn't risk missing you. Here's the list of things I need. Tell them it's desperate. I wouldn't give ten cents for Art Morrison's chances if he doesn't get that heart medicine. God speed you boys! I wish I could go with you. We'll all be waiting and praying."

It was three miles to the lodge, uphill all the way, and the road was completely obliterated by snow. Ed led the way, sometimes walking, often stumbling, and often floundering through drifts so deep and soft that even their snowshoes sank. In other places where the wind had clear sweep, the snow was packed hard and they made good progress.

It had been shortly after noon when they started, but the sun had begun to curve sharply downward before the lodge came into view. It was buried to the eaves in front, but Ed led them to the back where a covered shed gave entrance to the kitchen. Inside was warmth and comfort. Ed busied himself in getting a meal, and for an hour they rested and ate. There might be a long night of work and tension ahead of them. George Perry had been working all day, but was eager to get at the radio, so when they had rested he asked to be shown the way to Terry's den.

"We'll all rest better after we get out a call for help. You fellows can just leave me alone here and I'll study this thing out. He seems to have plenty of batteries, but I'm going mighty careful. I want every ounce of juice we have to count."

Neil and Ed looked at the tangle of wires, tubes, and connections, and shook their heads.

"We'll be more useful downstairs playing checkers by the fire," Ed said. "Call us if there's anything we can do."

"Don't worry about me. I have everything I need. There's a pageful of call letters here, and I'm bound to get somewhere eventually."

Downstairs Neil and Ed played a few games of checkers then sat by the fire talking. Neil learned that Ed's father owned the inn at the far end of the lake which was the attraction for the summer visitors who were the main support of the valley. As there was little for him to do in the winter he was glad to spend a month each year caring for the lodge and enjoying the opportunity to study the correspondence course he was taking.

"We have plans for making the inn much larger — into a really big thing. Dad is a good practical manager, but we know we should learn more also about modern methods of management. One of our regular summer people owns a hotel in the city, and he thinks this is an ideal spot for winter sports as well as summer vacationists. He's willing to help us finance it, but insisted that I take a course in a school he recommended. So all winter long I dig in."

"It's a shame we have to bother you. But I think the thanks of the doctor and all the others will convince you it was worthwhile. That is, if we get through. You may be the hero of the day before our emergency is over."

"You say 'our emergency.' What's it all to you, Mr. Abbott? You'll leave as soon as you can, won't you?"

"Yes. I'll be mighty glad to get back to my own apartment and my own job. But being here in such an emergency, I can't help but feel a part of it."

"I heard on the street today that you are going to get out the *Advocate* for Uncle Dick. That could turn into something big for you since you work on the *Ledger*. Mr. Rossiter will be mighty pleased when he finds the *Advocate* has come out as usual."

"What does Mr. Rossiter care about that little one-cylinder sheet in that little one-horse town?"

"He cares an awful lot. Just like Uncle Dick Richardson does. You know they own it, don't you?"

"Who are they?"

"Harry Rossiter and Uncle Dick."

"Well! And another well! Can't you cue me in? I've completely lost my place in the script."

"I don't know all the script, but during the summer the Rossiters come over to our place a lot, and I hear them talk. Here's the pitch as I see it. A Richardson ancestor founded that paper when the valley was first settled. It has descended through generations until now Uncle Dick and Harry Rossiter own it. Uncle Dick is much older, and I think he raised Mr. Rossiter. Anyway he sent him through college and helped him get a job on the *Ledger*. I guess he hoped he'd come back and help with the *Advocate*. Mr. Rossiter had sense enough to know that it would never be anything but a smalltown sheet, and he loved the daughter of his boss. So — he married her, inherited the *Ledger,* and there you are. But he still has a soft spot in his heart for the old home paper. It's rumored that he contributes generously to keep it going. Folks call it his pet."

"I only hope my pay goes on while I'm on this tour of duty."

"Are you doing the school articles, too?"

"What *are* they? Everyone is too busy to tell me about

them. They seem to be mighty important."

"They are, in their way. Uncle Dick is fond of history, thinks it's the most neglected subject in the present-day curriculum. Believes that if all our children were well informed in the story of our country, its beginnings, its various peoples, we would raise a generation of patriots who would put us back on our appointed course and hold us to it. He began writing editorials along that line. Folks read them and smiled. Dear Uncle Dick! But the state superintendent of public instruction got hold of one of the editorials, and while he probably wasn't quite so optimistic about the future as Uncle Dick was, he thought it was a mighty good plan. He got an appropriation for a subscription to the *Advocate* for every grade and high school in the state. Uncle Dick promised to publish a historical article every Friday. He does, and very attractive they are. We save them all at our house. It's history in a form that kids like. Like a dose of medicine wrapped up in a juicy hamburger."

"So that's why the mailing list is so large. I thought it surely must be padded."

"I have to feed the animals. Then maybe we'd better go up and see if George has gone to sleep on the job."

They found him working hard. "I'm still working on some of the connections. Terry seems to have been rebuilding it, for it's quite a mess. But I think it's all here. I'll let you know when I'm ready to start exploring. I don't know what Terry's call letters are, but if I can reach someone else I can find out. I'll try all these he has written down. Let's hope it will be someone in the U.S. that answers, rather than Mexico or Puerto Rico. Just any old place that can contact someone who can bring us some help."

He worked so industriously and soberly that Neil knew he was thinking of the sick children back in town. They returned to the living room, leaving him to his solitary task.

7

FEELING USELESS, AND yet not willing to go to sleep and leave the teacher working alone, they whiled away the hours with low-toned conversation, and a friendship was formed that was to prove a lifelong joy to both. Occasionally one of them would go up to check on the patient George. When they learned that he was finally "on the air" they waited tensely for the result of his efforts.

Over and over he called, listening intently to catch any answer. "Calling for Appleboro. Calling for Appleboro. Can a helicopter reach us? Not safe to try to land. A drop can be made at ball field west of town." Then would follow a list of the drugs needed, and a request for flashlight batteries, also batteries for the short-wave radio.

Over and over this was repeated. Neil and Ed offered to relieve the weary man, but he refused to give up.

"You aren't used to it. A faint call might come through and be gone before you caught it. I'll stick to it until morning. You fellows don't have a kid who needs that medicine. Few operators can work in the day time, so I'll get a little sleep and try again later on."

They left him and went back to their chairs, talking

despondently of the disappointment it would bring if they had to go back to town and report only a failure. Last night they had been jubilantly sure of success. Now they faced defeat. A gray dawn coming through the windows found both asleep in the big chairs while the fire burned low. The sound of George's feet on the stair wakened them, and his joyous shout brought them to their feet.

"I got it! I got an answer. I could hardly hear it, but it was real. He says they've been hearing me since midnight, but I didn't get them. He called the *Ledger* and talked to Mr. Rossiter. A helicopter is ready to start as soon as they can get the medicine. Let's get going back to town. It ought to be coming before too long, and I want to greet it. I told them we'd all be lined up around the field so they'd know where to make the drop. I can't wait to break the news!"

The return trip was easier since it lay downhill, and even so early there were watchers at the edge of the town who sped to tell the news at the first jubilant wave. Quickly the word went from home to home, and by common consent all work was suspended so that everyone who could struggle through the drifts might make his way to the ball field. There must be no chance of the precious bundles being dropped in the wrong place.

A small boy was the first to sight the helicopter, and his squeals of excitement alerted the crowd. Hats and caps, scarves and mittens were waved in salute as the big bird flew over, circling the field. Slowly it drifted over again, and down floated a bundle, then another and another. With a salute from the men who had brought such welcome relief, and with cheers from the crowd, the helicopter rose and was soon lost in the glare of the sunshine.

The doctor and Marvin were the first to reach the precious cargo, and guarded it from the too-zealous efforts at helpfulness. A toboggan was ready, and a triumphant procession made its way back to town.

One of the packages had carried a message. "We'll be back before dark." So by midafternoon a squad of young men with several toboggans were waiting, and came back with the second load. Sleep would be sound in Appleboro that night. They were still snowbound, but help was on the way.

After his little girl was out of danger, George Perry went to the lodge with Ed so that he might get any incoming messages and send out any requests that might come. Four high school boys agreed to act as messengers, two of them being at the lodge each day and two in town. The second day they brought a message for Uncle Dick which gave the sick man both satisfaction and amusement.

> Keep a stiff upper lip, Dick. We're all for you. The nation is watching the fight to get to you, and you'll be back in circulation before you know it. One of my careless reporters got stranded up there and must be in your midst now. If you can contact him, tell him to get over to the lodge and send in a good story. When a thing like this happens to my own home town I have a right to a scoop. How are you feeling? Are you getting out the *Advocate?* Keep the flag flying!

The next afternoon Neil made the trip back up with the boys and sat for several hours while George Perry took down news reports from the outside. When an hour came that Neil figured would give tomorrow's *Ledger* the desired scoop, his story was sent in. No mention was sent in about what he himself was doing, nor of Mr. Richardson's illness except to ask that Mr. Rossiter be informed that his cousin was doing nicely and that the *Advocate* had come out as usual.

Despite the age of helicopters it was not possible to live normally. There was no state of emergency, but there was lack of many of the accustomed adjuncts to living. The schools were opened, but some of the younger children from the outlying farms had to stay at home and learn their lessons from the assignments carried to them by older ones. The milk problem had been effectually solved by the boys from the Hollow. With the packing and hardening of the snow the farmers joined in the operation, and the milk from the three big farms in the valley came in to the dairy as usual. The boys were paid for their services and the dairy took over the distribution except to out of the way places. Food and other supplies were being dropped regularly. After the second day the mail also came. Later a "lift" was arranged that mail might be taken out. It was a happy day for Uncle Dick when he was told that even the back numbers of the *Advocate* were on their way.

In the Harding household Uncle Dick had been moved to the little bedroom off the kitchen where the big range, supplemented by the oil stove, provided sufficient heat for his safety. Mrs. Harding slept on the couch in the dining room that she might be near her patient. The other members of the household had to sleep in bedrooms upstairs, rooms so cold that they were habitually called igloos.

Each night they went shiveringly up to the frigid rooms carrying bricks that had been heated thoroughly in the oven and wrapped in any available old woolen garment. Neil joined this parade without protest, thinking that as well as thanking God that the supply of oil was enough to insure comfort for Uncle Dick for many weeks, they should add to this their gratitude for the supply of bricks.

The January thaw arrived on the last week of the month, and the snow began to disappear on the exposed places where the high winds had blown it off before it could harden. But in the cut where it had drifted to a depth of many feet and was mixed with the rocks that had fallen, the problem was an appalling one. Every day groups would climb to the hilltop overlooking the cut and watch, through fieldglasses, the workers below. On either side of the laborers the cliffs rose forbiddingly. These marked the line where the great glacier that had once covered this part of the state had met the warm air from the south and given up its onward march. It had melted, leaving a barrier of gigantic rocks at the valley's entrance. It was through the only break in this barrier that settlers had come to the pleasant valley and that the highway and railroad had reached the town.

Neil thought later, in trying to assess the damage, that his own loss might not be evident and certainly couldn't be counted with the tangibles, but to him it was very real. The night for his meeting with Jane had come and gone and he had been unable to get word to her. He had thought of asking B. Franklin to meet her and explain. But B.'s gift for joking might not lend itself to helping the situation. The best way would be to write her when she had reached home. Maybe she had already written him. There would be a letter waiting for him when he got back to the city. Perhaps he could arrange to visit her soon. After all, it *was* rather funny. Jane never made any allowances for natural disasters, and she had been sure that she would get the right leading and be ready to follow it after she had met him. Let Miss Jane wait awhile. But, oh, how he wished that he had met her and that they were even now planning their marriage!

The work on the Gap was discouragingly slow. The pass was so narrow that the huge rotary plows had no place to throw the snow, and it had to be hauled out by truck. When the area of the slide was reached it became more difficult, for the rocks brought down by the blasting and the slide could not be handled except by power shovels, and the still threatening walls had to be watched closely and appraised for safety with each thrust of the giant scoops. State engineers were on the job, assisted by experts from the railroad, even into the night hours when the work went on by aid of floodlights. Each time the workers returned from the hilltop, however, they had reports of progress, and the spirits of the beleaguered village began to lift. Help might be slow in coming, but it was on the way.

8

ON THE DAY when the linemen came scrambling over the last big drifts, bringing with them the equipment for repairing the telephone and electric lines, there was rejoicing on every side.

"Won't it be great to have the furnace and the power press running again?" said Marv with a tired sigh.

"And wonderful to be able to talk to folks again!" cried Lissa.

"To talk to folks again? Will you tell me what you *have* been doing all this while?"

"Very funny! Very, very funny! Well, I'll tell you. I've been out tramping the snowy streets, wading in ten foot drifts, risking my neck on slippery slides, and listening. *Listening,* I said. Not talking. All for the sake of getting news for your grubby little paper. And when it goes out do I get any thanks? No. Nobody thinks about the person who really does the work around here!"

"Help, help! I give up. You do it all. But don't forget that I'm the engineer and without me you can't run — nor walk. Just talk."

Marv dodged as Lissa shot a barrage of paper clips in his

direction, then ran downstairs to work again on the old press for what he hoped would be the last time. The linemen had assured him that by tomorrow night the electric power would be back.

Neil had been watching the two in amusement. Their badinage had helped greatly to lighten the atmosphere around the office during the tense days just past, and had sent many a worried townsman or woman back to his home with a smile. Surely things couldn't be *too* bad when Lissa Harding and Marv Stebbins could keep up their wrangling.

The door opened to admit an excited high school youth. "They got through a half hour ago, and the train's coming in tomorrow night, on time."

As the next afternoon drew to a close the station was crowded with those who felt that the occasion deserved their attention and attendance. They came until the platform was full and men and boys were perched on the fence along the tracks. Marv had locked the office with the excuse that he had to get some pictures and he knew the others would desert the ship if he left. The only persons who missed it were the ones who were too ill to be up, or who had to care for the sick. Neil wondered if even a visit by the president would have called out such a crowd. He thought that his days of newsgathering had brought him in contact with most of the residents but he realized his mistake, for the larger number were strangers to him. One couple interested him especially because they, too, seemed not to be integrated in the community. He was a man of middle age who looked like any prosperous business man might. She was a strikingly beautiful woman. Many greeted them in friendly fashion, indicating they were well known and liked, but no one stopped to chat or exchange pleasantries. Neil watched them for a few minutes and decided that he must ask Marv about them. Such personages could be profitably used to add human interest to the story he intended to send in to the *Ledger* tonight. That story would be a real scoop, and would mark his return to his old life. When the train pulled out tomorrow Neil Abbott would be on it!

The excited squeal of Ruth Harding and the whoop of

Pug alerted the crowd to the smoke rising just around the bend. When the train came into view Neil was torn between his desire to wave and cheer with the rest and the urgency of getting into his notebook the reactions of the crowd.

"It must have been some such scene as this that greeted the first string of cars that came down this track," he thought.

The train was coming slowly, moving cautiously over the track that had been subjected to unusual strain and moisture. Heads could be seen at the windows, and hats and hands waved to the waiting crowd. The first person off was the governor, followed by some railroad officials. Mr. Rossiter, with Terry and B. Franklin close behind him, was smiling and greeting them all. Then came the engineers whose wisdom and skill had made the rescue possible, then the work crews and even the drivers of the trucks.

Neil had been busy with his camera, regretting that he had only the small one he had used at the house party, but when he saw Ben and Terry he gave a whoop of delight.

"Oh, you camera boys! Get busy and get everything. I've got the story here. You take the pictures."

"We're already busy," said B. "Terry has been at the Gap taking pictures all week, but I've just got the prize of them all. I've just snapped a doozy of the *Ledger's* dumb reporter, the hero of the strip, the little boy that missed his train!"

Neil grabbed for the camera, but B. stepped out of reach, and he found himself almost catapulted into the arms of Mr. Rossiter who was talking to the governor.

"The very chap I want to see. Governor, this is the reporter I've been telling you about. When we first missed him we thought he had been thrown off the train or been kidnaped. Then word came that he had climbed off the train after once being on, and just let it go off without him. He's been marooned in this place trying to prove to the world and himself that he can run a newspaper. Do you care to meet such a chap?"

"I certainly do," and the governor reached for Neil's hand and pumped it vigorously. "We've been hearing all about you from that ham radio friend of yours, and although you couldn't hear us we've been cheering you on. You and all the plucky folks here.''

"They're the ones who deserve the cheers." As the governor turned to greet the couple who had interested Neil previously, he asked Mr. Rossiter self-consciously,

"What I'm concerned about just now, sir, is whether or not I still have a job."

"We'll try to fit you in some place. Maybe as a relief janitor. Maybe as assistant editor. You seem to have varied talents. But what I'm concerned about is Dick's condition. How is he?''

"Not very well, I guess. He wanted to come today, but couldn't. He hasn't been out since you were here last. The doctor doesn't seem very happy about him.''

"While the rest of these guests hang around and compliment themselves and each other over their achievement and take pictures of every snowdrift in sight, I'll go out to see Dick.''

"I'm afraid the road isn't cleared for a car yet."

"Who wants a car? I was using snowshoes when you were learning to ride a kiddy car. I can take to them again if the going gets too heavy for me. I'll be seeing you after I've talked to Dick.''

"Ready for your confession?" he asked later that evening after the dinner Neil had shared with the governor's party in the private car on the side track. "Let these other young blades go out and see the night spots of the town. I want to talk to you.''

Neil approached the interview with trepidation. Mr. Rossiter's tone was casual, neither dispelling nor confirming the fear he felt. Knowing his employer's strong convictions on the subject of responsibility and promptness, he could hardly imagine him doing other than disapprove of the carelessness that had brought about this situation. He sat waiting silently for the blow.

"You're a crazy irresponsible fellow, aren't you?"

"Yes, sir.''

"In all my days I never heard of anything so brainless. I saw you get on the train. I saw you put your luggage in the rack and settle down as if you intended to go back to sleep. I *counted* you before we left, and you were there! Then we got to The Falls and found a message that you'd been left behind. How did you manage it? A girl?"

"Nothing of the sort. Here's the story. It isn't creditable, but it's true."

When the story was finished Mr. Rossiter grunted. He made only one comment.

"Well, you managed to land in quite a bed of trouble. What are you going to do now?"

"I'd — I'd like to go back to the *Ledger*."

"I suspected as much. And for the sake of your self-respect I'll tell you that I'd like to have you. But that isn't the way it's going to work out."

"I'm sorry, sir. I've liked working for you and — "

"You'll still be working for me. You are going to stay here and work on the *Advocate*."

"Oh, no!"

"Oh, yes! It will be a long time before Dick is able to carry on — if ever. He's almost twenty years older than I, and has never been strong. He did a lot for me as a kid, and I'm going to see that he's happy now. The little paper is his life. He loves it. He loves the community. One of our ancestors was the first white man in the valley. There's always been one of us here and we've had the paper for almost all that time. I had hoped there'd always be one of us to run it, but Dick never married, and I don't think my kids would be interested."

He sighed and was silent a minute before he went on.

"You've seen how shut away the valley is. Even in summer the only entrance is through the Gap, and we're almost a world of our own. We've been able to hang onto the customs and habits of a healthier age. The *Advocate* has a reputation that reaches far. Folks like its provincialism, its back country language, its clingings to the old traditions that the world in general has dropped along the wayside. Dick has

60

saved all of these. I don't want them changed. I want the paper to come out every Tuesday and Friday as long as the valley lasts. You're to keep it rolling until someone else takes over."

"When will that be? Forever? I do want to help. I love Uncle Dick and the other folks here. They've been mighty good to me. But I want to go back to the city. There's surely someone else who can do it better. I'm no small town chap. I belong in the city."

"What are you going to do there?"

Neil caught the implication of the question, and his heart sank in quick foreboding.

"I had hoped to go back on the *Ledger*."

"Well, I'm not going to force you. And I won't fire you. You're a valuable man with promise for the years ahead. I am asking you to stay here, however. I know it will be a sacrifice on your part. But Dick has taken a fancy to you. He needs you. You've already made a place in the community. Dick has been telling me all about it. You can do the job better than anyone else we can find. I'll see that you get your salary regularly and you'll not lose anything in the long run. Dick may not live long, and we'll probably have to sell then to someone with a different idea. I made my choice long ago and could never fit in here again even if I wanted to. Terry is all that's left and what he will be is anyone's guess. But I'm afraid it won't be anything that's worth much to the world. I'm asking you to stay and help Dick out. I'm not forcing it though. Think it over tonight and let me know in the morning."

As Neil swung off the steps of the governor's car, Terry stepped from the shadows.

"I'm going out with you. I called Mrs. Harding and she said that your bed would hold two in a pinch. So I'm spending the night with you. B. knows about it and will explain if Dad asks any questions. Okay?"

"It seems to be arranged, so it will have to be okay. What do you have up your sleeve?"

"I want a chance to talk to Uncle Dick. He's my favorite

relative. Mrs. Harding says he won't go to sleep until he sees me, so I'm dropping in for a few minutes. Then I'm spending the rest of the night briefing you on an idea I have. It's a good one and you'd better be prepared to approve. It's the last hope of a dying generation.''

It was not literally the rest of the night that Terry talked, but it was so long that Neil had no time to think of his own problem at all. And when Terry had finished, the problem existed no longer. The decision had been made.

They went into town very early the next morning for Mr. Rossiter would be waiting for the decision, and Neil anticipated a discussion that might be lengthy. Terry joined B. in a last minute hunt for pictures, while Neil joined Mr. Rossiter in the lounge.

"Well, you're early! What's the decision?"

"That depends on you."

"On me? What do you mean?"

"I want to make a bargain with you."

"Holding me up for a raise, I suppose."

"Nothing of the sort. I'll stay here and carry on for an indefinite period, as long as Uncle Dick needs me. On your part you are to quit working on Terry about the *Ledger*. I had a long chat with him last night, and I wish you'd get him to talk to you as he did to me. He's afraid of you, sir. He does want to please you, but he hates the city. He told me about his mother's brother, and he's afraid that if he goes into the life of a reporter in the city he'll wind up the same way. I can understand the temptations he would meet and I hope he gets out of it. He is another Uncle Dick in his love for this place and its traditions. He wants to finish his work and take over here. He has big plans for the old paper. He wants to make the historical sheet a national thing. No one has ever known it before, but he has written many of the articles for Uncle Dick. And he sends in big envelopes of notes and stories often. He has more source material available than Uncle Dick has. Think about it and talk to him, sir. If you agree I'll stay until he can take over.''

Mr. Rossiter had been gazing at him in astonishment.

When Neil finished he grasped his hand, and with tears dangerously close to brimming over, said, "I've been trying for years to get close to that lad. He's afraid of me and I'm afraid of him. I'll talk to him, and if it turns out as you think, you can come in and take over the place I've been labeling for him, after you've done your stint here."

"Save that one for Ben Franklin. A son-in-law can inherit as well as a son, can't he?"

"Sure. I ought to know. But there will be a big place for you."

9

As HE WATCHED the train disappear around the bend, Neil's heart was heavy. He had enjoyed to a limited degree the enforced stay here, and he had grown to like his fellow workers and many others of his new friends. But not for a minute had he expected to stay here, and the sight of the cars growing smaller, with B. and Terry waving from the back platform, was a bitter sight.

He wished many times during the following days that he felt as happy over it as Uncle Dick, or even as Marv and Lissa did. To everyone else it seemed the ideal solution. To him it was a completely inexplicable situation which was to be borne with such grace as would not be a betrayal of the promise he had made to Mr. Rossiter. He would give nothing but his best to the task. His fellow workers should not know how he hated it. Only in his own room would he indulge in the despondency that was always within sight, just hiding in the shadow, ready to pop out at an opportunity.

"If I just had room enough for my desk and books and big brown chair. I suppose B. is having a picnic with that chair, and *I* paid for it. I'd send for the things, but where could I put them? I can hardly get between the bed and dresser now. And there's barely room for this one straight chair.''

Mrs. Harding must have sensed his unhappiness, for she stopped him one evening as he came in.

"Neil, I know that room can't be too comfortable, and I hadn't ever thought of renting it. I've just used it when the children were sick. For Uncle Dick's sake we want you to be close, but I didn't know how to solve it. Lissa came up with an idea last night that might be worth thinking about. Those old tourist cabins across the road are ours but we haven't operated them since my husband died. They are winterized and we used to do a good business with winter hunters. Now the boys have their den in one in the summer and the girls use another for a playhouse. The front one I've used only for storage. It's larger than the ordinary bedroom, and there's a small kitchen and smaller bath. We call it the guest house, but we don't have overnight guests often. We have plenty of furniture for it, and the boys could clear out the rest and put it in the attic. Do you think you could consider it?''

Her voice was anxious, and Neil realized that the strain of having a stranger in the house, coupled with the care of the sick man, must be a heavy burden for one already laden with family cares.

"I think that sounds great! I've been feeling that I was imposing on you good people, but Uncle Dick —''

"I know about Uncle Dick. We all spoil him, but we love him, and we don't want to worry him. He is very frail. If he wants you close to him, that's what we all must see to.''

"When can I look at the place?''

"Bud can take you now. The electricity and water are off, but Bud has an electric torch. If you decide to take it we can have it ready in a hurry.''

Feeling almost as great a thrill as if he were exploring a propective purchase, Neil examined the little cabin. Each moment his interest grew. The larger room would provide space for his desk, his radio and record player, a work table and the beloved big chair. Instead of the bed he would buy a studio couch which would serve for both bed and lounge.

He'd get a rug, too, and have his books and pictures sent on. The heater between the west windows ought to be sufficient for any weather.

"I like it! I'd like to get busy at fixing it up tonight. Can you put up with me a little longer until my things come from the city? I have almost everything I'll need, I'm sure," he said to Mrs. Harding later.

"You may stay until you're ready to go. We like to have you, but I know the little room is a dreary place. I ought to buy the bedding for this, though."

"No, indeed. I'll just write Ben to send mine along. We had all our own things back in the city except the big pieces of furniture. I see there are pans and dishes in the cupboard over there. I'd like to use them for the little cooking I do. I'll probably get my own breakfasts. Don't you worry about me. That cabin is going to be my house of dreams. What are you going to charge me?"

She looked embarrassed, as if she would have liked to tell him that the cabin would be free but was constrained by a need for the rent.

"Would ten dollars a month be all right?"

"It would not! That isn't enough to charge for a hen coop. Lissa, what do you think it's worth?"

"Twenty-five dollars a month — ten for the cabin and fifteen for the privilege of living across the road from us!"

"It's a deal!" He reached for his wallet.

"No!" cried Mrs. Harding in horror. "Lissa, you're awful! Why, I wouldn't think of taking so much for that kind of place."

"It's worth it to me."

The argument was ended by a mutual agreement that he should pay fifteen dollars and do any desired decorating himself.

"I'm eager to get it ready. I'll call B. tonight and tell him to ship the things, and I'll go shopping for my couch tomorrow. I like setting up housekeeping."

The process of furnishing the cabin and getting settled was stimulating enough to carry him through the next two weeks, but when the last book was on the shelves and the last picture hung, a mood of depression settled on his spirits.

"Here I am. But where am I? Is there any purpose in it all? I seem to have lost control somehow, and everyone else has his hand on the wheel."

Was this the result of his desire to find the answer to the questions the group had discussed that night last fall? Or was it the thing Jane had been talking about? Was a Christian supposed to be led around by a blind sort of chance and call it the Spirit's leading? What would Jane say? And where was she now? Probably having a real time with her friends, and too busy to even send a postcard. He would show her!

He did not have the opportunity to put his plan into action, however. The desired message came from Jane — not a mere postcard, but a letter that looked, even from the outside, as if it held a promise of reward for the long wait. He put it in his pocket where it gave a reassuring feeling of anticipation to his day. Such a letter could not be read except in the privacy of his own room. The day, which was a cloudy one with a raw east wind, became to him so bright that Marv, who had brought the letter, wondered aloud what the reading of it would do for him if its mere receipt held so much happiness.

He was more glad than he could express that he had saved reading until he was alone, for when he had finished he sat in the darkness of his little cabin and tried to realize what had happened to his life. He had turned out the light lest Bud and Pug decide to pay him one of their frequent visits. The letter lay on the floor where he had dropped it when his hands had become slack and could not hold it. He did not want ever to touch it again except to burn it. He wondered bitterly if he would have to make a bonfire in the road to dispose of it, for an oil burner was not designed as a rubbish incinerator. Blizzards that brought out old ranges and wood stoves had something in their favor after all. Well, oil stove or not, he would get rid of that letter, and as he watched it burn he would erase all thought of Jane Barr from his mind forever.

It hadn't been an unkind letter at all. He had to admit

that. It had just been completely foolish and completely final, although she hoped he would think kindly of her and some day they might meet again in mutual understanding.

"Not if I can help it," he muttered as, long after midnight, he wearily picked up the letter and put it in the wastebasket. "No, I don't want to see you, Janie. Somewhere along the way our paths parted. I wonder if I will ever know just what did it."

He threw himself into the work at the office, determined that the others there should have no chance to note his depression and comment on it. He needed not have worried on that score, for each seemed engrossed in his own affairs. The gay spirit of the days of isolation from the world had vanished. Marv was having dental work done and was in no mood to be concerned about another's troubles, while Lissa had lost the happy energy that had carried her through the grueling days of January, and was so moody that it was a relief when she went out on a news-gathering tour of the town.

What a bunch of little sunbeams we are, thought Neil one afternoon as he was preparing the papers to go out with the mail next day. *I know my trouble, and anyone can explain Marv's grouch, but what's ailing her? She has nothing to worry about.*

Lissa was troubled, but her friends could not help when they could not understand. It was apparent to Neil who kept up his daily visits to the Harding home, that the mother was concerned but as much in the dark as the rest of them. She inquired if anything had happened at the office to cause her daughter distress, and shook her head in perplexity at the negative answer. Lissa tried very obviously to throw off her despondency when at home, but the mother eye saw through the attempt.

On a day in March while Lissa worked on subscriptions and Neil was laboring over an editorial which Uncle Dick had suggested, a large car stopped in front of the office. Lissa saw it first, and without making a comment, left her desk and joined Marv in the shop. Neil rose to his feet as the door opened, and found himself facing the man who had attracted his attention at the station the day the train came in with the triumphant workers.

"May I help you? I'm Neil Abbott. I've been asked to help out here while Mr. Richardson is ill."

"I've heard about you, even before Harry Rossiter told me of the occurrence that brought you to us just in time to aid in our emergency. My son came home every day with reports of your doings."

"Your son?"

"Yes, Howie Winchester. I'm Howard Winchester, Senior. Dick called the other night and asked me to get him some information about a couple of bills that are coming up in the legislature. Can you take him these papers? I'm short on time and can't get out there today."

"I'll be glad to take them. And I'm happy to have met you. If your son is the handsome young chap who loved to wield a snow shovel better than he liked going to school, I remember him well."

"I'm sure you do," laughed the father. "Those boys thought it great fun to pile that snow up to the top of the doors of the high school, didn't they? But it wasn't quite so funny when they had to shovel it all away again. Well, I must be going. My wife is outside and is getting impatient. I told her I'd be only a minute."

As the car drove away Neil had only time for a glimpse of the beautiful lady inside. He thought he had never seen a more beautiful face, nor a sadder one. Lissa came back and worked more industriously than before on her books. Her cheeks were unnaturally red and her eyes overbright. On her lips, in place of the usual impish smile, there was a twist of bitterness. For the rest of the afternoon the only sounds in the office were the tapping of the typewriters and the hum of the press as Marv ran an order of sale bills for a farmer.

As the spring days grew warmer and the last of the heavy snow could barely be seen in distant hollows, the atmosphere of the office changed. Lissa's trouble had apparently been overcome or filed away for a more convenient time for worry. Uncle Dick got the doctor's permission to spend an hour a day out of doors, so, bundled in overshoes, muffler and heavy coat he was taken for a drive by either Lissa or Neil. While they gathered news he happily greeted his old friends, and received such a welcome as one might expect for a dignitary of the realm. To Lissa it was just what should have been expected. To Neil it was a revelation of love, and a lesson in human relations. No wonder the little paper was queer! You just couldn't handle the news gathered from friends like these in the impersonal manner of the *Ledger*. Speaking of the fourth estate couldn't explain the *Advocate* at all. There must be a fifth estate!

Neil accepted the friendship of these people as it was offered him, with a growing wonder. It was different from his friendships in the city. After years there his circle of friends was limited to a few very choice companions on the *Ledger* staff, and the group at the church. True, there were many on the staff who knew him casually, but they knew little and cared less about his life outside of working hours. In this valley it appeared that he was known by every resident, and their interest in him was, he knew, not an evidence of idle curiosity, but of real regard. He soon knew their names and most of their problems. Occasionally he saw Uncle Dick give just the assistance that was needed and, as the weeks passed, he found himself sharing the problems and giving, when he could, the encouragement or tangible help that meant more than they could often express. He would not admit that he was enjoying the role into which he had been cast, but it gave him a weariness of body and a peace of soul that sent him to bed each night to sleep rather than brood.

That this was for the best was shown to him the day the big envelope that could be nothing but an invitation of some sort, came to him. He left the opening of it until he was alone in his cabin and there, with no curious eyes to see, read the announcement of the marriage of Jane Olivia Barr to Gregory Rowe Lowrey. He stared in unbelieving amazement.

"Oh, no! Not Greg the Grind! What can she see in him? What's he got that I haven't? Janie, how could you?"

He spent a few bitter hours realizing that he had not accepted her letter as final but had been clinging to a thread of hope. Now that was severed and he must forget it. At midnight he took a large picture and an envelope of snapshots from his desk and dropped them into the wastebasket. In the morning he would have a splendid bonfire behind the cabin. "So ends the story of Janie!" he mumbled as he sleepily drew up the covers.

10

HAVING DISMISSED JANE from his life and having nothing to fill the gap, Neil gave more of himself to the *Advocate*. After all, it was here, something to be conquered before he could go on to bigger campaigns. It could stand a lot of improvement, and that must be the reason he was sent here if one could believe the proponents of the idea that all things were directed for good.

"Surely for such a day as this I came into the kingdom," he repeatedly sarcastically. "Today begins a new day for the *Advocate*."

"Printer man," he said to Marv, "doesn't this paper ever change its ads, its set-up, its layout, or what have you? There hasn't been a new ad except in the classifieds since I came. Don't we ever get any new ones? I asked Uncle Dick about it once and he said for me to wait until he was back before thinking of such things. But he's back for a while every day now, and everything stays just the same. What gives?"

"We like it the way it is. Just remember that you're not working on the *Ledger:* Remember also, that the *Advocate* was an institution when you were in rompers or whatever you

72

wore in your infancy. You can find plenty of *Ledgers* and their like in the country, but there's only one *Advocate*. Its popularity lies in its uniqueness, its difference from the *Ledger,* if you will. It clings to the old ways as well as the old standards of moral uprightness in personal and civic life. And after you've been here long enough to get the reactions to Uncle Dick's human interest historical articles, you may change your ideas rather than the *Advocate.*"

"The lecture is free," said Lissa from her desk, "but we're taking a collection for the Fund for the Education of Overly Confident Young Newsmen. Drop your greenbacks in the secretary's basket."

"You're both mighty cute. But I still insist the people of this town need an up-to-date paper. They're just like other folks and they need to know more of the world than they can learn through this antiquated sheet. As a museum piece it's fine. As a newspaper it — well, it just isn't!"

"Oh, we get other papers. Why don't you go over to the post office and watch the sorting some day? Almost every family gets a copy of the *Capital Star* or the *Ledger.* We get about mentally even if we do stick close to our valley."

"Our paper has a personal touch the others lack," said Lissa as she turned from the phone and tossed a piece of paper on Neil's desk. "Can you imagine the *Ledger* printing an item like that? Of course not. But it's news here."

"Oh, no!" with a groan Neil looked at her. "Twin calves! Well, who cares? And we don't have cows in the *Ledger* stable so how could we be expected to have twin calves."

"We care here. Jim Haddon borrowed money from the bank to buy that cow, and she is paying him mighty good interest in those calves. He's just getting a start and we'll all be glad for him. We wouldn't think of leaving it out. Everybody wants to know it."

"All right. But what are you going to leave out? I told you not to bring in any more news."

"I didn't bring it in. It came on the phone. And leave out

Mother's iris. I just used them for a filler that I could take out if a really important item came in."

"Just as you say, folks. It's your paper, not mine. I wish I could carry a banner across the top of the front page disclaiming any responsibility for it. Or better yet, I wish I had never come to that house party last winter. Life has never been the same since."

Lissa's answer made him meekly ashamed of his outburst. "Many of us here in Appleboro have often thanked God that you did come. We think He sent you."

After this sermon and rebuke he tried to keep to himself his regrets and gave himself wholeheartedly to his task. Determining to become a part of the community upon which he had been so unceremoniously "dumped," he attended the village meetings and tried to feel a sympathetic interest in its business. He played baseball with the young businessmen, and found in the group a few congenial friends. He visited Ed at the lake and was surprised at the extent of the project of preparing for summer guests. He became a faithful attendant at the church on the corner of the square, and joined the class of young people taught by Mr. Horne.

As the days grew warm enough for the ground to be tilled, he liked to watch Mrs. Harding in her flower garden. All day long she was busy at other things, in the house where her many duties gave little chance for thought of her own pleasure, or in the vegetable garden where she supervised the efforts of Bud and Pug. The evenings, however, were her own, and often she could be seen at work there while the children played on the lawn and Uncle Dick sat on a bench at the garden's edge.

"She's an artist," said Neil one Sunday afternoon as he sat with Uncle Dick and looked across the garden where tulips and iris were a blaze of color, and where the lilac scent made the air so heavy with sweetness that it seemed almost more than one could bear.

"Grace Harding is a remarkable woman, any way you look at it," answered Uncle Dick almost belligerently. "Don't ever let anyone tell you otherwise. She's one of

God's rare saints, and I hope to be on hand when she gets her crown up yonder. I just want to add my Amen to everything the Lord says when He awards it."

"I'm admiring her arrangement of those flowers. It must take a fine imagination and a great knowledge of flowers to be able to plan and plant so far ahead that the right colors and types of flowers will be blooming together and setting off each other's beauty as those tulips and iris do."

"Yes, they have to be fed and watered and *loved*. Grace has done all that in good measure. Those flowers have been watered in years past with the tears of a heartsick and shamed woman, and nourished with the prayers she sent to the Throne as she dug and weeded and strove to find grace to go out and smile again at a world that had frowned on her."

His voice had been rising, and Neil wondered how he could halt this emotional display that could not but be harmful to the frail old man. Before he could speak, however, Uncle Dick arose.

"Forget what I said, my boy. Please forget it. I'm tired and not quite responsible. I'd better go in now and go to bed. I want one of you to drive me out to the Hollow tomorrow. The boys out there are troubling me a bit. Will you help me up the stairs? And don't intrude on Grace when she's in the garden. The Lord is with her there and they'd rather be left alone."

Forgetting the remarks of the old man was not easy, for they had wakened his interest in this family. The mother, "one of God's rare saints" as Uncle Dick had called her, was a source of amazement to him as he observed the prodigious amount of work that she managed. He became increasingly aware of the tender love between her and Lissa, a love that seemed deeper and stronger and more understanding than existed between her and the other children.

One day when Bud and Pug had taken their loads of *Advocates* to deliver, their report cards were left lying on Neil's desk. Picking them up to place with their books, he noticed that they were made out for Wallace Duncan and Louis Sheehan.

75

"Hey, what's this?" he asked Marv. "Aren't these Bud's and Pug's cards?"

"Yes, why? Oh, the names. Those are their real names, though folks always call them Harding. Why look so startled? Didn't you know those kids, all five of them, are foster children? They're not related to Mrs. Harding or even to each other in any way. They're wards of the state, and she's paid to care for them. They get pretty good value for their money, don't you think?

"I surely do. I never dreamed that they weren't her own. I can see now why she and Lissa are so close. Lissa is all that's really her own. How long has Mr. Harding been dead?"

"I don't know. I've been here over eight years and he was dead before I came. His death was accidental, something to do with a farm machine of some sort. That's all I know about it. Uncle Dick could tell you more. He is related in some way, a cousin to Lissa's grandmother, I think."

That evening when Neil went across the road to talk over the day's business with Uncle Dick, he observed more closely than before the five children who had been taken into the home and heart of this woman. There could be no doubt that all had been given a happy and normal home, probably a better one than they could ever have known before. Here they were cared for and loved in an atmosphere that enabled them to develop as God meant that they should. The boys were normal adolescents, careless, noisy, ofttimes lazy. But they were obedient and good-natured, showing signs of a growing sense of responsibility. They would go out from here prepared to make their ways through life.

"If I get a chance I'll tell them how I got my education on my own," he resolved. "Maybe it will help them."

The girls, about seven, nine and twelve years of age, were happy and unspoiled, inclined to petty quarrels, but showing in their manners and speech the effects of a refined home atmosphere. Neil, while he waited for the drink of hot milk and crackers that Lissa was preparing for Uncle Dick's bedtime snack, found his eyes following Mrs. Harding as she moved about the room. She bent over Pug's shoulder to help him with a difficult algebra problem, then encouraged Bud to try again on a diagram for science class that would not come right. She stopped to give June some instructions in the use of the dictionary, to hear Ruth recite a poem, and to correct René's hand position as she toiled at a page of writing. Then her eyes lifted to Lissa preparing the tray. The girl seemed to feel the gaze, for she turned and smiled in a way that made Neil wish that in his life there had been someone with whom he felt in such accord as existed between these two. He took the tray and went to Uncle Dick, wishing as he listened to the old man that there were someone to greet him in the cabin across the road.

As he lay waiting for sleep the thought of the woman stayed with him. What an unusual woman she was! She was probably not over forty-five years old, slim and graceful as a girl. She was not beautiful, if one thought of such beauty as Mrs. Howard Winchester possessed. But Grace Harding had another quality that was a more noble attribute than mere facial beauty. She was handsome, with her heavy straight hair wound in braids about her head, and she carried her shoulders thrown back, her back straight, as if to be ready at any time to add to the burdens already there.

"Nothing can reach through that peace to trouble her," he thought. "It isn't because she hasn't known trouble. She has lost her husband who Uncle Dick says was one of the finest men he ever knew; she has been shamed and has shed heartsick tears as she walked in the garden with the Lord. Why should she ever have been shamed? Who could see her as anything but noble? She works like a slave and never goes out except to market and church. She seems to have no close friends. But she has all that is required for peace of soul, which is more than most of us can say."

Later when he learned her story it increased his wonder.

11

UNCLE DICK'S CONCERN about the boys who lived in the Hollow spread to others in the last weeks of the school term. The resort on the lake ten miles away was preparing to open and the area hummed with a degree of activity that gave promise of a busy summer. In this activity Bill Banning and his pals, the same crew that had given immeasurable help by running the "milk train" during the days of the emergency, contributed more than their share. They had two old cars they had built from parts assembled from various wrecks and junk yards, and during the evenings the cars, loaded with boys, seemed to be everywhere on the highways. They managed to keep inside the law as far as Mr. Horne, who was still trying to find a point of contact with them, could determine. They did however, manage to make complete nuisances of themselves, according to some of their critics.

Across the lake from the resort lay the swamp which as yet had never been conquered by man. But what man had failed to do these boys had ventured. In its depths they had found an island that could be reached by those agile enough to progress by leaping from tussock to tussock, and in places swinging from one tree to another. Here they established their headquarters and built a shack. What went on in its shelter, one could not discover and dreaded to guess.

Reports of trouble began to come in from the half dozen dairy farms, and from the small fruit and garden farms among the hills. Chickens and eggs were missed from the coops and fruit from the orchards. Sometimes the cows would have been milked when they came into the barn at night. Tires were punctured on cars and gas siphoned out. Everyone felt sure that the Bushwhackers, as they called themselves, were the miscreants, but no one had ever seen them in the vicinity of the happenings.

There had been several heated discussions about the Bushwhackers in the *Advocate* office, and Mr. Horne had mentioned them several times in conversation with Neil, who found himself thinking about them with growing concern.

One evening the lights of a car turning into the drive aroused him from a reverie, and he opened the screen door as Mr. Horne stepped up onto the little porch.

"Come in, friend. Never was guest so welcome. I'm so bored I was just wondering if I could challenge the youngest Harding girl to a game of jacks. Sit here where you can hear the music of my private brook, and try to forget that I didn't go to church last Sunday morning."

"I'm not here to chastise you for neglecting church. Anyway, I happen to know that you sat with the Stebbins' sick boy so that they could both go. No, I came tonight on a different errand. I came to ask you to take a class in the church school."

"What kind of class? You said boys, didn't you? How old? Kindergarteners or deacons?"

"A class that is as yet nonexistent. Its life depends on you."

"On me? How come?"

"I've persuaded Bill to bring his gang in from the Hollow if we will keep them in a class to themselves and if we will have you teach them."

"Where did they get such an idea?"

"They liked you when you helped them with their 'milk

79

train.' Bill says he would have never offered to help that time if he had not seen you with Marv delivering papers that first night. Said if a stranger could pitch in that way he thought they should also. Then when they did come he says you treated them as if they were just as much a part of things as anyone else.''

"They were. A mighty important part, if you believe me. I think anyone who has a baby who got that milk knows that.''

"They ought to, but memories are pretty short. On this mild May evening last winter's blizzard seems a hazy occurrence. Since the gas thefts, tire damages, and troubles on the farms, the Bushwhackers are in pretty bad repute. Will you make an effort to help them?''

"Where are you going to find a meeting place for such a class?''

"Here's my idea. For the present it won't be a Sunday class. We don't have a classroom for them. I think they'd rather come at night anyway. They'd be willing to come to my place. We've had them in for hot dogs and cokes twice when they were helping me fix a playground for the little folks in the Hollow. They are fairly friendly with our Don. We have a room in our basement; the old coal bin is empty since we changed to gas heat. It can be made into a good meeting place. I think the boys would be glad to do the work if we pay for the materials. We could line it with wallboard, paint it, put up curtains at the window, and get a linoleum rug to cover the cement floor. There's an outside entrance, so the boys wouldn't be embarrassed by having to come through our house. Now, I've told you everything. Come across and relieve my suspense. Will you do it? Thank you. I'm sure you will.''

Neil laughed. "You haven't left much room for refusal, have you?''

"I didn't intend to. If somebody doesn't do something about those boys soon there's going to be real trouble. They aren't bad. I don't know why they aren't accepted by the town people, or why they carry such big chips on their shoulders. But I do know that they need help, and I think God sent you here to help them."

"Uncle Dick says He sent me here to run the paper while he was sick. Now you're saying this is the cause for which I came to this part of the kingdom."

"Maybe you came for both."

They sat listening to the purl of the brook as it flowed over the rocks below the window. Twilight had faded, but the full moon was so bright that Neil turned out the light that they might better enjoy the charm of the night. They talked of many things, some pertaining to Mr. Horne's work, some to Neil's life in the city. Before he realized it he was telling of his days as a reporter in Juvenile Court and the longing he had to do something to help the lads who passed through its doors, some to a new effort at good citizenship, but all too many back to the old temptations and failures.

"What made you so interested in them in the first place? Your assignment to the court?"

"Yes and no. The real beginning was longer ago than that. You see I was a ward of that court once myself."

"You?"

"Yes, I. When I was three my mother died very suddenly. No one knew anything about my father, so I was taken to the Detention Home. A reporter from the *Ledger* took my picture and wrote quite a story about me — the little boy whose only possession was a name. They hoped the story and picture would bring forth some relative. But none appeared. I did get foster parents who later adopted me. They gave me all that any parents could of affection and careful training. Both are dead now, but I've never forgotten their kindness or the things they taught me. I have the clipping of the story and picture. All my life I've wanted to write something like that, a story that would stir someone to something for another boy who needed it."

"That's a good story in itself. Some day you may write it up and find it effective in helping another lad."

"I don't worry much about the *little* chaps anymore. Plenty of people want them. The ones I can't forget are the teenagers, the ones who got a bad start somehow and now can't get back on the right track even if they want to — the kids like the Bushwhackers whom no one likes."

Mr. Horne laughed delightedly. "Caught in your own trap, my friend! Now I know you won't refuse me. I'll expect you tomorrow night when I get the boys onto the job of cleaning up that coal bin."

Mr. Horne rose to go, and Neil walked to the car with him. The moonlight showed both faces sober.

"I'm going to be praying for you, Neil," said the minister with a parting handclasp, "that you will not only be a blessing to the Bushwhackers, but that you will find for yourself the thing your heart seeks." Neil watched until the car was lost in the distance.

"Now what did he mean?" he pondered. "How does he know what I want or what my life lacks? He couldn't have heard about Jane, and he certainly couldn't know my spiritual problems when I can't even formulate them myself. At that, I guess it won't hurt to have him praying for me. He's the kind of fellow I like to have on my team."

12

By the time he had slept on the idea Neil thought of at least a dozen good reasons why he should have refused Mr. Horne's request. One of these would have to be considered seriously. That was the possibility that he might soon be recalled to the city. There was no excuse for him to be exiled here any longer. Any day might bring release. This thought so lightened his heart that he was whistling happily as he went down the drive to where Lissa waited in Uncle Dick's little car.

"Why so happy? Did you dream of her last night?"

"You're the only her in my life."

"What pleasure it gives me to be the only woman in the life of a man who never looks at any of them."

"I've looked at you and decided that if I had a little sister I'd want her to be just like you."

"The old line. 'I want you for a sister.' Don't you know a better one than that?"

"No. That's the only line for me and any girl. I thought I had another one once, but the fish went off with the bait and line both. I have nothing left."

She gave him a sidelong look even while seeming to

keep her eyes on her driving. His mood appeared to have changed, and the smile had been replaced by a frown. Impulsively she put out her hand.

"I'm sorry. I'm always blundering into things that aren't my business. I've made you feel badly. Want to talk about it, or am I just blundering farther? I'm a good listener, and I *can* keep my mouth shut even though Marv would never believe it. Don't talk if you don't want to. Just pretend I asked about the price of fat hogs."

"You're quite a little honey, you know. I really meant what I said about wishing I had a sister like you. If I *were* lucky enough to have such a sister I think I'd want to tell her about my troubles. But we'll be at the office soon and I don't want Marv to see me weeping on your shoulder."

"We aren't going to the office now. Mother is going to drive in to do some shopping and she'll take Uncle Dick in. Marv will call her if he gets tired before we get back. You and I are to go to Mendon, you to get the court records for the month, and I to go shopping. When you finish at the courthouse you are to go to the library and look up these items. Bring back the books you find them in. They're for the school article Uncle Dick is working on now. If you get through with all of that, come and help me shop."

"Fine. That should be great fun."

"I think so! I'm going to spend maybe one hundred dollars!"

"In Mendon? Why not help out the economy of Appleboro?"

"Appleboro is all right for ordinary occasions. But for extraordinary ones like a class reunion I shop at a *big* city. One where they have parking meters and elevators and three dime stores. A *real* city."

"And a dinky little courthouse, and a library that opens for four hours each day. Where is this wonderful reunion to be held?"

"In Pendleton Hall where they all are held."

"Pendleton Hall? Do you mean a *college* class? Did *you* go to college?"

84

"Why else should I go to a reunion? Are you surprised that the child of Grace and John Harding should be admitted to an accredited college?"

Her cheeks were blazing and her eyes filled with tears. She drew off the road and stopped the car.

"Now you are going to explain."

"I don't know what there is to explain," he protested. "I presume I owe you an apology but I'm afraid I don't know for what. I honestly never dreamed you were old enough to have gone through college. Is it an unforgivable sin to misjudge a gal's age even when you think her several years younger than she must be? How old are you anyway?"

"Twenty-five. I'm sorry, Neil," she said shamefacedly. "I truly am. If I could only remember to leave the chip off my shoulder when I dress! I'm always going about fighting windmills because I think they've attacked me."

He laughed at the sight of her woebegone little face, and spoke reassuringly. "I still don't have the dimmest idea how I offended, but let's table that discussion for a while. Did you really go to Marshall? That's my college!"

"I know it. You were a senior the year I was a freshman."

"How did you find that out?"

"Remembered it. You were editor of the *Green and Gold*. Everybody knew you. I used to almost swoon when you met me in the halls."

"I'm sure you did — *not*. I wish I had known you then. I'd have taken a good look at you, and maybe taken you to the Lookout."

"I worked there that year, and I spilled water once in Jane Barr's lap when she was with you. She was always with you and — Oh!" she stopped in dismay. "Neil, is *she* the girl that ran off with your fishing line, hook, sinker, pole and everything? I'm sorry. I should have kept my mouth closed, but I never do! I'm really sorry if I hurt you."

"You don't need to be sorry. I'm trying hard not to pity myself and I don't want anyone else feeling sad about it."

"But I *wanted* Jane to marry you. She was a wonderful

girl and I'm sure she's a beautiful woman. I used to try to be like her, so calm and sweet and gracious all the time. But I'd just be getting a good start and something would come along and raise my temperature, and I'd find myself acting just like Lissa Harding. I never have admired *her*."

"I admire her — tremendously. Someday I'll tell you more about her. She has some mighty fine characteristics."

"If you knew her as well as I do you might be ashamed to be seen riding with her. Let's talk about something else. Do you still want to talk?"

"Yes, I'll tell you about Jane. I've wanted to talk to someone about it. You probably know that everyone linked our names together at Marshall. I was crazy about her, and she admitted she liked me. I couldn't think of getting married after we graduated since I didn't have a thing to offer any girl but a lot of debts. I didn't even have much of a job. I wanted to be a newspaperman and I'd majored in journalism. But I couldn't get a job at first. I worked in insurance for six months and almost starved to death. Then I got on the *Ledger,* and I made good right from the start. But it's a long pull up from the very lowest step of the ladder and the pay wasn't enough to pay off the debts and support a wife at the same time. So we had to wait.

"We weren't engaged. We agreed that we'd be just friends and that each would feel free to date others. But we wrote often and neither of us dated anyone else often. I'd see her once a year on vacation and I thought everything was going fine. I realize now that we never had any time alone so I didn't have a chance to see how she was changing.

"I saw her at Commencement last year. Our class had a reunion then. The whole gang of us had a big time together and, although I realize now that Jane was awfully quiet, it didn't mean much to me then. She just seemed to me more desirable than ever, and I made up my mind that the next time I got a raise I'd ask her to marry me. I got the raise in September and wrote her. She answered right away but it wasn't what I expected. She didn't say no, but just that she didn't know. That was the first crazy idea. She wanted us to spend the next four months praying about whether we loved each other enough to get married! After all those years of waiting! Why wait so long to decide? It was just plain crazy!''

"Did she say that was what you were to pray about?"

"Well — not exactly. She said for us to find God's will about the matter. How can anyone judge God's will in such a case except by the feelings he has toward the other person? She wanted a sign of some sort, I suppose. It was all beyond me. It made me feel as if she doubted our love, or as if she thought I didn't measure up in some way. Jane didn't used to be so squeamish. She was a fine Christian girl, but she certainly didn't go around parading her piety like that. We had a fellow in the class, Greg the Grind we called him, who was afraid to make a decision at all without asking God's advice. He was a fine fellow, but I couldn't get his wave length. I wouldn't want to think Jane could be like that."

"Don't you believe in praying for guidance?"

"Sure. But not to the exclusion of the brain God gave me. My mother, the woman who raised me when I was left alone, used to tell me to pray each day for guidance for the day, and I've done it ever since. But I still say God expects me to go into that day and use my brain to make my own decisions."

"Don't be silly. Of course He expects you to use your brain. But brains are pretty tricky, too. Don't you think it would be advisable to put our brains also into His keeping?"

"Are you on Jane's side?"

"I'm on nobody's side. I want to hear the rest of the story."

"There isn't much. She suggested that I meet her on a certain date in January when she would be going through the city, and if we both felt then that God meant us to marry we would make definite plans. Maybe you know the answer to that. I was shut in here on that date and couldn't even get a message to her. When there was opportunity she wrote that she had been there and waited two hours. When she left she *knew*, she said, that she and I should not marry. God had

87

another and better plan for each of us she was sure. Apparently, she already had an idea what His plan for her was, for recently I got an announcement of her marriage to Gregory Lowrey, Greg the Grind, if you please. What do you think of that?''

"I still think Jane Barr was pretty much of a gal, and I'm sure she'll make just the right kind of wife for the kind of man Gregory Lowrey is!''

It took some time for him to digest this statement, then he questioned anxiously, "Will you explain that remark, please? Am I all wrong and you other folks way ahead of me in spiritual discernment? Why do you think Jane was right?''

"That's easy. If she hadn't had her doubts she wouldn't have hesitated when you asked her. 'In case of doubt or uncertainty, take the safe course.' And she hadn't decided even when she got to the city. She was probably pretty sure she didn't love you the way she should but didn't know how to meet the issue. When you didn't appear that, to her, was God's way of showing her. Probably she was asking for a guidepost of some sort. That was it, for her.''

"Completely crazy.''

"Maybe not. You hadn't really been together much since you graduated, and each of you had surely changed in that time. A college chum may not at all be the one a girl wants to tie to for life. I *know* that.''

"Sounds as if you had to meet the same issue yourself.''

"I did. And it hurt for a long time even though I knew I was right. He knows it now. I have a date to go to dinner with him and his wife the evening before the reunion.''

"I suppose you're hinting that some day I'll be dining with Mr. and Mrs. Lowrey and enjoying it.''

"Could be.''

"Couldn't be.''

"Time cures all. I'm serious when I say I believe you will one day thank Jane for saying no to you.''

"That'll be the day! Well, it's all water over the dam now. Jane has her Greg and I honestly hope they are happy. I couldn't stand to think of Janie unhappy. I'm trying to forget it all, and of course I will. But it is a bit hard to give up a dream that has been the sustaining motive of my life.''

''I hope it helps a bit to know that someone cares.''

''It does. Just don't say anything about it to anyone else, please. And thanks for everything. You're a real tonic.''

They rode along in silence until Neil broke the silence.

''Now that I've opened my heart to you, when do I get to asking questions? There are several that are waiting.''

''I can't think what they might be, but you may ask. *Maybe* I'll answer. Let's not start now, though. Mendon is just around this corner.''

''All right. We'll table Lissa. But on the way home—''

''It's a promise. I'll answer any questions I feel like answering.''

13

WHEN THEY WERE ready to start for home Neil got behind the wheel of the car.

"I'd better drive. You're going to be answering questions."

"If I feel like it. Remember?"

"Yes, only if you feel like it. First, why did you get angry when I was surprised that you'd been to college?"

She sat unanswering until a full mile had rolled behind them. When she spoke her voice was low. "I'm ashamed to answer that because I know now that you did it only because I'm unfortunately so childish-looking that you thought I couldn't be going to a college reunion. I should have known you'd never be casting a slur on me or on my family, but I'm so used to being defensive that I assumed you were challenging me to battle."

"I'm glad you know now that I didn't mean that. But why do you think you always have to be on the defensive? In all the weeks I've been here I've never seen any signs of an attack headed your way. Is it anything you can talk about?"

"Is that the truth, that no one has told you anything?"

"Anything about what? I've heard many nice things

said both about you and your work on the *Advocate*. But not one derogatory word."

"I don't mean about me. Folks have come to accept me. 'After all, the child isn't to blame.' I can hear them say it behind my back. But haven't you heard something about my mother?"

"Your mother? Of course not! What could I hear about her?"

"Think back. Think hard. Haven't you seen or heard something that puzzled you, something that you wanted explained?"

He shook his head, troubled by her words. He reviewed the weeks that he had spent in Appleboro. He went over every remembered contact with Mrs. Harding, every mention of her name from another's lips. Only one remark could hold a suggestion.

On one of the early mornings when the town was snowbound he had heard some of the women talking of the work of the mission circle in the church. An additional member was needed on the committee that had the task of corresponding with their missionaries. Mrs. Horne suggested Mrs. Harding. The work was something she could do at home, and her interest in the missionaries was deep. There had been a silence then, one that apparently puzzled Mrs. Horne as it did the listener. Then Mrs. Hunter spoke nervously.

"That's Mrs. Winchester's committee. It would be better if someone else were named."

He hadn't understood it then, but had forgotten it. Now it came back to trouble him. But knowing Lissa's moodiness when Mrs. Winchester was in the office he decided not to mention it. It couldn't mean anything.

"I can't think of a thing significant."

"I'll ask you another question then. Have you never wondered why my mother never goes any place except to church and shopping?"

"No, I haven't. She's so busy all the time that I assumed she didn't have time. If she doesn't go out socially I'm sure the loss belongs to society. She'd be an asset any place."

"Thank you! I'm very glad to have anyone appreciate my mother. I think she's the grandest woman on this earth, and I don't mean maybe!"

"I agree with you that she's something pretty special. But why the heat over it? Doesn't the world in general agree?"

"No. This little corner of the world probably considers her their black sheep, their horrible example, the girl who went wrong."

He stared at her in amazement. The thought of Mrs. Harding in such a role was so incongruous that it must be only a figment of Lissa's imagination. Probably she had misunderstood some careless bit of gossip or irresponsible remark, and because her mother did not have the time or money to take an active part in the town's social life, had thought it applied to her. There could be no real foundation for such a belief.

"I think you are going mildly insane," he said. "You don't know what you're saying. No one, and I mean *no one* could think anything wrong of your mother. She is the finest woman I ever met."

"We've already agreed on that. I've always known it. But there is something I have to tell Mother someday and ask her forgiveness. There was a time when I believed what folks said about her. I hope she'll forgive me. I never shall forgive myself."

"Can you give a little more light please? I don't want to be too inquisitive, but you have me dangling in a pretty uncertain position. I'm glad you came out of that belief. I can't see how you ever got into it."

"Neither can I. But the proof seemed irrefutable. I'll tell you if you will give me your solemn promise never to tell a soul."

"My lips are sealed."

Drawing a long breath, Lissa began. "Until I was about fourteen I never thought anything about the way we lived. My father was alive then and my grandmother lived with us. We had wonderful times together and I never thought to

92

wonder why we didn't go out much. One day I had ridden my bicycle to town and in turning a corner on the square I accidently collided with a woman and knocked a bundle out of her arms. I stopped to pick it up and she jerked it from me and called me a name. I knew it was an ugly word, but I had no idea of its meaning. I just stood there with the tears running down my face. Mrs. Sperry came past. You know her. She's president of the mission circle, and she's nice. She kissed me and I saw tears in her eyes.

" 'Try to forget what she said, honey. She has a lot of trouble of her own and it makes her sharp. Don't let yourself be hurt by what folks say. You're a dear girl.' I've never forgotten her kindness or the comfort of her kiss. Mrs. Sperry ranks high with me.

"When I got home I went to the dictionary and looked up the word. At fourteen I knew what being 'born out of wedlock' meant. I went out into the woods and stayed all afternoon crying by myself. I was determined not to let Daddy or Mother know what I'd heard, and I wasn't going to believe it. I couldn't forget it, however, and I knew I'd never be satisfied until I'd proved it was a lie."

She stopped as if waiting for more strength. Then she continued.

"One day when Mother and Daddy drove to Mendon and Grandma was asleep, I made a search. I knew where to look for I'd seen the folks put important papers in a certain drawer of Daddy's desk and then hang the key on the back of the kitchen cabinet. It didn't take me long to find the paper I wanted. It was my birth certificate and my parents were named, John Harding and Grace Lennon. There could be no mistake. It was my name and my birthday, and I knew Mother's name had been Lennon.

"Next I looked at their marriage certificate. They were married when I was six months old. Well," she drew a long breath, "that's the story. Folks in Appleboro can't help but know it because both lived here all their lives. They went to high school here. Everybody *must* know it."

"Now tell me the end of the story."

"What makes you think that isn't the end?"

"I know it isn't. You said there was a time when you believed the things folks said about your mother. I'm sure you don't believe them now. Come across with the rest of the story. Don't I deserve the explanation?"

"I don't know the explanation. I know that for all of my life my mother has borne the stigma of having done wrong. A year ago I stumbled onto the fact that my mother is just as pure and good and blameless as anyone could be. I *know* that, and I know who could prove it to this town if she would. But I haven't the least idea what the rest of the story is."

"How could you know so much and so little?"

"By hearing Mother talking to someone one day, someone whose sympathies are with another woman and who wants to give all the profits to that other woman while Mother carries the shame as she has done for twenty-five years."

"Did you know the woman who was talking?"

"Yes, but I don't know who the other woman is. Mother knows that I heard them that day, and she has made me promise I'll never tell. She cried when she begged that promise from me. I've only seen her cry twice. The other time was when they brought my father home after the accident. This time was worse because I'd made her cry. I promised her I'd keep still, and I have, except to you. I'm sure she won't mind if I tell you. She loves you. She said so. But you have to promise, as I did, not to defend her if someone speaks against her. That's what she insisted on.

"I'll never forget how she looked that day. She put her hands on my shoulders and looked into my eyes. She said, 'Lissa, you're a woman now, but you're still my baby. By every standard by which God will judge, you are my dear child. For all your years you have been the joy of my life. If you love me at all, please promise me you will never try to find out more than you know now. That's enough for me and I pray it will be enough for you. You have obeyed me for twenty-four years. Don't go against my wishes now.' With

94

her feeling that way there was nothing I could do, was there?''

"No. Nothing to do but to honor her wishes and love and reverence her all your life. It's evident she's shielding someone. And she has earned the right to keep that one's name to herself."

"It seems like that. But I don't understand. How could that birth certificate be wrong?''

"I don't know and you may never find out. We do know that your mother is innocent, and we know she loved and married your father no matter what his part in the affair is.''

"His part is pretty plain. No one could ever doubt that. I look too much like him for there to be any doubt at all. He surely was a part of that big mistake, but he was a good father, and Mother loved him. He almost adored her, and Grandma Harding seems to feel that way about her. I'm sure Grandma knows the story."

"Is your Grandmother still alive?''

"Yes. She lived with us until two years ago when she had a stroke. Caring for her was too much for Mother with all the rest of the work, so she went to live with Aunt Mildred in Iowa. I miss her. We were *such* good friends. I'm sure she knew that I had found out something about my birth. Maybe she woke up and saw me at the desk that day. She made every opportunity she could to tell me what a wonderful, good mother I had. Well, that's all this time. There's no more and never will be, I suppose. But how I'd like to stand on the high school roof and tell the world that no matter what I am, my mother is completely blameless. It burns me up to think that anyone should have a single evil thought about my mother. And to think that some other woman is going about the world posing as a — a — a *white* sheep! I'm sure she is a regular termagant. Where else could I have gotten this temper?''

"Cool off, Lissa," Neil said gently. The story he had heard had moved him more than he cared to admit. He, too, felt that with small opportunity he could "burn completely up." But Lissa must not see his perturbation. Her own was too great.

"I know how you feel. But I don't think folks are talking about it now. They may have done so long ago, but that's forgotten. Your father and mother lived fine Christian lives in this community and his name is still spoken with love by many. Your mother's life has long ago wiped out any criticism of her supposed error. The whole town loves you, and if they knew the truth as you know it they'd put up a victory arch for your mother. Let's put it all aside. I've told you my story, you've given me yours. Is there anything more?"

"Not today, thank you. There are a lot more questions I want to ask you, but we're almost home. We'd better get to the office and get these things typed up before closing time."

"Okay, office, here we come."

14

JULY CAME ON with its flood of summer folk. The cottages around the lake, the lodges in the hills, the motels along the highways were filled. The high school girls found jobs clerking in the stores or working in the eating places that sprang up like mushrooms. The boys were working as helpers at the Inn or in the camps and parks nearby. Only the Bushwhackers and a few young people whose parents could afford to let them play through the summer, were idle. The former appeared at the Inn each morning with fish to sell, then disappeared again into their swamp fastness. On Saturday nights they came to the Horne home to gather in the renovated coalbin for an hour, then to eat the refreshments that had been prepared as a drawing card. Bill was always there but the others were irregular in attendance. They listened in comparative quiet as Neil or Mr. Horne talked and prayed. They ate the doughnuts or cookies that Mrs. Horne or Mrs. Harding had made, drank the lemonade or cokes, and left. The next day, if Neil met one of them on the street he was apt to be passed up as a total stranger.

"I don't get it at all," he said despondently one night as he sat with the Hornes, Lissa and her mother after the boys had gone. "I just plain don't get it! What's eatin' them? We've done everything we can, and they keep on acting like a crew of pallbearers. Why do they come at all?"

"They come because they like you," said the minister. "But they don't know how to show it."

But Neil was not satisfied with that answer. Later he talked the situation over with Uncle Dick, who counseled him to have patience and sympathy.

"But what good will sympathy do? If they'd cooperate as they did in January we'd be all right. But we can't produce another emergency for them."

"Can you do something for me then?"

"Surely."

"Just hold on and pray a little longer. You *have* prayed, I presume?"

"Yes, but it doesn't seem to do any good. My praying and my teaching seem to be ineffective."

"Could be, son."

Neil looked up in astonishment at this agreement, but Uncle Dick went on without noticing his perturbation. "Promise me that you won't give them up for a few weeks. Surely you will see some sprouts by them. And I'll be scratching my head for an idea."

Neil made the promise, more for Uncle Dick's sake than because of any hope of his own. The sign they hoped for came unexpectedly. It was only a small sprout, but it held promise.

He and Lissa had been over to the resort to spend the evening on the beach with Ed and some friends. Returning to their car as midnight neared, they found two flat tires. It was not a case of the air having been let out. It was deliberate puncture. Two at one time was too much of a coincidence to be an accident. He might have dealt with one flat, but two were beyond him. Ed took them home and promised to have the tires repaired and the car delivered next day.

As Neil waited for the car his anger mounted. That the Bushwhackers had done it was almost unbelievable, yet who else would have? His confidence in their innocence was shaken. He did not say anything to Uncle Dick about it, but Lissa had told the story at home and Uncle Dick was already on the defensive for the boys. Neil preferred to remain silent rather than subject himself to another lecture, so took no part in the discussion that developed in the office.

When five o'clock came and the car had not been delivered, he prepared to call Ed and inquire about it. Perhaps other damage had been done. At that moment, however, Ed himself called to report that the car was just ready and would be delivered after supper. A friend was coming into town and would leave it at the cabin about seven-thirty.

Mrs. Harding and the girls had gathered on the porch to watch Lissa, Neil, Bud and Pug in a game of badminton. When the car was driven in by the cabin across the road Neil waited, hoping the driver would come across. When there was no sign of such intention, he tossed his racket to Ruth.

"Take my place, Ruthie, and show Lissa and Bud who's the best player around here."

As he approached the car, Bill's long form slid out from behind the wheel. His face was anxious and red with embarrassment. Thinking that the boy had become remorseful and wished to apologize, Neil greeted him soberly. However much one wanted to gain the confidence of this leader of the young rebels, it would not do to let such a prank go unrebuked.

The boy stood as if undecided whether to stay or run, but Neil noticed with a twinge of sympathy that his chin was quivering.

"What is it, Bill? I won't hurt you. Want to tell me about it?"

"Well — well — er — Ed said you thought — you thought we did it."

"What do you say? Did you?"

Bill looked up and his desperately anxious eyes were filled with tears which he blinked back vigorously. His voice was husky.

"No, we didn't. Honest. We weren't near there. We wouldn't have done such a thing to *you*."

"I'd like to believe you, Bill. I'd hate to think my own boys would do such a thing, either to me or anyone else."

"We didn't, Mr. Abbott. We don't do things like that. And if we *did* do them to someone we wouldn't do it to you."

"Why?"

"Well — we — we like you!"

"Do you mean that, Bill? Then why do you treat me like a stranger when you meet me on the street?"

Bill looked so uncomfortable and self-conscious that Neil thought of the interested spectators across the street, and decided on a change.

"Let's go inside my diggings. I've been on my feet so much today that they're crying for rest. I have some cold drinks in the refrigerator. Mrs. Harding sent over some lemonade awhile ago and it just hits the spot on a night like this."

He gave no chance for refusal, and Bill followed with obvious reluctance, fearing the unknown. The lemonade and some cookies seemed to ease the tension a bit, and Bill looked around the room with interest. From the books on the shelves, the pictures on the wall and the stack of records beside the player his gaze wandered with appreciation.

"It's a swell hangout," he conceded. "When I get through school and go away I'm going to have a nice place."

"Where are you going?"

"Don't know. Any place to get away from here!"

"Why do you hate it so much? I think it's a nice little place."

"Yeh, for folks like you. For me, no!"

"Going to college? I noticed by the reports in the *Advocate* that you're mighty good in science. You should major in that."

"Fat chance."

"Why not? I got my education without any help from anyone. You could do the same."

"Maybe you didn't have any hindrances either."

"Plenty of them. But they can be overcome."

"Maybe. And maybe some of them can't."

"Can you tell me?"

"Oh — not having the kind of home you can take folks into. My mother and father are okay. They both do the best they can. They're as good as anybody even if we don't live in a house with white porch pillars. But we have just four rooms and eight people in them. You can't ever have folks in when your're that crowded. And you can't learn how to act so's you could get along in college."

"That shouldn't hold you down. You can keep your eyes and ears open and learn how to act. My adopted parents were immigrants, and they never did have the kind of manners or customs that most American families have. But I learned. Your parents are Americans for generations back, and I'm sure they came from good stock. I've talked to them and I think I know. You can make your own future, Bill."

"Not when everybody is bound to think you're bad. Like thinking our gang has been stealing and busting up things. They ought to be looking close to home!"

Neil was staring at Bill in astonishment. "Bill! What are you saying? Do you know who has been doing all those things?"

A car had driven into the driveway, and Bill showed an immediate urgency to be off. Overlooking the question, he hurriedly left to join the boys in the Bushwhacker car that had arrived for him. Neil watched as they went down the road, then turned and went back into his room. He had things to think about that made him forget all about the group across the road. No more games for him tonight.

15

Neil was sitting alone on his porch one evening when Lissa came slowly across bearing a loaf of fresh bread.

"Why so glum?" he questioned. "You've been under a cloud all day. I'm sorry when you feel badly and don't give any of us a chance to help."

"You couldn't. Nobody can. It's a fight between me and the devil. Just now he seems to be in the ascendency, but I'll win out yet. With my mother praying for me I can't lose. But it will take a lot of even her praying. I haven't yet got to the place where I want to do what I know I have to do to be able to live with my conscience for the rest of my life. I'm an awful person, Neil. Were you ever so bad you didn't want to be good?"

"Let's leave my dark past out of it. Can you tell me about the thing that's troubling you?"

"No. That's part of the toughness of the problem. If I could just talk it over with someone who has just a little bit of earthly clay in his make-up, I believe we could reach ground where I could wage a creditable fight. But the only persons who have any suspicion of it at all are my mother and Uncle Dick. I haven't told them, but they're good guessers. But both of them are so far beyond me in surrender to the Lord's will that I don't even understand their language at times. I need someone of the earth, earthy.''

I ought to qualify there.''

"You do, as far as that's concerned. But I'm afraid you'd encourage me to go on in my own way, and that isn't what I need. I need someone who knows I should accept a certain thing in a Christlike spirit, and who will help me to do it even while feeling as strongly as I do about it. But I have to go now. I promised the girls I'd show them how to make fudge. Uncle Dick wants you to come up before you go to bed.''

"I'll come along now and get in on the fudge. I'm willing to try your cooking.''

While they waited for the fudge to cool, Neil told Lissa and Mrs. Harding of a promise Mrs. Brown had made to braid him a rug if he would buy the material.

"My foster mother made one once out of her old dresses. I used it by my bed for years. I'm going to buy new cloth for Mrs. Brown, so it should last indefinitely. What colors would you suggest?''

Mrs. Harding showed him one her mother-in-law had made from denim in several soft shades, and they agreed that a combination of two shades of blue with soft rose would be good. Lissa agreed to buy the cloth for him.

"Thanks for your help,'' Neil said. "I don't know much about such things. When I get married I'll let you furnish my house.''

"How will your wife take that?''

"She'll take it and like it.''

Mrs. Harding laughed at him and Lissa said, "I hope that when that time comes you decide to remain in the cabins. You could connect them and have one of those strung along houses like they have in New England. I'd decorate all of them for you.''

"You'd better find me a wife first,'' he said, suddenly sober.

"I'm sorry,'' she said contritely. "I wish I could find

you a girl that appreciated you. Jane just doesn't know what she missed. Let's not think of her anymore."

"Agreed. That's so easy to say."

"I'll be looking for that other girl to fill the vacancy. In the meantime you'd better hike up to Uncle Dick. It's his bedtime."

Uncle Dick was already in bed, but wide awake and impatient to get to the business that was on his mind.

"Did you hear that they're going to send a bus into the Hollow and bring the grade school children into town this fall?"

"No. Is it something I should be interested in? I saw the schoolhouse today and it isn't a place that would ever inspire a kid. Why haven't they been coming into town before this?"

"Because they raised such a fuss about staying there that the county board let them. Now the building has been condemned and the board won't fix it. It's cheaper to bring the kids into town, and a lot better for them, too."

"I think that's fine. Maybe it will break down that silly barrier and when these kids grow up we won't have Bushwhackers."

"It'll be good for all. I'm glad for it. Now I have an idea, and I can't go to sleep until I've talked to you about it. I want to buy that building. I think they'll be glad to have it taken off their hands."

"You want to buy it? May I ask what for?"

"Can't you guess?"

"Not an inkling."

"You're slower than I thought. What do they need most at the Hollow? What do those boys need to hold them at home and keep them out of trouble?"

Neil thought of his talk with Bill and of the yearning in the boy's eyes when he admired the cabin room across the road. He thought of the shack back in the swamp where the boys met safe from interruption or meddling. He thought of Bill's explanation that he had no place to take a friend. He looked up at Uncle Dick in dawning understanding.

"Do you mean what I think you do? Would you buy that

place and fix it up for that gang of boys? Go to all that expense for the Bushwhackers? Why?''

"Because I want to. Isn't that reason enough for an old man to have? And not for the Bushwhackers alone, but for all the folks there. There are two big rooms. We could do a lot with that space. The women could meet and have their branch group of the mission circle there. We could have a Sunday school for the children who can't get in here. We could fix up a gym for games, and Bill could make a laboratory of the old coal shed eventually. Don't you think it's a good idea?''

"It's an astounding one. But it would cost a lot of money.''

"What's money compared to boys and girls?''

"It's nothing if you happen to have it. The lack of it can be quite a hindrance to good works.''

"We'll worry about money tomorrow. I'm already planning to put a big squeeze on Harry Rossiter. And I have a few shekels salted away that ought to be working for the Lord. Put out the light as you leave.''

Neil took his dismissal with a grin and went out. The light was dim in the lower hall, and the silent house indicated that its occupants were in bed. But as he softly closed the screen door Lissa spoke from the shadows around the porch swing.

"All through? Come over and sit a while.''

"Okay. Something on your mind?''

"Yes. What's the matter with us?''

"You and who else?'

"You.''

"You've apparently thought through the thing. What *is* wrong with us?''

"We are two unhappy people. You're fretting at being held here when you want to be in the city. Sounds crazy to me, but that's it. And I'm unhappy because there's a big lump of bitterness in my heart and I won't get rid of it. We're both Christians. Why don't we act like it?''

"Do you think we've been acting *un*like it?''

"Yes, I do. No Christian should ever coddle a grievance the way we are doing. How can we expect our testimony to be what it should? I'm not joking, Neil. I'm troubled. I don't feel a bit like the victorious Christian that I should be."

"I know you're not joking. What should we do to change the picture?"

"Your case is a lot simpler than mine. All you have to do is to look things in the face, admit the truth and then accept it. But I know the truth, I admit it, and I won't accept it. The only way I can win would be to get down on my knees and stay there until I'd let go completely of Lissa Harding and all her bitterness, her resentment and her desire for revenge. And I can't make myself do that! Oh, Neil, help me! I just can't want to forgive her!"

He reached for her hand and gave it a reassuring grip. He didn't know in full what was bothering her, but he knew that he wanted to help her in any way possible. Never before in all his life had another human being clung to him for support as she was doing now. He longed fervently to be just such a prop as she needed, but he felt more like a pillar of crumbling sand.

"You said 'her.' Have you found out who — who she is?"

"Not for sure. But I have some strong ideas. Maybe if I did know I could meet the thing more squarely. Maybe I could find some explanation or extenuating circumstances. But I can't do that. I just go on wondering and the hate builds up. I have to admit it, Neil. There are times when it is really hate. And that's wicked. I don't want to be wicked, but I don't want to forgive her! Please help me. What she did to Mother was terrible, but Mother doesn't hate her. Why should I?"

"Probably because you love your mother more than she loves herself. Maybe she has had her times of almost hating, also. None of us will ever know what she endured through the years, or how often she was tempted to tell what she knew. She knew something else, though, that was better. She knew what to do to cure hate. I don't believe she carries even resentment now."

"I know she doesn't. Isn't she a wonder? Why can't I be like her? Or don't I want to if it involves giving up my private grudges? Can't you help me?"

"How can I when I'm so unfit? You have an indictment against me also, haven't you?"

"Your trouble is much more simple. You see, you just don't understand. You're not acknowledging Christ's leading, or feeling the need of it. You ask for leading in a general way, but you don't see its necessity in the little details. Some day you will. And when you do, you accept it and live it. That's the kind of person you are."

"I'm grateful for your good opinion, but I'm not sure it's deserved. I'm beginning to have a very humble opinion of Neil Abbott."

"Then you're learning. That's the way we all start. The trouble with me is that I *know* what's right, and I don't in the least want to do it. And at times I don't want to."

Lissa rose from the swing and he knew it was time to go. She looked up, and the moonlight showed tears on her cheek.

"We do need help, both of us. Don't we?"

He stood at the window of his cabin long after he had seen her light go out. Over and over he reviewed the conversation, and he prayed for the troubled girl who couldn't want to forgive. Then, when the moon had sunk behind the trees by the creek, he turned wearily to his bed.

"Oh, if I could only realize Him!"

16

UNCLE DICK GREETED Neil excitedly as he came into the office after his lunch hour two weeks later. "Good news, boy! I saw Mort Kinney go past a while ago. He says the school board met last night and voted to sell me the old schoolhouse for a song, if I feel like singing."

"Are you going to sing? And what are you doing here at this hour? Aren't you supposed to go home and lie down after lunch? Does the doctor know how you're behaving?"

"I'm old enough to take care of myself! Anyway, the doctor was in while you were out gallivanting this morning, and he gave me a clean bill of health. Lissa is out on an assignment, and I want you to go on another. I'll stay here and keep the ship afloat."

"What would Mr. Rossiter say if he came in and found you alone? I promised him I'd take care of you."

"Harry Rossiter knows me well enough to understand that I can stand a very limited amount of this 'taking care' business. He won't blame you, because he told me you were to do as I say. Even the doctor knows it would be impossible for me to rest with this bee buzzing in my bonnet."

"Okay, I'll be good and let you have your way. But may I go and help you hive your bee?"

"You can be very useful."

"Fine. I've felt like a fifth wheel ever since you came back. What's my assignment? I'll do my best to perform it, but I hope it doesn't call for too much in the way of brain power."

"It's your legs I want, not your brains. I flatter myself that my own brains are still in fair working order. I aim to take care of that end of the business. But my old legs are beginning to wobble a bit. That's where you can help."

"With Mr. Rossiter's approval? I'm still on his payroll, remember."

"I remember. I'll guarantee not only his approval but his cooperation. Here's the first step. Go over to Charlie Kent's office and tell him to get things ready for the legal end of it. I don't want to lose any time."

"Fine. And while I'm out I'll run up to the resort and see what I can pick up there. Will you want me back before closing time?"

"No. Marv isn't busy just now and you may consider yourself dismissed for the day."

Just outside the door he met Lissa returning from an errand.

"Where to now, big boy?"

"I've been elected as Uncle Dick's official legs. What that will advantage Mr. Rossiter I fail to see. But I've been assured he'll like it. He's paying the bill, so what can I say? I'm going out to collect a schoolhouse for Uncle Dick."

"A schoolhouse! You *are* crazy."

"Nevertheless that's it. It's not for publication, though."

"My lips are sealed. Where are you bound now?"

"To the Hollow. I wish you could go along."

"I can, part way. I'd like to ride along as far as the Winchesters'."

"*You* want to go there?"

"Don't want to. Just am."

109

She said it so shortly that the question he was about to ask died on his lips. Later as they rode along she explained to him.

"I know you're wondering what this is all about. Here it is. I am this day starting a campaign to make Lissa Harding do what she *should* do rather than what she wants to do. You see I have decided that with the Lord's help I can control my actions and, I hope, my words. If I do that, maybe in time I'll be able to control my thoughts and emotions. Do you think that's a good assumption? After our talk that night two weeks ago I decided I had to take some definite step. This was the only one I could see."

"Yes, it is a good idea, but one that will take a lot of courage to go through with. What's the plan? Are you going out there and tell them that you've been waging a war with yourself as to whether to let them live or not?"

"What a sweet way you have of putting things! Of course not. That will come later. No apologies today for slights that they probably haven't even noticed. This is just a little ice-breaking expedition. I heard Uncle Dick say that he wished someone would find time to ask Mr. Winchester to make a more detailed explanation about that bill he is trying to get through the legislature. Also he thought we should have some more word about her illness, something more than we have had from Howie. I had asked the Lord to give me a chance to behave myself as a Christian should, and I thought this was it. I don't like it, not a little bit. But I'm doing it. I'd surely appreciate some prayer help."

The shake of her voice and the quiver of her chin betrayed the fact that her heart was still burdened by her problems. For some reason her whole being rebelled against this self-assigned task, but she would carry through.

"I'll be praying," Neil promised. "I don't place much value on my prayers, but I'm there to try."

She gave him a weak smile as she started up the long walk that led to the mansion set back amid the trees. Neil watched her until she reached the steps, marching resolutely along with shoulders squared. She turned and waved, and he drove on with a prayer in his heart for the valiant girl.

Neil always enjoyed his visits to the Hollow. It was as if he had stepped into a different country. It lay so near to Appleboro, yet so far away. Today, however, he wondered if it might not be just a little bit too peaceful. Trying to look at it through the eyes of an adolescent boy, he saw that it held little interest. Boys were not seeking peace, he knew. They wanted action, and the Bushwhackers were out to get just that. Mr. Horne was worried about the situation, for the school bus was rented and came out every Sunday for those who would go into church and Sunday school. Many of the children went regularly, but the older boys not at all. Few of the adults were interested. Somehow Appleboro had failed to reach a mission field that had been planted at its door. Uncle Dick's plan might have much to recommend it if it could be worked out.

Neil spent a busy hour going over the old building. The playground, with its weeds and trash, was an eyesore, but could be made into a parklike lawn with a small outlay of labor and money. The building was a more difficult problem. He examined beams and studding, window sills and door frames. He climbed into the space under the roof and inspected the wiring there. He knew too little of such things to make any appraisal of cost. All he could do was to make notes of repairs needed or alterations to be made. He could not judge how much of the old material could be reused. He did, however, take measurements that would give Uncle Dick some idea as to use for the rooms. He hoped the larger room might be long enough for a basketball court. If this project proved successful perhaps the Bushwhackers would eventually meet the town boys in the field of sports. As he worked he became more interested in the plan that had seemed at first just a plaything for his old friend. There were real possibilities here if one had money enough to develop them.

It was time for him to start for the resort, but first he must see Mrs. Brown. She had sent word by Bill that the rug was finished, and he had brought a basket of apples to show his appreciation and Mrs. Harding had sent a bag of beans and a cabbage. He would have just time for a short visit with his old friend before going on to the other end of the lake.

The beauty of the rug was a breathtaking surprise to him. Mrs. Brown had refused to let him see it during the making, and he had prepared himself for something which would be dear to him because of the love back of the gift but which would be relegated to an inconspicuous place in his small home. He found it hard to believe that this oval of soft, beautifully blended colors could have been made from the few yards of denim he had left there less than two weeks ago, and he was voluble in his admiration. Mrs. Brown's eyes shone at his words, and she insisted that he stay for some milk and gingerbread a neighbor girl had prepared.

"Dottie is so good to me," she said. "She does altogether too much for the small sum I can pay her. I *must* be able to get about soon so that she won't have to spend her time on me. She needs to get a job that will bring in money enough for her clothes and books for school this fall. She's so pretty and clever that she could get a good place if she didn't think she had to help me."

"Let me put my brain to work on the problem," Neil said reaching for his second slice of gingerbread. "Maybe we can find someone who can come in for a few hours a day so that Dottie will be free for work at the inn. They need girls there, Ed says."

He did not go back to the highway to reach the inn, but took a short-cut that ran along the lake. He had traveled it before and found it a pleasant drive in spite of the rutted road which did not tempt many drivers. He found his heart lightened by the short visit he had had. He must do something to help solve the problems of the little woman who had been one of his first friends in this north country. He would like to pay Dottie's wages so that she could continue as helper, but Mrs. Brown would not accept a gift, he knew. If he could find some work that she could do at home she would be happy to provide the salary herself. He must give it real thought. In the meantime the rug would not be relegated to any dark corner.

The breeze was brisk and the ripples on the lake danced and shone in the afternoon sunshine. Water always fascinated him, and he found his eyes turning often from the road to the sparkling wavelets. On one of these quick glances he thought he discerned movements on the other side where the steep cliffs and the deep woods behind them formed a natural obstruction past which the summer colony had not spread. That area was the habitat of the Bushwhackers, and he wondered what activity could be occupying them now. They would have delivered their catch of fish to the markets, and the afternoon would be their own. He hoped the activities were peaceable and legitimate, and was reassured by the knowledge that such an isolated spot could not be interesting to anyone else. Only a Bushwhacker could reach it. He could see them now on a great rock that lay by the side of the cliff as if it had fallen after the winter's weathering. These were his boys, he was sure. But what were they doing?

He drew to the side of the road and stopped the car. In the glove compartment were the field glasses he had purchased several weeks before when Uncle Dick had interested him in the various birds they saw in their trips about the countryside. By the time he had adjusted them the boys had gone from the rock. He watched for their reappearance, but the rock remained vacant. Then he saw them on top of the cliff. They must have made or found a trail at the rear. What could they be doing in that practically inaccessible place? Unless he was mistaken they had left most, if not all, of their clothing below.

He could see Bill lining them up. No one could mistake that gangling length. Neil counted them. All there, twelve of them, no, thirteen. Was there a new Bushwhacker? Were they conducting some weird tribal ceremony? Bill stepped to the head of the line at the edge of the cliff, raised his hands above his head, poised for a moment then, before Neil had time to grasp the significance of the pose, sprang into the air and, in a long, perfectly executed dive, plunged into the lake below. Neil held his breath as he watched. Surely no one except some professional could make such a dive and live! It looked as if another boy were preparing to follow. Was this a strange suicide pact among the group of antisocial, maladjusted boys? What could he do to stop them? Even if he could be heard at this distance they would not heed his call. With sick heart he saw the second lad make the dive and followed him with his eyes until he struck the water and disappeared as Bill had done. Would the rest go the same way?

His eyes roamed over the surface of the lake, and with a relief so great that it made him weak, he saw the flash of white arms as the two swimmers circled the spot where the others could be expected to cleave the water. One after another twelve boys made that splendid dive while Neil sat entranced. This was no group of maladjusted youths. They had adjusted in their own way to their surroundings, and they were stronger for it. The thirteenth boy stood alone on the cliff as if waiting for a signal. Back in the water the twelve were arranged in a semicircle some yards from the spot where he would disappear. Up on the cliff alone the boy seemed to hesitate, then, as if at a signal he was off. When he struck the water the other boys disappeared also. Neil waited tensely through seconds that seemed endless. Then one dark head broke through the water, another and another. He counted anxiously until the full number had risen and the "school of porpoises" as he mentally dubbed them, were headed for their landing place below the rock. He saw them clamber out of the water with their wet bodies glistening.

Back on the rock where their clothes had been left they clustered around one boy with much back slapping, apparently of congratulation.

That must be number thirteen, Neil thought. *I've witnessed an initiation ceremony. I'll warrant that fellow wishes they'd save those whacks until he gets dried.*

Drying did not seem a part of the program, however. Before he realized how it could have happened the clothes had been donned, and the group disappeared into the thicket. The rock and cliff sat empty in the sun. The show was over and the audience could now leave. He drove away, but his thoughts stayed with the boys. He almost envied them their carefree existence. What a thrill it must be to poise for a minute on that high point, then with an upward and outward spring, cut the air in a long, clean dive, part the water with his outthrust hands, go down and down into the cool depths, to swim back again to the surface and take in deep breaths of the pine-scented air. What an experience! There was much to be said for the wild, free life.

"I'd like to join them. But what a sorry spectacle I'd make of myself in an attempt at such a dive. I'd better limit my swimming to Grade One, Class C. That's where I rank alongside those fish."

17

WHEN NEIL DREW up to the door of the inn, Ed Walsh greeted him with a grin.

"Go right down to the dock. Your little playmates from the city got in this morning and have been asking for you."

"Which ones?"

"Sara and her crowd. It seems there's a shortage of males here and they want you to come over and play with them."

"Tell them I'm busy."

"Tell them yourself. I have to make my living by catering to them."

"And I make mine by catering to Sara's dad. All the same difference."

"Yep. But it's you they want. I'm going back to talk to the cook."

"About a piece of pie, I suppose. Okay, I'll go with you and gather what Uncle Dick calls gleanings from our summer harvest. Marv calls it 'songs from our birds of passage,' and Lissa says it's crumbs from the upper crust. Got anything for me?"

Over the pie which the cook served to both, Neil managed to get most of the news he had expected, the names of recently arrived guests and the departing ones, special notice of a minor celebrity or two, and the report of a near tragedy when a novice swimmer had to be revived by the lifeguards.

"Now I'm ready to face the gals. Thanks for the pie, Mrs. Kline. That's really what I came for, but don't tell my boss that."

Sara Rossiter greeted him with a squeal of delight and began at once to make plans for him. He firmly refused all, even when a half dozen girls added their pleas.

"Can't do it. I'm due back at the office right now, and I'm busy for the next month. At that time I get a week's vacation. I'll see you then."

"You don't want to come," said Sara sulkily as she followed him to the car. "You're just itching to get back to Appleboro and Lissa Harding. What's she got that I haven't?"

"A job, Sara, just like I have. We both work for a living. So you run along with your dolls and duds and I'll get me back to the salt mines. B. will probably be out for the weekend."

He had started the engine and reached to close the door which Sara still held open, when another of her squeals stopped him.

"What now?"

"That rug! That beautiful rug. May I have it, Neil?"

"You may not. It's mine."

"Where did you get it? I want one just like it. Won't you sell it to me?"

"Nothing doing in that line. This rug was made for me by a lady who loves me for myself alone, and it is *not* for sale."

"Did Lissa make it?"

"She has never even seen it."

"Please sell it to me. You used to like me, Neil. Why won't you do this for me now?"

"Because this particular rug was made especially for

me. It's not for sale at any price. Try to get that through your determined little noodle.''

"Then get me another one just like it. If the lady made one she can make another, can't she? I'd pay a big price.''

He stared at her for so long that she scowled impatiently and was turning away, when he laughed and said,

"Sara, you're the joy of my life. Thank you for an idea. I'm sure I can get her to make one, and I assure you you'll pay all it's worth.''

He drove back along the highway at a rapid pace. The office would be closing soon and he wanted to get these items typed and on Uncle Dick's desk, ready for approval before going to Marv. As he neared the Winchester house he thought of Lissa and wondered how her day had gone. She was not at the gate where she said she would meet him if she did not decide to walk into town, but as he crossed the bridge over the creek she arose from a big rock at the water's edge and lifted her hand with thumb upturned.

"What are you doing here? Caught any fish?''

"Not even a tadpole. I didn't want to go to the office now for I don't want Uncle Dick to see me and draw any conclusions. Anyway, he said I needn't come back there if I had anything else to do. Bless his simple heart, he's probably picturing me dining with the Winchesters this evening.''

"Didn't they ask you?''

"Don't joke, please. I can't stand it. Will you take me for a ride before suppertime? I'm in no mood to go home.''

"I wish I could. But I promised Uncle Dick I'd have these items on his desk before I go home tonight. Marv goes to press early. And after that I promised Bud and Pug a night on the town — all the gourmet delights of the best drive-in, then twilight baseball. It'll be quite a session.''

"Gourmand delights, you mean. And I'm sure it will be a big time. But I need you, Neil. If you'll take me for a drive before supper I'll do the typing for you while you and the boys eat. Then you can take me home before the game. I just *have* to talk to you now.''

"I don't know what it's all about. But if it's advice or

counsel you're after, I'm apt to hand it out with frankness.''

"That's what I need, someone who can give it to me straight.''

"Let's go to the office first and get the typing done. Four hands will make quick work of it. Then I'll call your mother and say we're going for a ride and that I'll pick up the boys at six o'clock. Also that you'll be going with us. You need the outing and I'm sure I'll relish some adult company. Here we go!''

When they reached the office the call was made, and by the time Marv was ready to leave, the notes were on Uncle Dick's desk. The old editor himself had given up in midafternoon and caught a ride home with a neighbor. He was not there to notice Lissa's nervous despondency. Only Marv observed it and he, in spite of his love for teasing, was tactful and unquestioning when he saw a need.

They drove off the highway on the graveled road that led to the dairy farms and in a quiet place by the wayside, where a picnic table had been placed under a great tree, they sat for their talk.

"Now out with it. Didn't the call go well? Wouldn't he give you the news?''

"I got the news all right. So far, so good. The rest was awful. Neil, I flunked right out!''

"What do you mean? You didn't get into a fight, did you?''

"Of course not. Neither did I remember to be the sweet, poised, calm young lady I intended to be. I didn't act a bit as Jane Barr would have.''

"Fine. No one wanted you to. I prayed for you, but I certainly didn't ask God to help you act like Jane Barr.''

"But she'd have been in control of herself and the situation all the time. I wasn't.''

"Can't you tell me? Was it bad?''

"It was torture. The minute I stepped in that house I knew I was out of bounds. I should never have gone. So of course I was nervous and all confused. Mr. Winchester was kind, though. I think he wants to be really nice. He gave me the notes all typed up and told me some things about the importance of the bill. That part was interesting, and I think if I'd just stayed and talked with him I'd have forgotten my nervousness and enjoyed it all. But then the awful part came!"

"Which was — ?"

"He said Mrs. Winchester wanted to see me. I tried to excuse myself, said I had to go back to the office. But he didn't even listen to me. Very politely but very forcefully he took my arm and marched me right into the sunroom where she was sitting, or maybe you'd call it lying, on a chaise lounge. I felt as if my heart had stopped beating, I was so frightened."

"Right here I think I have the right to get this straight. Was she the woman you heard?"

"Yes, the one who was talking to Mother. Not the one they were talking about. At least I don't *think* she was that one."

"Surely they weren't the same."

"I don't know. I'm all mixed up. I can't remember a single name being spoken. And both of them spoke several times of the mother and of something 'she' did. Do you want to know just what I did hear?"

"If you care to tell me."

"I have to tell someone. I'm so tired of puzzling over it all alone, and I don't want to bother or hurt Mother. I'd been in the attic and came down unexpectedly. Mother was in the front room talking to someone and as I came down the stairs I heard Mrs. Winchester's voice, but couldn't understand what she said. When Mother answered I stopped for I could tell she was disturbed and I didn't want to break in on them. When I tried to move the stairs creaked and so I just froze there, intending to apologize to Mother later. Then when I realized what Mother was saying I *couldn't* move. I simply went into deep-freeze! This is what Mother said: 'For twenty-four years I have had Lissa. I've paid the cost in full in shame and loneliness. For the first six months I accepted her money because I had to. I couldn't work with a young baby to care for. I was among strangers, and I was a very frightened girl. When John Harding found me and learned the truth we decided never to accept another cent. After we were married we went to court to legalize our right to have her. It took us two years and cost a great deal of money in lawyer's fees and lost time, but we won. We had the hospital records, testimony from the nurses and a doctor, and some pictures of me to prove that *I* was Grace Lennon. We told the whole story and the judge believed us. We got full adoption papers. Lissa is mine!'

"That's what my mother said, Neil. Now listen to the rest of it. From Mrs. Winchester, 'Don't you think the real mother has *some* rights?' And Mother's answer, '*I* am her real mother. There is no motherhood in letting another woman bear such a stigma. Aside from the cost in shame and misjudgment, I have borne the financial cost also. The day John found me he insisted that we buy her a complete new outfit for which he paid. Not one penny of Farrell money has been spent on her since. Nor will the Winchester money be accepted.'

"Then Mrs. Winchester said, 'I wish you'd believe, Grace, that I had no idea of what she did. I never knew it until more than ten years later when we came back to Appleboro. She wouldn't tell me and I couldn't help you when I didn't know. I wish you could forgive her.'

" 'I do forgive her,' Mother said. 'I can never forget what she did for me. There isn't a day passes that I don't thank God for my strong body and straight limbs. Then I thank Him for her and for Lissa. She is the child I could never bear John Harding, and she is mine by all the laws of God and man. I'll do anything else you want, Nita, but the Farrell family can't have any part of my daughter. At any time in all the years since I came back with her in my arms I could have made the judge's findings public and the world would have known she did not belong to me. I chose to keep her as my own. I don't want to grieve you further, Nita. Forget about Lissa. She is happy as Alicia Harding. I am happy as her mother. Go back to your fine husband and your equally fine son, and forget it all. Remember, as I do, that the one who planned it this way was a frantic and sick woman. I have forgiven her long ago. You must do the same. Had you been in her place, perhaps you would have acted as she did. Don't condemn. Try to remember her as she was before tragedy struck her. And let's bury this forever. Lissa is mine!' ''

Lissa sat twisting her hands together until Neil reached for them and held them in his own.

"Quiet, little girl. Wait a few minutes until you have relaxed a bit. Then tell me what this has to do with today. Is she still trying to get hold of you? That's silly. You're twenty-five, even if you do look and act like sixteen. No one can make you do what you don't want to do."

"God can."

"Only if it's right. He wouldn't be in anything that is wrong."

"May it *is* right. Maybe I need just the thing this is meant to teach me."

"What does she want of you? Did she say anything about a claim on you?"

"Oh, no. She acted as if I were one of the village girls she wanted to befriend. She wants to give me a better job."

"Where? And what?"

"In her home. They are going to move to the capital for the winter and she thinks she will need a companion-secretary. I'm chosen for the honor. She says she will pay much more than I'm making, and Mother will not have to board me! As if my mother thinks of me in terms of board!"

Did you tell her you'd think it over, or did you do what I think you did?''

"I did what you *know* I did. In spite of all my good resolutions I blew up like an honest-to-goodness volcano! The maid came in and said Mrs. Winchester must not talk longer. I was politely ushered out of the room and shown from the house by a polite but distressed Mr. Winchester. I felt sorry for him and I think he felt sorry for me. He asked me to be patient with a sick woman who was distressed because she fancied I was the child of a relative. We were both relieved when he closed the door on me. That's all of it, Neil. Doesn't sound like so much when I tell it but it was plenty of 'unfun' to go through.''

"I know it was. I wish there were something I could do about it, but I can't think of a thing except to put you in the car and take you for a drive up to the inn and back. You're to fix your thoughts on me and entertain me with your best conversation. By the time we get back you'll look calm and happy enough to greet your mother when we pick up the boys.''

"But I don't want to talk. Let's sing.''

Sing they did as they drove, and when they drew up at the Harding house at six o'clock Lissa greeted her mother with a kiss and a promise to behave herself at the ball game. This last was explained by the mother with a story of how, when her daughter was sixteen, she went in as substitute when the home team was losing, and saved the day but became the talk of the town for a few days.

Bud and Pug were waiting with three envious little girls looking on, and Neil promised that next week they should all go out for some fun with him.

"You're the nicest thing that ever came into our lives,'' said Pug solemnly as they drove away.

18

To THE TWO boys the meal at the drive-in was a real occasion. They had heard some of the older folks speak casually of eating here after some game or function, but had never been able to afford such expenditures of money for themselves. Bud, unknown to even Pug, was saving such coins as he could accumulate after he had bought the things Mrs. Harding required for school, from his pay as paper carrier, and hoped some day to be able to take a girl there. He did not know who the girl might be, for he had small use for them all, but taking a girl to the drive-in seemed to be the thing that marked a fellow as one of the important ones at school. He would get his driver's license soon, and when the purse was large enough he would take a girl to the drive-in if it killed him! He was glad of this chance to find out how a man treated a girl when he took her out. He would watch Neil closely tonight, and when his time came he would be prepared.

To Pug the occasion was thrilling for a different cause. Neil had said he could eat all the hot dogs he wanted with mustard, pickles, catsup and everything! And he could finish off with a banana split if he felt able. Pug had no doubt about feeling able, but he did wonder a bit if Neil had brought along enough money. Lissa probably could help out if Neil ran short, for yesterday had been her payday. He hoped she had brought her money along. Anyway he intended to hold Neil to his promise. Such a chance might never come again.

When the pert little waitress had brought their trays (while Bud watched closely every move that was made), and the boys were so busy that they had no ears for the conversation in the front seat, Neil turned anxiously to the girl who sat quietly beside him.

"How's it going now, lady? You're looking at that sandwich as if it were made of rattlesnake. Give it to Pug and we'll order something else."

"No," she said with an embarrassed laugh. "The sandwich looks really wonderful, and I'm going to eat it. Pug can order another when he wants it. It's just that I keep thinking of things."

"That is what you are *not* to do until this evening is over. This is my party and I don't want you to spoil it."

"I'm sorry, and I'll be good. I'll eat the sandwich. I didn't feel like eating lunch. Maybe I'm just not hungry."

At the ball park the boys joined a group of their friends while Neil and Lissa found a place high on the stands where they had a view, not only of the players but of the crowds that filled the stands on either side. More interesting than the game were the people who enthusiastically supported their little town's team as it battled against a team from "outside." Neil guessed that very few of Appleboro's population had been left at home tonight. He saw every merchant from around the town square, the doctor, the dentist, the town's one lawyer, and every member of the high school faculty. Even the minister was there in a rakish cap that bespoke his loyalty to the team on which his son played shortstop. What a fine, friendly bunch of people they were! But how could they be satisfied in this dead little village shut away from the realities of life, behind the hills that hemmed them in? Any one of them could have done better for himself outside, yet here they were, apparently fixed in provincialism and liking it!

From this unhappy thought Neil turned to the game and tried to become interested in it. Lissa was cheering with the crowd for the home pitcher who had just struck out a player, and Neil joined his voice to the uproar and forgot his introversive troubles. It was a thrilling game as small town sports go. The visitors were fighting valiantly to overcome a two-run lead of the Appleboro lads, while the latter strove just as valiantly to increase it. From the volume of cheering for both sides an uninformed listener might have inferred that the world series was being played.

The brilliance of the floodlights began to tire Neil's eyes. He had been reading too much lately after going to bed, and his eyes felt sore and strained. To relieve them he turned his glance to the leafy branches of the surrounding trees, and was just beginning to feel relaxed and sleepy when a movement above him brought him to attention. He chuckled inwardly, recognizing the lanky form of Bill sitting far out on an oak branch, from which eyrie perch he had an excellent view of the whole field.

"The Bushwhackers' version of the traditional knothole," he thought. "I wonder if all of them are here. It gives one a queer feeling to know they are there and yet never to hear a sound. Only a Bushwhacker could do that."

One by one he counted them, picking them out from the shadows as he used to find hidden figures in a picture puzzle.

Thirteen. That's all of them. But that dark shadow in this tree could be another. Maybe the fourteenth candidate is in training. "Lissa," he whispered softly, "I wish you could see what I'm seeing in the branches of these trees. It's almost as interesting as the game."

"I saw them," she answered softly. "I got curious about your silence and when I saw you looking so furtively around I followed suit. It's Bill and his friends, isn't it?"

"Yes. I've counted fourteen, I think. I'm glad to see that they are regular boys. They pretend to be interested in nothing except their own pursuits, but they couldn't stay away from a ball game.''

"How still they've been. I haven't heard a chirp out of them.''

"They're a well disciplined bunch. They know when to keep still. What a wonderful top sergeant Bill may make some day! If those kids were found they would be routed out. Let's not tell on them.''

"Of course not! I'm for those boys any time, any place, anyhow. I wish I thought as highly of some of the other boys in this town.''

He wondered to whom she referred, but an exciting moment in the game claimed their attention and there was no chance for further conversation. The home team retained its lead, and when the final score read 7-5 the weary young pitcher was carried off the field on the shoulders of his mates while the band played a triumphal tune.

"That was *some* game!'' said Pug with a happy sigh as he climbed into the car.

"Yeah,'' agreed Bud. "But if Ernie and Howie could play the score woulda been 7-0. There never was another pitcher in Appleboro like Ernie, and Howie can sock 'em like nobody's business.''

"Why can't they play?'' asked the puzzled Lissa.

"Their mothers won't let them. Ernie got hit by a ball a long time ago when he was a little kid and his mother said he couldn't play anymore. That scared Howie's mother and she said the same. They do play lots of the time, though, when the team is just practicing, but they can't be on the team 'cause then their mothers would have to know it. Boy, are they sore about it!''

"I don't blame them,'' said Lissa under her breath. "Someone ought to teach those mothers something about boys.''

"Second that motion,'' said Neil. "They're fortunate that the boys have accepted it so well. I'm afraid I'd have broken loose some place else just to prove my manhood.''

By the Harding steps as Bud and Pug rushed away to tell

the happy outcome of their evening to the girls who were hanging over the stair rail in robes and slippers, Lissa turned and gave her hand to Neil.

"Thank you for — well, for everything," she said with a smile.

"Everything all right? Will you go to sleep and not worry?"

"I promise. I'm going to sleep thanking the Lord for sending you here. I'm going to have a talk with my mother about it all. I should never have tried to walk alone in such a place. After that things will work out all right. She's so all right herself!"

"I'm sure of that. And may I add you're a little bit of all right yourself."

"I'm not really. I get pretty discouraged about me at times. But I'm glad you're fooled."

"Maybe I know you better than you know yourself." Then without waiting for an answer he stooped and kissed her. "Happy dreams," he said.

For a moment she stood as if stunned. Then she turned and ran quickly into the house. After he heard her steps on the stairs he walked slowly to his own cabin.

"I'm afraid she didn't like that. I mustn't do it again. I never meant a thing by it, but perhaps her mother is strict about such things. I certainly don't want to offend them."

19

NEIL WAS CLEANING the typewriters, whistling softly as he went about the unpleasant task, when Marv came into the office next morning.

"What in the world got you up and down here at this hour of the day? And why clean the typewriters? That's Lissa's job. If you're looking for work, grab the broom and start on the shop. *That's* worthy of a man."

"Go to it then, with my blessing. As to why I'm working, I couldn't sleep and decided to work."

"Then cleaning a typewriter is just what you need! What is it now, pal? Girl trouble still — or again?"

"Neither. The only girl I'd ever lie awake about is now another man's wife, and I've dropped her from my dreams. But there are other troubles in the world. Hadn't you heard that bit of news?"

"Still fretting about the job, I guess. Don't, my friend. I'm not in on the secret councils of this giant business, but there's one thing I'm sure of. You don't have to worry. Mr. Harry Rossiter has his eagle eye on you for some purpose. Ten years from now — what in the world? There must be news right under our noses. Let's go and see!"

He left his place by the window and was out of the door in one bound. Neil, following him, saw a crowd gathered in front of the drugstore on the other side of the square. From other doors along that block excited men were pouring, and by the time the two young men reached the scene the confusion was so great that it took the combined efforts of the two village constables, the minister and the village president to quiet them enough to find out what had happened.

To the little town the happening was serious indeed. Every store in the block had been entered during the night. The damage in any one place was not large, vandalism rather than burglary being the apparent motive. The accumulation of disorder and destruction in the eight stores was something that could not be passed over lightly. It was a shocked and sober group of people who finally dispersed to their homes and left the owners and constables to guard the wreckage until more officers of the law could be summoned from the county seat.

Uncle Dick and Lissa arrived and had to be told the one big piece of news of the whole summer. The printing of the paper was held up while they all worked frantically to make the changes necessary for the inclusion of the story in the issue. People dropped in as usual to see if the *Advocate* had any additional information to offer. There were grim expressions of determination to deal violently with the vandals if caught.

"A lot of folks are saying it's that gang of boys from the Hollow," said John Tripp, who owned the meat market next door. "What fun can they get out of such pranks? I think they'll find they went too far this time."

Seeing the meat truck from Mendon driving up, he left hurriedly. As the screen door closed behind him Uncle Dick turned to Neil with bewildered sadness. "Do *you* believe those boys would do something like that?"

"*I* don't!" Lissa burst out before Neil had time to answer. "I think it's awful the way everything is laid onto those boys just because they're not like the others. Maybe it's better they aren't."

"Just what do you mean by that crack?" asked Neil curiously.

"And what do you have against the town kids?" joined in Marv. "They're a swell bunch in my book. And what a game of ball they played last night. The Bushwhackers would be a lot better off if they'd mix with the town kids and let some good qualities rub off on them."

"Says Marv, the expert on Youth Guidance. Mr. Stebbins, what you don't know about nothing is all of it. Now I'm going out to gather up some good wholesome news that has nothing to do with breaking and entering. If anyone else wants to go to the scene of the crime and get the gory details of how much vaseline was smeared on Mr. Hunter's fixtures, and will the barber ever get his chairs cleaned after the shoe polish they got last night, he can do it. I'll have none of it."

Uncle Dick and Neil watched in amazement as she slammed the door and went out. Marv went silently back to the shop and started his press."

"Whatever started her on such a rampage?" Neil asked.

"I don't know. But you can depend on it that it was something that hit her pretty hard. Lissa's always had a hot temper, but she doesn't fly the track like this any more unless it's over something she thinks is serious. She resents having folks accuse those boys, but she can't really know anything about it."

"Unless she knows, or suspects, who did do it. And I don't see how she could do that. No wonder that man born of woman is full of trouble. He couldn't help but be with the inheritance he has."

"That's a fact," agreed Uncle Dick. "But I suspect that more than a few of his troubles come from his father's side, so don't blame the women too much. And what would we do without them? Tell me, boy, do you think those boys from the Hollow did that malicious thing?"

"No, I don't. And now that we're on the subject I'll state that I don't think they've been doing any of the mischief they've been accused of. They're a wild gang, but they aren't vicious, and they're having too much fun in their hut in the woods to bother with a fool stunt like this. I'm inclined to doubt the wholesomeness of some of their activities, but they're not harming the public. Only themselves."

"What do you mean by that?"

"The thing I'm most concerned about just now is damage to their bodies. I think they're conducting experiments of some sort. If it's rockets it could spell disaster. I've noticed all year that those boys get better grades in science than in any other study, higher than most of the town boys. And one night a book on rockets was left in the room at Mr. Horne's after the kids had left. If they're trying to make rockets they'll blow themselves sky high."

"And you don't think they were involved in last night's affair? Why?"

"It's entirely out of character. That was a very childish stunt. The Bushwhackers aren't childish. They are too mature for their years."

The people, however, who believed in the innocence of the boys from the Hollow were in the minority. By most it was considered that their guilt was already established. Even Marv, who was usually lenient in his judgments, shook his head sadly and admitted that there seemed no other solution.

"They're not fair at all," stormed Lissa when she returned from her newsgathering, angry and almost tearful at the things she had heard. "It's wicked to blame those boys when there isn't a shred of real evidence against them. That's just the way with this town. Everybody likes to hit the person that's down."

She sat down at her typewriter and began to list the obvious damage in each store. The machine made such a clatter that the men, after a look at her blazing cheeks, turned to their work in silence. Definitely this was not time for a discussion. Later, when Bud and Pug rode in with their egg orders for delivery she went out and sat in her car with them for twenty minutes, talking insistently and apparently urging something to which they would not agree. Neil, at the table by the window, could tell by the set lips and sullen head-shaking that she was not getting the thing she desired. When the boys drew away and left with their loads of eggs, she returned to the room still determinedly quiet and angry.

To the youth of the town the whole affair was a thrilling break in the regular course of existence, and they lent eager aid in straightening the merchandise. The summer people from the resort and the cottages among the hills came into view, to comment and to help. Bud and Pug spent an hour between their egg deliveries and time for their paper route work, toiling side by side with Howie Winchester and Ernie Hunter.

"You boys are worth your weight in gold today," said the druggist. "When we get all cleaned up again we're going to give you a recognition dinner. Recognizing your worth to the community, you know. In contrast to that Bushwhacker gang," he added.

"Oh, don't be so hard on them," said Howie, who was standing near. "They probably meant it all for fun."

"Fun nothing! They meant it for meanness, and something has to be done about them."

Neil had gone out to check on the progress in cleaning up the stores, and when he returned to the office Lissa was still cross and depressed, discouraging any attempts at conversation.

"What a temperamental and yet dependable girl she is!" Neil mused as he watcher her at the typewriter. "She's furious over something, and it has to do with last night's raid. Why does she care so much for the boys? She's so angry she won't talk, yet she's plugging away at those tiresome lists as if she were listing the bars of gold at Fort Knox. It's a thankless task. I suppose, though, that it will be the most widely read of any article in Tuesday's paper. Today's account is thrill enough of itself. Let them string out such an item of news as far as they can. Such a chance won't come again — we hope. I wonder if Lissa has settled her differences with Bud and Pug. Life won't be very jolly at the Harding house this evening if she hasn't."

Apparently she had not settled those differences and was loath to go home until she had, for as Neil left for the restaurant after closing time, the three of them were again in session in the car. Only when Uncle Dick came out did the argument cease. From his table at the diner Neil saw the boys get out of the car and start out again with their loads of papers. It was not evident that the battle had been decided. It was probable that a reluctant truce had been declared.

"Does she think those two boys had anything to do with it?" he pondered. "She's crazy if she does. Those kids went home with us, and I'm sure they couldn't have sneaked back to town on such a binge. Bud wouldn't tell a lie, and Pug couldn't. But it sure looks as if she is trying to get them to admit something. And as if they didn't intend to do it. Whatever is troubling her, I wish she'd let me help."

She did not ask for help, however, and Neil spent the evening alone in his room, thinking moodily of the events of the day and feeling resentment building up in him as he realized how strong the feeling against the Bushwhackers was. This emotion brought the return of his dissatisfaction with the whole situation. Since his talk with Lissa that night on the porch, he had made a sincere effort to accept the things that had befallen him and gain from them any values that might accrue. Tonight he felt that he had no further desire to adjust to this community with its harsh judgments and baseless prejudices. It was not worth the effort. Yet even as he reasoned, he knew he could not give it up now. If there were one chance in all the world that this was of the Lord he could but continue to seek for His leading and follow it.

"I guess I've really come a long way in being willing to acknowledge that," he murmured with a weary sigh. "With all my heart I want His will for myself, but how can I be sure what that is? If I had a sense of His reality I could pray with much more confidence that I'd be answered. I could trust Him more fully in this mixed-up situation. I'd like just now to be able to pray effectively about my boys."

He bowed his head in his hands and prayed. He felt a frantic reaching out to God, and pled earnestly for himself and for the wild, undisciplined and yet strangely self-disciplined lads who had won his sympathies. Perhaps because he had always had a sense of loneliness himself he had understood the apartness of the clannish Bushwhackers. He wanted to help them more than he had ever wanted anything in his life, and had prayed with an abandon he had never before known. When he went at last to his bed he had achieved no sense of nearness to the Presence he desired, but there had come a calm that brought peace and a relaxation of tension. He could sleep now, and tomorrow might bring a solution of the problem that burdened him.

When he was wakened by a scratching at his window he thought a wind must have risen and tossed the branches of the big tree against the cabin. Then he heard a whisper at the screen door.

"Mr. Abbott! Neil! It's Bill."

Quickly he opened the door and drew the three lads inside. He knew from their size that the other two must be the Hawkins twins.

"Don't turn on the light, please. We don't want anyone to see us till we've talked to you. We've been hiding all evening waiting for folks to put out their lights. What's it all about, Mr. Abbott? Lonnie Stiles waited all afternoon for us to come out of the woods so he could tell us they were after us. He said there must be awful trouble. What's it about?"

"What did you fellows do last night after you left the ball park?"

There was a quick drawing of breaths as the lads realized they had been seen in their perches on the trees, then Bill laughed.

"Somebody saw us? Guess we'll have to practice harder on camouflage. Who was it saw us? Were they gonna make us pay?"

"Lissa and I saw you and we didn't tell anyone. That's not what the trouble is about. What did you do afterward?"

"We just went home, honest we did. We were at home till half past four when we got up to go fishin'."

"Can you prove that you were in your homes all night?"

"I don't know about that. Our folks can say our beds

had been slept in, but I don't know if they really saw us in them."

"It would be a lot better if you chaps would keep in touch with your families. Your parents are too busy to chase you and you run wild like a pack of — of — mountain goats!"

Bill laughed softly. "I'll bet those goats have a lot of fun."

"And so do you, eh? Well, it might not be fun now."

"Can't you tell us what you're getting at? We can't make sense of all this quizzing."

He told them briefly what had happened and that it was generally believed that they were responsible. To this the boys gave indignant answer.

"We didn't go near town at all after the game. Wasn't it a doozer? It'd been even better if Ernie and Howie could have played. Yeh, we went right home and stayed till we went fishin', like I told you. Who says we did it? Do you believe that, Mr. Abbot?"

"No, I believe you. I don't think you'd do a silly thing like that, just as I don't believe you've been pulling the jobs all summer that you've been blamed for. But we have to *prove* it."

"Seems to me it's the other folks that have to do the provin'." In his earnestness Bill forgot his former meticulous care for his final g's and spoke with the language of his boyhood.

"Pretty shrewd, Bill. The burden of proof rests with the other side. But it would help everybody to get things straightened out if you'd do something to help yourself. Have you any idea who is causing all this trouble and letting you fellows be blamed for it?"

The silence that greeted him gave assurance that if they knew nothing, they had some definite suspicions. Bill as usual, spoke for all.

"We don't know anything, Mr. Abbott."

"But you *think* a lot, don't you?"

Again there was silence, and he knew it would be

useless to pursue that line of questioning. "Okay. I was a boy not too long ago, and I know how you feel about telling tales. But think it over. There's a gang someplace in this community, that's going to get into real trouble someday, and soon. That sort of thing gets worse if allowed to go on. You might be doing those chaps, whoever they are, a service by helping us to get hold of them before it's too late."

Silence being his only answer, he drew a long sigh and said, "Let me help you then. Will you come to town tomorrow and tell your story to the police and some of the other men?"

"Will you come with us?"

"Glad to."

"Won't they grab us before we can get there?"

"I think I can arrange that. I'll promise to bring you in. I'll meet you in front of the old schoolhouse. Some of the boys can ride with me and the rest can follow in your own two cars. Is it a promise?"

"Yes, sir, if you're with us. Maybe Mr. Horne will come, too."

"I'm sure he will. Nine o'clock tomorrow morning. Don't fail me. I'll be waiting."

"With us a deal's a deal. We won't let you down."

They slipped away into the night, and Neil went back to sleep. He still did not know the answer to the problems, but he was sure of his boys.

20

THIRTEEN BOYS SAT in self-conscious silence before the group of men gathered in the high school classroom. They looked sullen and defiant, and Neil hoped nervously that they would cooperate with their questioners as well as they had with him. He was relieved when the school principal began the hearing. He briefly reviewed the reason for the meeting, and questioned the boys in a kindly manner, but they remained uncommunicative. Bill, as spokesman, gave curt answers to the questions, denying any part in the break-ins.

Finally the discouraged principal ended his questions, and said, "Well, I'm sorry you won't cooperate, fellows, and I sincerely hope that you can find proof of where you were after nine-thirty Thursday night."

One of the merchants sat up as if just awakening from sleep. "But, Marsh, where they were after nine-thirty doesn't mean a thing! We have just assumed that it was done then because no one noticed anything until morning. We were all in cars when we followed the band home, and we didn't go along that side of the square at all. It could have been done during the ball game. I've just thought of some-

138

thing. My clock was jerked off the wall and stopped a little after eight, and so was Hunter's. I saw him setting his. That dirty business was all over by nine-thirty."

"That's so," agreed Mr. Hunter. "I never thought of it till Jim spoke. I had to set my clock up only a little over two hours when I got around to it at ten-twenty-five. A fat bunch of detectives we are!"

Mr. Marsh turned to the boys again. His face was grave and troubled. It was evident he did not like the task ahead of him. "Can you tell us, Bill, where you boys were between eight and eight-thirty?"

"No."

"Can't? Or won't?"

"I'm just not telling."

Neil had been listening with a heavy heart. He did not believe the Bushwhackers had been involved in the mischief at all, but their lack of cooperation with the men was creating a prejudice against them, and the suspicion in which they were held was not dimished by their group attitude. He had hoped that Bill would answer frankly. Surely it would be better to confess the truth than to be so misjudged. When there was continued silence he stood and spoke.

"Mr. Marsh, may I have the chair for a few minutes?"

"Yes, indeed. If you think you can get any farther than I have, I'll make you a present of the chair and throw in the desk!"

With a laugh Neil faced the boys. "Bill, tell them where you were at eight-thirty last night."

Bill was still unready to commit himself. Perhaps he did not get the implication of Neil's smile, or guess what the statements of the men could mean to him and his friends. His voice was as gruff as before.

"I'm not talking. We hadn't a thing to do with that business. Believe that or not, it's true. That's all I'm saying."

"Well, I'm saying more. Friends, if the damage was done between eight and nine — and I think we will all admit the evidence is pretty conclusive — I can give an alibi for these boys. So can Lissa Harding. She and I were together on the top row of the east bleachers, right under the big oaks. There were fourteen boys in those three trees, watching the ball game. The only ones I actually recognized were Bill, the Hawkins twins and Sandy McGuffy, but I think you will all be willing to admit that the others are surely the ones who are with them here. If you want me to I'll get Lissa on the phone and have one of you ask her about it. Or I'll ask her to come over and tell you. She'll back me up in the statement I've made."

The men sat in astonished silence, which was broken at last by Mr. Marsh. Speaking soberly with what seemed to Neil an air of self-conscious shame, he spoke to the boys.

"I'm sure I am speaking for all of us when I say that we are very sorry to have made this mistake. I don't think a single man of us here can claim never having watched a ball game from a knothole or a tree. For all the men here I want to beg your pardon. Will you, Bill, as representative of your group, shake hands with me to show that you've forgiven us? I hope we will never make such an unfounded accusation again."

Bill looked at the outstretched hand doubtfully, as if he had no desire to touch it, but he caught Neil's glance and grudgingly returned the clasp.

They were dismissed, and as they filed out of the door Neil was there to give each a friendly slap on the back and remind them that he would see them at the Horne house at eight o'clock. When the clatter of their shoes had died on the stairs, Mr. Marsh took the floor again.

"That seems to be it, friends. I'm turning it back to the village board. We seem to be right back where we started, except that now we don't have anyone to suspect. We'd better turn the matter over to the law."

Finding the culprits, however, did not prove to be the easy task the villagers had thought it should be. It had been assumed that the Bushwhackers were guilty, and no other investigations had been made until all clues, if there ever had been any, had been destroyed. The loss had not been enough to justify the hiring of a detective, and gradually the interest in the case died. The annual regatta at the resort became the focus of attention, and it would have taken a major calamity to overshadow it. The constables gave closer attention to the square and its stores, and the people forgot their apprehensions.

21

ON A DAY in August when the heat in the office had been almost unbearable, Lissa approached Neil as he prepared to leave at five o'clock. She had been in one of her unpredictable moods all day, and had had some near-angry words with Neil over an item she had brought in and which he did not think deserving of front page space, so he was surprised when she stopped him.

"Forget everything that happened today, please, Neil. I need you. I'll brief you a bit while Uncle Dick is busy on that phone call. Mother wants you to come for supper tonight. I was talking to her while you were helping Marv with those laundromat bills. Will you come and will you do something for me afterward?"

She looked sick and tired, and Neil's heart smote him for teasing her.

"You know I'll do anything I can to help you. All that stuff today was mostly in fun. We're ashamed to admit it, but we like to see you get hot and bothered. I never want to hurt you. How can I help?"

"Take me for a ride tonight."

"Of course. Couldn't have happened at a better time.

I'm to get my new car after work. Wait and ride out with me."

"Can't. Have to take Uncle Dick home. The doctor hasn't told him he can drive yet. Ooops! I'll have to go. He's ready to leave and he'll try to beat me to that wheel."

She was gone and slid in behind the wheel of the car seconds before Uncle Dick reached it. Neil smiled with amused compassion at the disappointment on the old man's face. The poor fellow knew he should not drive, but how he longed to do it! It would make him feel vigorous and able again, Neil thought.

It was a pleasant assignment that had been handed him, he decided as he showered in his tiny bathroom. Probably Lissa had called her mother and arranged for the invitation. Whatever was in her mind for the evening could not be a very pleasant prospect, for the strained look on her face told of anxiety, almost dread. What was she afraid of and how could he render helpful service? He hoped he could have a large enough assignment to be fit payment for the good meal he knew he would have. It would be simple, something hot for nourishment, something cool for refreshment, with a dessert of berries from the rows of everbearings in the garden. He had heard Lissa tell about how the children liked to pick them.

He wondered anew, as he did every time he entered this house, how Mrs. Harding managed to accomplish all that she did. A big house to keep, eight people to feed three times a day, five children to train and discipline, chickens, garden and fruit to be cared for, a semi-invalid to watch over and a dear daughter to cherish and cheer in what must be, to her, distressing circumstances. As he ate his eyes wandered again and again to her face, worn and tired at times, yet never losing its expression of quiet peace. Remembering the story Lissa had told of the tragedy in her mother's life, he knew, with the understanding he always seemed to have of another's feelings, that this comparatively young woman had passed through a hot fire of soul agony and had come out into peace.

While Lissa washed the dishes afterward, he wiped them, giving the little girls a much appreciated relief from the task.

"When I get married I hope you're my husband," said René, the youngest. "Don't you think that would be nice?"

"Not bad at all. But let's put that on the shelf until you're a bit older. Now you girls put away these dishes and I'll give you each a dime for a big ice cream cone next time you go to town. I have a date with Lissa tonight. You won't mind that, will you?"

"Oh, no. That's all right. You're just a brother to Lissa. She said so."

"Sure. I'm her big brother, and you don't need to be jealous."

"I'm not jealous. I spoke for you first so even if she wanted you she'd know I had dibs on you. Anyway, she always gives up to other people. Pug says we walk all over her."

Lissa's face flushed and she said hastily, "All right, girls. You're excused. I'll put away the pans after Slowpoke gets them wiped."

"Slowpoke will be finished by the time you are," Neil retorted. "There! That's the last. Better take a sweater. It gets cold down by the lake and I want to go down and show off the car. I may even let you drive it. Mrs. Harding, did I remember to tell you I'm running off with your daughter for a few hours?"

"She told me. I'm glad. Both of you need more play than you're getting. Have a good time, and be careful with that new car."

"Fun!" exclaimed Lissa as the car turned out of the driveway. "If she knew what I have to do tonight she'd spend the evening on her knees. I need her prayers, I'll admit, but I'm not going to let her carry my burdens. This one has nothing to do with her."

"Could you share a bit of that burden or problem?"

She did not answer him, and he said no more. This

problem seemed to belong only to herself. As they passed the square she spoke.

"Go to Winchesters'. I guess I'll have to tell you some of it. I hope you won't try to guess any more than I'm telling you. I have to see Mr. Winchester tonight, and I have to tell him something that I'm afraid will make him furiously angry. He'll hate me more than ever."

"Now what wild idea has set up housekeeping in your little brain? Why should Howard Winchester hate you? He has bigger business than that to concern himself with, and he seems a decent sort. What have you done?"

"It's usually what I won't do that disturbs him. He's still working on the companion-secretary deal, and I think he's distressed to find I'm not interested and mean it! I've found out who he *thinks* I am, and if it's any comfort to his pride I'll let him believe it. He thinks I'm the child of a cousin of Mrs. Winchester. Both parents, he says, died when I was a few weeks old and I was out for adoption by the grandmother who couldn't keep me. Nice story, isn't it? Wonder who thought it up."

"Whatever the real story is, I hope for the sake of that home that he never finds out differently. The truth is something his wife doesn't want him to know. The 'real mother' is still living, to judge by what you heard, and she did something that may have been illegal. Maybe she forged that birth certificate and Mrs. Winchester knows it."

"It's a crazy mess, and I'm in the middle of it. But that's not my problem tonight. This one hits Howard Winchester right in the middle of his existence. Here we are. Let me out here at the front walk. It will work or it won't. In either case I won't be long. I'll not stay for any polite conversation afterward, nor even for a spot of tea."

"You don't think he'll hurt you, do you?"

She laughed and seemed to lose a bit of her tension. "You're a dear old granny, but I like being worried over. He won't hurt me, but you can do some praying that I'll act like a lady and not disgrace the cousin he thinks I belong to!"

He watched her as she marched up the walk, and

thought that just so must prisoners have marched to the executioner in the days of Bloody Mary. A line from a poem read long ago went through his mind and he repeated it softly,

" 'Steel true and blade straight.' Now what was the rest of that? I'm sure there was more of it, but I guess it wouldn't apply. That first line sure fits Lissa though!"

As he waited it occurred to him that he might help by praying even though he still felt a hesitancy about asking the Lord to concern Himself over details of life that Christians could handle alone. Perhaps Lissa's temper was not a thing that could be handled without His help, however. With his arms crossed on the wheel, he bowed his head on them and prayed. He forgot about the errand or the need for temper control. The only prayer that came to his lips was that Lissa might find the peace that made her mother's face beautiful.

He did not see the slim boy's figure that came from the back of the house and made its way down the driveway to a car that had been waiting in the shadow of a low-branching maple across the road. It was only the sound of tires on the concrete that roused him, and he watched the car pick up speed and disappear in the distance.

"Did that car drop from a parachute? I never heard it coming until those tires squealed. It couldn't have come out of the drive. Something funny here."

Lissa came running down the walk and climbed breathlessly into his car. "Well, that's over, and I'm here to say that Mr. Howard Winchester is one decent gentleman. He gets my vote when he wants to run for senator, if he does."

"He didn't hurt you?"

"He thanked me. Thanked me, Neil, for hurting him so badly I almost cried for him. Well, it's over. Do you mind taking me for a real ride in this dreamboat? I don't want to go home until I've done something to tell mother about when she asks questions."

"Where do you want to go? This is supposed to be a date, you know, and I want to give you a good time."

"Let's go and see Mrs. Brown at the Hollow. I have two more rug orders for her. You really started something there. I don't know how many people are helping her. They come in whenever they can and she keeps a strict account of their hours. Several of the high school girls are kept busy cutting and folding and pressing the rags, and a lot of the women are helping her sew. Those rugs are absolutely beautiful, and Sara keeps sending orders from all her friends. Mrs. Brown told us last week that we'd better tell folks she's taking orders for winter work now. She has all she can do for the present."

"I don't see how she does it. It looks like real drudgery to me, but she says she's happier than she has been for years. She feels she has a purpose in life now."

Mrs. Brown gave them a delighted greeting. She had folded her work away for the day and was rocking alone on her porch when they drove up. When Lissa asked how the latest rug was coming she showed them the almost finished piece. Then she took them into her bedroom to show four others that were ready for delivery.

"These things must take a whale of a lot of work," said Neil gazing in admiration at the beautifully blended colors. "They are almost too beautiful to walk on, but they look as if they would last forever."

"They *will* wear well. I never had a chance to make one of new material before nor to choose the colors. The idea of making them of denim is something I'd like to patent. The colors are so soft, and the goods will wear like buckskin. That Sary can give some of these to her grandchildren. I sewed them with that nylon cord I saw advertised in the catalog. You just can't break it."

When Lissa gave her the two new orders she gave a delighted laugh. "I wanted to make her a rug just like yours," she explained to Neil. "But she says she won't let me until she's brought me five other orders. This makes four. See, I keep track in my notebook like this."

There were four names in the notebook with AH after them. "That's for Alicia Harding," she said. "When there's another one I'm starting on yours."

After tea and cookies, they prepared to leave and Mrs. Brown followed them to the front porch.

"Now you drive real careful. It's dark on the creek road, and you've got Lissa to look out for."

"I'll do just that. She *is* pretty valuable cargo!"

They drove past the old schoolhouse which showed signs that someone had begun the work of rehabilitation.

"People are probably beginning to get curious," Neil said. "Uncle Dick says he's not going to tell anyone outside the office and family just exactly what he is planning until he's ready to turn it over to some management that he will decide on. Says there will be too much free advice handed out and he wants to do it his own way."

"I don't blame him. I get pretty tired of too much oversight myself. Like when I think the new baby at Hodges' deserves front page mention more than Warren Tolliver's new porch does. Like when the men all gang up against me and put the baby on the back page while the porch has the middle of the front."

"You don't get the point at all. You're too feminine in your outlook to ever be a good newspaper man, but worse than that, you're deceitful."

"What do you mean? Am I supposed to like *that?*"

"What do you think of a girl who keeps her identity hidden from her own fellow worker for months upon months?"

"And what do you call it when he doesn't recognize her?"

"I call him pretty dumb. Now tell me. Are you really the sophisticated young lady that I escorted home from our church that rainy night last September? And if so, why haven't you identified yourself to me before this?"

"I never recognized you that first day you came into the *Advocate* office. I hadn't really had a good look at you that night in the city. I was glad for the ride, I enjoyed the conversation, but not even your voice seemed familiar. I'm not good at remembering things like that. If you'd been able to leave with the rest of the party I'd never have thought of it again. But later my mind got to working. You've spoken often of Bruce Franklin as your roommate. It didn't take much brain power to figure it out from there."

"Why didn't you let me in on the secret? I feel like a chump. Why didn't Sara tell me?"

"Because I told her not to. We've been having lots of fun over it. You can expect some razzing when they find out you finally woke up."

"Woke up is right. I've been in a regular coma. But what *I* want to know is, how you came to be so intimate with Sara. How do you get invitations to the Rossiter home? Are you, like Uncle Dick, related to them?"

"No. But because of Uncle Dick we've seen a great deal of them. This summer I haven't seen much of Sara because we agreed not to be seen together until you knew who I was. Even if you didn't get wise I was invited to spend my vacation with her and her mother on a trip to Yellowstone. We used to be together a lot before I started to work. That *does* make a difference in any girl's life."

"Were you in Sara's class at Marshall?"

"Yes. That's why I chose Marshall. You didn't know Sara then so naturally wouldn't have noticed her roommate. I was invited to that party last winter, but Uncle Dick was very sick that weekend and I didn't want to leave mother. I wanted to go though. Mr. Rossiter taught Sara and me to ski on those hills, and I didn't get a chance to go skiing all winter."

"You had plenty of exercise on snowshoes. . . . Well, well. So it was you who believed that all things do work together for good to the elect."

149

22

FOR SEVERAL WEEKS things in the little town ran along
smoothly. The boys played ball with neighboring teams and
spent their evening hours in practice. Their days were taken
up with summer jobs in store, shop, or farm. The girls
worked as waitresses or as clerks at the resort. The
Bushwhackers fished in the morning, sold their catch as
usual, then retired into the woods for their secret sessions
which were becoming a matter of deep concern for those who
were interested in the lads. No one knew how to interfere
without causing more trouble.

Uncle Dick was determined to get the Youth Center, as
he called it, ready for use as quickly as possible. A carpenter
friend was entrusted with the secret, drove out to inspect it
and decide what must be done to make it safe and attractive.
Two floor joists had been weakened by borers, and several
rafters were sagging and would have to be replaced. The
window and door frames were sound, but the sashes had
rotted until they would no longer hold the glass. Under Uncle
Dick's questioning the man agreed that after these things
were taken care of, the rest of the work could be done by
unskilled labor under proper supervision.

During the last two weeks of August, while the town's young people were still too busy with their other affairs, the carpenter finished his work and Uncle Dick hired the Bushwhackers to put on the roofing and fresh paint inside and out. Neil, as he had feared, was chosen as supervisor.

In spite of his avowed dislike for the task, however, he was faithful to it and put his best efforts into seeing that the Bushwhackers learned how to lay roofing and paint, and then put their knowledge into effect. He succeeded so well that when the rain came that the dairymen had been praying for, the old schoolhouse was weatherproof. By that time the summer people were gone and the boys and girls back in school. The town was settling down to its seasonal routine, and there was an air of relaxed enjoyment of the quiet that brooded over the lake and hills. Uncle Dick was as happy as a small boy with his first bicycle.

"I haven't had so much fun since I helped build a tree house when I was in knee pants. Neil, do you think you and your boys could lay some new floor boards? The ones right in front of the door are so worn that the knots could trip somebody. Mr. Hawkins said he'd help if you don't know how to go about it."

"I'll be glad for Mr. Hawkins' help. If he hadn't arrived in time I'd have been putting the roofing strips on upside down. The twins knew I was doing it wrong but were too polite to tell me, so they went after their dad."

"The furnace man from Mendon will come in with his figures sometime this morning. I'm going out to the Hollow with him. If he gets busy right away we ought to have the place ready to open by snowfall."

"If the snow doesn't come too soon and the boys have the time to fix those floorboards and finish the painting. Bill and the twins are talking of trying to get jobs after school. They need the money, they say."

"We'll pay them as much as anybody can. I don't know where they could get jobs around here anyway. The town boys probably have them all spoken for."

"They'll do anything and do it fairly well if they want

151

money for their experiments. They should be able to find work as easily as the other boys do. But there's still a prejudice against them, they think. Is there another gang or clique around here that's stirring up feeling against the Bushwhackers?"

"Not that I know of," answered Uncle Dick, and Marv agreed. "The boys like to gather in front of the drugstore evenings, but there doesn't seem to be any gang spirit."

"Oh, yeah?" came a derisive voice from the corner where Lissa was working.

"What do you mean?" demanded Uncle Dick, quick to come to the defense of his town. "There aren't any young gangsters in this town, and you know it!"

Lissa looked abashed at this reproof from the usually gentle old man, but she held her ground staunchly. "I haven't said there's a gang. Nor will I say there isn't. How many does it take to make a gang? It would be good for some of the parents of this town to wake up and look at their kids with open eyes. Some of them might be surprised."

Turning her back on the astonished men she took her notebook and went out to gather the news around the square. When the door had closed after her the men looked at each other in bewilderment.

"Wow!" said Marv. "What ails that child these days? Gangs in Appleboro! She's off her rocker."

"Women!" was Neil's contribution to the conversation.

"Don't blame her," came Uncle Dick's soft voice. "Lissa doesn't mean to be so touchy. She's not that kind of girl at all. But she is troubled now with a problem she won't share, and it's too big for her. She doesn't have an easy life, and she hasn't yet learned to ride with the storm."

By the first week in October the new floorboards were laid, gleaming paint covered the walls and ceiling, the shutters were repaired and in place, and two floor furnaces were ready for operation. All that remained to be done was the buying and placing of equipment and furniture, and advice was needed for that. It was time for the community to learn the purpose of all the activity in the Hollow. Mr. Rossiter asked for the privilege of writing the announcement for the *Advocate,* and of paying the expenses of "Open House," the night of the dedication. This event was set for the last Friday in October.

The announcement which Mr. Rossiter asked to be placed in front page center, gave the whole story of the working out of Uncle Dick's plan and concluded with a eulogy of Uncle Dick's life and work in the community, causing the old editor acute embarrassment and secret pleasure. Mr. Rossiter's name signed at the bottom gave it unusual prominence, and added importance to the entire project. Below this was the announcement that a friend had made a gift of ping-pong, basketball and badminton equipment, as well as an electrical kitchenette which could be used for preparing refreshments for meetings, then could be wheeled out of sight in the old cloakroom. Many who read the announcement, with its statement that its purpose was to serve all the youth of the community, read into it the hope that it might erase the caste lines which had been drawn.

Another item in the same issue stirred almost as much excitement. The banker at Mendon had written that he had received a check for payment to the merchants who had suffered from the damage by vandals in the summer. Claims from each merchant were to be submitted to the banker, with an endorsement by the village lawyer, and payment would be made promptly. The name of the one who wished such restitution to be made was not made public and speculation about it brought no solution.

"We will put our thank you note in the *Advocate,* and hope he sees it," the merchants agreed. "He couldn't be the guilty party. No man with that much money is going around slinging nails and screws all around or unrolling yards of cloth just for fun."

Between interest in the football season which had opened with a win over the supposedly strongest team in the league, and in the news about the new Youth Center, Appleboro had no time to think about the Bushwhackers. The latter were too busy, however, to miss the attention to which they had become accustomed. They had a project of their own, and Neil was their sponsor and only confidant, having earned that honor by advancing the money needed for the working out of their plan.

Some distance back of the schoolhouse in the Hollow was an old shed where wood and coal had been kept for the two big stoves that formerly heated the class rooms. The boys saw in this a place where they might, if it could be made to pass inspection, have a laboratory in which they could perform experiments beyond the capacity of the hut in the woods. It must be repaired and cleaned to make its possibilities evident to those who would have to pass on it, so every afternoon when they were not busy at other tasks they spent on the shed. It was straightened and braced, old boards replaced by salvage from the discarded flooring of the schoolhouse, the roof repaired, and the interior swept clean of bark and splinters. One end had been left open for easy unloading of the fuel, and this was envisaged by the boys as the place where they might, if all went as they planned, roll out a rocket that would be the answer to the national defense problem. There must be doors, however, for the work would of necessity be of a secret nature. For this purpose Neil's money was used, and the door frame and wide doors that resulted were a source of pride to Neil as well as the boys.

"We'd better wait a while before we try to get permission to have a lab here," counseled Bill. "We don't have enough money for the equipment anyway. Let's just let Mr. Richardson use it for a garage when he comes out. Then when we're ready Mr. Abbott can ask him for it."

The broken glass, rusty cans and other unsightly accumulation had been hauled from the yard that it might be used for parking on the night of the dedication, and the improved appearance gave the girls an idea of their own. They would rake the yard and cut down the old weed stalks that gave it a ragged appearance. Several of the children were inspired to such an extent that they cleared certain unattractive spots in their own dooryards. Two days before the dedication there was nothing left for them to do except wait, which was the hardest task of all.

On Thursday Mr. Rossiter drove in with Terry who was bursting with pride over what Uncle Dick had done. The three of them went out to the Hollow to inspect the Center and direct the men who were delivering the furniture, and returned glowingly happy over what they had seen, and especially over the part played by the Hollow's own boys.

"What makes folks think those kids are bad?" asked Terry over the coffee that Marv had made on the plate in the shop. "I think they're a pretty sharp crew."

"They're sharp, all right," agreed Neil. "And I don't let anyone say that they're bad. But they are undeniably antisocial."

"I don't even think they're that. While Dad and Uncle Dick were tinkering with that kitchen gadget the school bus rolled in. Some of the boys came over and showed me the shop they've been working on in the back. They talked plenty about that."

"That's because they recognized you as another non-conformist," said Neil in an undertone and Terry grinned in comprehension.

"Those boys have changed a lot in the last few months, and Neil deserves most of the credit. He and the minister teamed up and really went after them. That's what inspired me with the Center idea. Thought maybe we could get a line on what makes them so wary. The only people they really trust are Neil and Mr. Horne."

"They trust you," protested Neil.

"Let's say they are beginning to."

"What happened to make them that way?" asked Mr. Rossiter.

"Nothing that anyone can figure out."

"Something did happen, though. Somebody said something or did something that didn't mean a thing to the fellow that did it. Or maybe he meant to push 'em over," said Terry. "Whatever it was it meant a lot to some of those kids. And

155

they got the others off on that same track. Kids don't act like that just for fun.''

"You're right, they don't." This from Lissa at her table in the corner. Only Neil heard it, for the others had turned to greet Mr. Horne who had just come in. He wished he dared ask her the meaning of the remark.

23

NEIL HAD FALLEN asleep in his chair listening to his records when a knocking at his door awakened him, and Bud burst in saying almost incoherently, "Have you seen Uncle Dick? Mother wants to know. He's not at home and he's not at Rossiter's. Will you take me to the office?"

"No, I haven't. Yes, I will. Are you sure he's not at the lodge? Lissa said he was going there."

Neil was pulling on his coat as he went. As they came out of the cabin they could see the lights blazing in the side lot of the Harding place, and Mrs. Harding was backing the small truck out of the drive.

She stopped only long enough to explain hurriedly, "We all thought he was at the lodge. He said he was going there. Then just a while ago Harry called and wanted to talk to him about something. Thought he was here. It seems he called about five-thirty after you folks had all left the office and said he didn't feel like going. But he didn't come home. We have to go and hunt him. He's sick or hurt someplace, I know. Harry is coming in and will meet us at the office. But Uncle Dick won't be there, I'm sure."

She drove off, Pug in the seat beside her. Neil and Bud

followed, desperately trying to think of anything that could have detained the editor until this late hour. Would he have lain down on the old cot and fallen so soundly asleep that even the telephone on his desk could not waken him? Would they find him in a condition that was more than sleep? It wouldn't be in character at all for him to lie down at such an hour unless he had been too ill to call Mrs. Harding.

They opened the office door, dreading to look at the cot lest their fears be realized. It was empty, however, and although they searched every corner of office, shop and basement they found no clue to help. Neil called Marv to see if he had any knowledge the others lacked. He knew nothing, but promised that he would be down in ten minutes to help in what promised to be a real search.

The two constables, seeing the lights, came one after the other to inquire as to the cause, and the Rossiters arrived simultaneously with Marv.

"He had planned to spend the night with us," explained Mr. Rossiter. "We left with Mr. Horne and went over to see the new lights they've put in the Sunday school rooms. Dick said he was going to Tichnors' to see how Elmer was getting along, then he would drive out in time for supper. It's such a short distance no one could have dreamed he shouldn't go alone. He called about five-forty-five and said he'd been to Tichnors' and had decided to go on home. Said he was tired and if he came out we'd talk until all hours and he'd better go home and get his rest. That's all I know except that Grace said he hadn't been home."

"Wherever he is, he is sick or hurt," Mrs. Harding's voice quavered with the concern she felt. "We *have* to find him, and I don't know where to hunt."

"None of us do. We just have to go every possible place. Abbott, do you or Marv know of any place where he *might* be?"

Both young men shook their heads.

"Then we'll have to go everyplace that little car of his could go. Grace, you had better go home and wait by the telephone. Terry and I will go together. You young fellows each take a boy, and we'll get busy. The sooner we start the better.''

''Where do we come in?'' asked one of the constables. ''Seems like this ought to be our job.''

''You stay in town. Look back of all the stores, in every alley and every backyard. Look behind the trees. Look every place!''

Mr. Rossiter had taken leadership of the group and was deploying his forces. His brusque manner showed that he was deeply shaken by his cousin's disappearance.

''Shouldn't we get Dr. Anderson?'' asked Mrs. Harding. ''If Uncle Dick is sick or hurt the doctor should be on hand.''

''He can't be with all of us. We don't know which team will find him. Call him when you get home, Grace, and tell him to stay where we can reach him. You and Lissa stay by the phone and each team will call in occasionally so that we can all keep informed. Marv, you and your lad go to the Tichnors'. Maybe he was calling from there and they can tell you something that will help. Abbott and the other boy go to the Gap. Look all around here, then stop at the farms on the way back. Terry and I will go to the Hollow, then if nothing has been heard we'll head back toward the lodge. He may have started there after all. Stop at every farm. Don't be afraid to wake folks up. Nobody will mind being disturbed for Dick.''

As he drove along the road that led to the Gap, Neil watched on one side and Bud on the other for car tracks that might tell them something. It was slow work, for the night was not bright and often Bud had to get out with his flashlight to examine a spot that looked suspicious. On each side the ditches, filled with water from a heavy rain the day before, looked forbidding and dangerous. Had the little car gone into a skid on this muddy shoulder of the highway Uncle Dick's weak arms could not have righted it. But in such a case the car would be seen for the ditches were shallow.

When they came to the Gap itself Bud drove the car

while Neil walked along the right-of-way in the deep shadow cast by the cliff. Back on the other side then, beyond the railroad tracks where the debris left by the blasting still made shadows where a man's body might be hidden. The implications of such a thought made him sick at heart, but Mr. Rossiter had said to look every place, and it should be done. But neither here nor in any of the byways beyond could any trace of the old man be found. At the first house they passed on their way back, Neil roused the sleeping occupants and made his telephone call. Lissa answered.

"No news yet. Mr. Rossiter called a few minutes ago and said for you to report at the office. They're getting the state police out. I've persuaded Mother to go to bed. Uncle Dick will need her when they find him. Don't you think the boys had better come home?"

"I'll bring them out and then get back to the office. I'm staying on the job until we find out what this is all about. If we find that any harm has come to Uncle Dick from someone's meanness or even carelessness I'm staying on awhile longer just for my own satisfaction."

"I know how you feel. But Neil, please be careful."

To the farmer who had been standing by he made a hurried explanation and got the promise that as soon as morning came a posse would be beating the fields and the brushy land along the foot of the hills. Back at the office the others were waiting, their sober faces telling the story he had already heard from Lissa. One of the constables volunteered to take the boys home and Neil stayed to answer any questions the police might want to ask.

"Did you talk to any of the boys at the Hollow?" he asked while they waited.

"Yes. A man told us that Bill Somebody would know if anyone did. So we woke him up. He said none of them had seen him since he left with me this afternoon. I guess it's yesterday afternoon by now. That clock there says two-forty. Bill wanted to come with us but we told him there was nothing he could do."

"Did you look at the Center?"

"Yes, that was the first place we went. Everything was just as Dick and I left it. Both doors padlocked, shutters fastened from the inside. No one had been there since we left. Terry went out to that shed in the back, but it was locked tight. Dick had said only he and the electrician had keys, so no one could have got in without leaving some damage. We'll have to look elsewhere for Dick. I think he had a heart attack someplace."

"And then hid himself and car?"

"I guess I'm just not thinking straight. Maybe it's because I don't want to discover that there's anyone in the world mean enough to harm Dick. Whoever it was I'm sure he never knew the old chap. No one who knew Dick could harm him."

"If anyone ever did, this state wouldn't be big enough to hide him," said one of the constables.

Marv and Neil had been talking together and now Neil spoke. "Marv and I think we had better go back to the Hollow in time to get the Bushwhackers up and out as soon as it is light enough. That swamp back of those cliffs on the lake shore has to be searched, and those boys are the only ones that can do it. Anyone else would be hopelessly lost in fifteen minutes. But we think it has to be done."

"It does. Everything possible has to be done. When those police get here I'm going with them. I can't sit still and do nothing. Maybe Dick is suffering right now and calling for help. If he's been kidnaped I wish the brutes that did it would hurry up and demand a ransom, so I could pay it."

Mr. Rossiter's voice broke and he drew a long quivering breath and wiped his eyes. The silence that followed was broken by Marv.

"We keep coffee here for when we need a break. The chap who took the boys home is back with some sandwiches Lissa sent. Let's eat something before we start out again. We'll do a better job for it."

Over the coffee they planned their further search. It seemed probable that the police would want many helpers, for the woods, hills and small canyons would require close search. In the midst of this discussion the police arrived, two cars and two motorcycles, eight men in all.

"Who's the missing person?" asked the officer in charge. "Man, woman, boy or girl?"

"Man. A frail man who ought not be out this chilly night. It is Mr. Richardson, the editor of the newspaper."

"Uncle Dick?"

"Yes, do you know him?"

"I'll say I do! We stop for a chat every time we meet on the road. He came to see two of us fellows in the hospital after we were hurt in an accident last year. All us guys are for Uncle Dick. To him, everybody's people. What happened to him?"

"That's exactly what we want you to find out."

The story was told, the pitifully scant information they had. Uncle Dick's plan to go to the lodge, his subsequent call that he had changed his mind, the discovery that he was neither at the lodge nor the Harding home.

"I thanked the Lord at first that I had made that call," said Mr. Rossiter. "Now it doesn't seem to have made much difference. We haven't done Dick an iota of good in all these hours."

It was agreed that as soon as dawn had come men and boys should beat across the fields and the hills so thoroughly that nothing could be overlooked. The officer suggested that high school be forgotten for the day, that the boys might assist in the search.

"They tire less easily than the men, and they can go places some of the men would be afraid to look at," he explained.

Marv and Neil would go again to the Hollow to enlist the aid of the Bushwhackers. The police with Mr. Rossiter would use all their skill and experience to direct and extend the search. The sergeant in charge would go to the Harding home to question everyone there and to search Uncle Dick's room for clues.

"You folks probably think that's far-fetched and completely unnecessary. It may prove just that. But in cases like this we have to do a lot of things that seem foolish in hopes that one of them may furnish a clue. Just because we know Uncle Dick, we can't take these things for granted. We have to do everything we can think of. Someplace we will find a lead. I promise you we won't quit till we do."

By dawn a crowd had gathered, men and boys eager to be out on their appointed task, the women anxious and often tearful. The proprietor of the restaurant opened early and declined pay for the coffee and rolls he served. It was arranged that the news of discovery of Uncle Dick (or of his body, they admitted shudderingly) should be telephoned as quickly as possible to the fire station that the siren might recall the other searchers. Mrs. Horne came, suggesting that the women come to her home for a prayer meeting. Later, if the hunt continued, they could prepare and take out lunches to the crews.

Marv and Neil drove to the Hollow, their hearts heavy with foreboding. The thought that Uncle Dick might have spent the night in the swamp was intolerable.

"If he's in there I could almost hope he's dead," said Neil. "I get sick just at the thought of undertaking such a hunt."

"We don't know that he's there. Let's not borrow any trouble."

"You're right, of course. But where else could he be? We've looked every place he'd have gone of his own will. Terry and his dad even drove clear to the resort last night before they came in. Nothing there. There's been a criminal attack of some sort, and anyone who would attack a frail old man like Uncle Dick wouldn't hesitate to pull any other dirty trick he could think of, in order to hide his guilt."

Bill and his boys were waiting for them, looking frightened and miserable. "Look, Mr. Abbott, folks don't think we've done this, do they? I'll — I'll swear we had nothing to do with it. We haven't seen him since he left with Mr. Rossiter and his son yesterday afternoon."

"I know you haven't. And no one else thinks so. Don't get to expecting that you'll be blamed for everything that goes wrong. The folks in town are all right, once you get to know them. And nothing could do more to raise their esteem for you than for you to go all out in this hunt. Bill, you divide the fellows into two teams and tell them how to work. I'll go with one and Marv with the other. Let's make all the haste we can, but do a good job. If Uncle Dick is in that swamp, even if he wasn't injured before being taken there, every minute's delay makes his situation more serious. Now there's another thing. Mr. Horne suggested that we pray before we start out. I'll pray now, then let each fellow pray as we go."

After the prayer they all managed to get into the boys' two cars, Bill explaining that he doubted if the larger car could "make it." They reached the hut, by car, then afoot, then Bill outlined his strategy. Each team was to take a designated area and work if thoroughly, then return to the hut where they would compare ideas before starting again. It was slow and tedious work, and to Neil and Marv, grueling labor. They marveled at the ease with which the boys made their way, leaping from one hummock to another and apparently knowing without doubt which ones would bear the weight of their bodies. In spite of his anxiety Neil was touched and amused by the care with which the young men were guided and safeguarded. The Hawkins twins were his leaders, and one of them was always at his side to prevent a stumble or misstep. Occasionally the other boys would disappear for what seemed a long time, but when a leader whistled there was a quick answer, and soon they would return to tell of their efforts.

The story was always the same. Nothing had been seen that could be considered unusual. The swamp lay under its blanket of autumn leaves, silent except for the dropping of acorns or the splash of an otter hurrying into a pool at their approach. There were no threads of torn clothing hanging on twigs, no bits of paper that might have been dropped by one being taken against his will. After three weary hours they all met at the hut to plan a deeper penetration or give up and go home.

"I don't like to give up," said Bill. "But honestly, I

don't think anyone could possibly have gone back further. We've only done it once or twice and it was so bad we decided it wasn't worth it. Nobody could do it in the dark. Wouldn't we be of more use outside helping cover the hills where the summer cottages are?"

"There are crews out there now, a lot of them. Let's sit here awhile and rest and try to get a new idea. I'm completely bushed."

It was a small hut and most of the boys stayed outside. Bill and the twins built a fire in an old stove at one end and soon the welcome warmth began to be felt. Water from their canteens was heated and mixed with powdered cocoa for a most welcome drink. These attentions had their effect and Neil's head was nodding when Bill jumped up with a sharp exclamation as another boy burst through the door.

"What was it?"

Before the lad could answer, it came again — two shrill blasts on a whistle.

"That's Minnie. I gave her a whistle and told her to blow if anything happened."

"Does it mean he's been found?" gasped Marv and Neil together as they started for the door.

"No. That was to be one long blast. This means that she wants us. She must know something."

Into the cars again, then the drive through the winding, brushy and poorly defined road to the big tree at the edge of the woods where Minnie waited. She was excited and crying.

"I came because we're scared, Bill. Us girls wanted to be doin' something, so we got the rakes again and worked on the schoolyard. Kate Hawkins and Billy were playin' around while we worked and they dug a knot out of the back of the shed. There's a car in there, Bill. I saw it. And the door's padlocked."

"Did you tell anybody?"

"No, the men are all away and the women are all crying or so busy talkin' they won't listen. I told the girls to stay there and I'd go get you. I'm scared, Bill!"

"So am I," said Bill. "Climb in and we'll get out of here pronto!"

How even a small girl managed to crowd into the car, Neil could not understand, but she did and they were off on a wild trip over a rough road. But they were arriving, which was all that mattered. They were tumbling out before the cars had come to a stop by the shed, and Bill rushed to the back to verify Minnie's story.

"It's true," he gasped. "I can just see a part of a wheel and fender. Get anything we can find. We gotta break in!"

Marv grabbed the jack handle that one of the boys produced and, without regard for the newly installed doors, attacked the padlock. It was only a few minutes, although it seemed an hour to the watchers before the wood splintered and the lock gave way. The boys, looking sick and frightened, drew back as Neil and Marv entered the dark shed. The silent, huddled shape on the back seat of the car told that the search was ended. Uncle Dick was found, but one look at his bloodless face and half-opened mouth told that it might not be a happy return to his village.

"Bill, call the fire station and tell them," said Neil as he hurried to his own car to which Marv was carrying the slight form. A feeble pulse told that life was flickering low. Hoarse, rasping breaths were so far apart that the watchers doubted if the next would come at all. From a gash on the head blood had flowed over the old man's face and clothes. He had made an effort to bandage it with a handkerchief, but that, too, was bloodstained.

"Drive like you never drove before," said Marv as he put his burden down on the back seat and climbed in beside it.

The group of boys and girls watched the car disappear down the hill road. As it passed from sight one of the twins, hoarse with anger, said,

"That was done by some low down — low down — oh, there's no name for them!"

"Maybe nobody meant to," Minnie ventured, but a chorus of boys answered her.

"Nobody could lock that door without seein' the car."

"I'll bet I know who it was."

"Shut up then if you don't want trouble."

They prob'ly thought they was lockin' us in."

Bill had come back from his errand and now took charge, drawing a long breath, then letting it out slowly.

"Don't anybody do anything till we know more. Just keep your mouths shut. If it's what we think we'll take care of it — good!"

24

In the big south bedroom of the Harding house Uncle Dick lay unconscious of the commotion he had created in the community. The doctor sat by the bed watching every labored breath. Mrs. Harding stood at his side, her eyes fixed on the thin face which was beginning to show a bit of color in place of the chalkiness that had been there when the men carried their unconscious burden up the stairs two hours before. The doctor's wife, in white dress and cap, stepped softly about with an air of efficiency that gave assurance to Mrs. Harding's troubled heart. Downstairs a group of men sat at the kitchen table drinking the coffee Lissa had made and talking over the strange occurrence.

What was Uncle Dick doing at the Center at that hour? Had he gone there purposely on some forgotten errand, or had he been carried there in an unconscious state? Who had driven the car in and then left, locking the doors to the shed? And *why* had anyone done such a thing? Who had struck Uncle Dick, inflicting that wound on his head?

"The question of *why* can wait," said Mr. Rossiter. "The thing we have to find out now is who did this dastardly thing! When we do — !" he left his sentence unfinished as if his thought were beyond words. Terry, by his side, was clenching his hands as if to steady them.

"Let's all get back to town," said Neil. "Marv left awhile ago saying that he was going to get some rest and then run off the *Advocate*. It will be a day late but it will be out by the time Uncle Dick wakes up enough to ask about it."

"If he ever does," muttered Terry.

At the office it was agreed to leave two of the high school teachers in charge to answer such questions that might come in, while Neil and Marv should go home and sleep for several hours in order to be back later to run off the issue of the paper that would carry the news of the accident. It would be up to Neil to make that write-up, while Marv would be readying the press. Lissa could not be spared from home but the two teachers volunteered their services in preparing the mailing that must catch the next morning's train.

It was five o'clock when Neil woke from a sleep so deep that he felt as if he had been drugged. A bath and shave refreshed him, and after a trip across the road to see what the latest development was, and a bowl of vegetable soup that Ruthie served to him in the kitchen, he felt able to meet the demands of the hours that lay ahead.

It was ten o'clock when the last paper was ready for the mail. "Let's call it a day," said Marv stretching his weary arms. "We can have the rest of them ready by the time the boys get here for their loads. I'll call them and tell them to report at nine in the morning. If anyone objects to his paper being late, send him to me."

As Neil approached his car a dark form stepped out of the shadow of the building and Bill's voice spoke softly,

"Mr. Abbott, can I come home with you? I want to talk about something."

"Sure. Hop in my car and I'll drive you out."

"I don't want anyone to see us together. My car's around the corner. The twins are in it and we'll follow you out."

He disappeared again into the shadows, but Neil had hardly turned off his engine in the cabin drive until they were beside him. It was evident that they were very much troubled lads. Inside the cabin they pled their case before the only person whom they knew who might listen sympathetically.

"Mr. Abbott, honestly we would never have done such a thing to Uncle Dick. He's always been good to us, and that clubhouse is a wonderful thing. We've worked on it with him and we like him! Why should anyone think we'd want to hurt him?"

"Does anyone?"

"Yes, they've been saying things about us all afternoon. Some of them think we fooled them on that burglary business. And they say they're going to turn us over to the sheriff at Mendon."

"How do you know all this?"

"Don Horne called and told me. Don's an all right guy and he knows we wouldn't do it. He walked around town and listened to folks and heard 'em say those things."

"I'm another one that doesn't believe a thing like that. You can count on Mr. Horne, too, and I think Mr. Marsh is convinced you are all right. But I'm afraid you're right in thinking you are being blamed. I heard a few things myself this evening. Sit down and let's talk this thing over. Maybe we can get to the heart of things. Will you answer some questions? You fellows get about more than we older ones can. And if boys like Don are for you it is probable a lot more are. If you will tell us all you know maybe we can find some clue to help you."

"We don't know anything. Not one single thing. We didn't know Uncle Dick was in the shed, and we never locked the doors."

"Where were you all evening?"

"In Macey's shed working on our car. He has a light there and lets us use it if we keep his car up, too."

"Does he know how long you were there?"

"No, I guess not. They all went into town and hadn't got home when we left."

"What time was that? Did you see any activity about the Center when you went past?"

"None of us noticed anything. We've talked about that. It was all dark and quiet. Cross my heart, Mr. Abbott, we don't any of us know anything about this."

"Do you have any suspicions?"

"We don't know a thing."

"You're dodging the issue, Bill. Now I want a straight and full answer. If you aren't guilty you don't have a thing to fear. I'm asking again. Please answer me. Do you have any idea who did this cowardly thing?"

Bill faced him, face pale and lips set stubbornly.

"We don't know."

Neil turned quickly and spoke to the boy nearest him. "Bryan, who did this?"

Bryan, the smaller and more reserved twin, looked beseechingly at Bill, then answered shakily, "I don't know."

"All right, Byron. What do you say?"

"I'm not saying anything."

"Bill?"

"Nothing."

Neil looked at them in exasperation. "You all make me disgusted. Uncle Dick, who has done the finest thing for you chaps that this community has ever seen, has been seriously injured. Maybe fatally. The ones who did it should be made to face the consequences. If it was an accident no one will be punished. If it were done maliciously the perpetrators *should* be punished. Yet you chaps refuse to help us. Do you want them to go scot free?"

When the continued silence had convinced him that he would get no answer he arose and turned to the door.

"I guess that's all we have to say to each other now, then. I suppose that you are all accessories to this thing if you hide knowledge of it."

This last was more than Bill could take from one he had loved and admired since he first met him. He grabbed Neil's arm.

"You don't understand at all, Mr. Abbott! We aren't hiding anything. We don't *know* anything. That's the truth.

We haven't a bit of evidence we could give to anybody. But we're going to find out the truth, and when we get our evidence, those fellows — " His voice broke with anger, and his face showed his consternation as he realized the slip he had made. Neil was quick to catch his advantage.

"What fellows, Bill?" he asked quietly.

"I'm not saying anything more."

That was all that could be learned from them, but Neil realized that he must make every effort possible to control his boys.

"I won't ask any more questions, but I want a promise from you. I want you to promise me that you won't take matters into your own hands. We older men will find out what we need to know, and it will be better for all if you stay out of it. Don't worry about what others say. Go home and assure your folks that you had nothing to do with it. Tell them not to worry. Stay close at home so that folks can see and know where you are. I'll get in touch with you later. When we get this thing settled it's going to be settled for all time. Don't you worry."

It was easy to tell the boys not to worry, but his own heart was heavy. There must be another gang of youth in the town who were as clever as the Bushwhackers and whose pursuits were not as harmless. But who could it be? The Bushwhackers knew about that gang, and although they could not connect them with Uncle Dick's accident they were sure the connection was there. The thing he feared was that they would find the evidence they sought and take justice into their own hands. That must not be.

His problem was still fresh in his mind as he worked in the office next day. Lissa was busy at home as the doctor had not been able to get a nurse from Mendon and his wife had duties in her own home that could not be neglected. Saturday was always busy, for the farmers came in from every part of the valley and this day most of them stopped to inquire about their old friend. Friday's paper was to be delivered and there was a large mimeographing order from the high school. In Lissa's absence the stencil cutting became Neil's task, and he found it an exacting one. It was late afternoon before he had time to talk alone with Marv and tell him of Bill's visit.

"Those kids had better be coming across with what they know," said Marv after he had heard the story. "They may be needing some evidence of their own innocence before long."

"What do you mean by that? Have you heard anything?"

"Enough. When I went home at noon a bunch of men were talking on the corner of the square. Most of them were the ones whose stores were broken into. They stopped me to ask about Uncle Dick and they said some pretty ugly things about the Bushwhackers. They're still thinking they were the vandals who messed up their stores."

"Haven't they any brains?" asked Neil indignantly. "Neither those kids nor their dads could have come across with that check to pay for that. And whoever did it, was the guilty party."

"Well, don't get hot at me. I believe in the boys. After last night I'm on their side. But somebody in this town isn't, and the talk is spreading."

"We've got to keep things quiet until Uncle Dick can tell us what happened. I hope it can be straightened out by Monday. I hate to think of the boys coming in to school and somebody making remarks about them. Those kids could break loose and really start something around here."

"I'm going to stop in at the Hardings as soon as I've had my supper. If the nurse hasn't come maybe I can sit with Uncle Dick while Mrs. Harding and Lissa rest awhile. I'll ask them if he has said anything that would give them a clue. Mr. Rossiter may know something by now. He's been there all day, I think."

"Terry went home without him, didn't he? Mr. Rossiter is the most devoted cousin I ever saw."

"Guess they're more like father and son. Terry said his dad would stay until Uncle Dick is out of danger. I'm glad that he can take the responsibility off Mrs. Harding. Well, I'll be seeing you. I'll call you if I learn anything."

When he entered the Harding house the girls were doing the dishes, Mrs. Harding was upstairs and Lissa was alone in the dining room. She greeted him and asked eagerly about affairs at the office.

"We got the paper out. The mailing caught the train all right. The others were all delivered by noon. Not half bad, considering what yesterday was."

"Nor considering that you were up all night Thursday and entertained until close to midnight last night."

"Who has been telling tales to you?"

"I make them up by myself. It was Bill that came to see you, wasn't it? I wasn't spying, Neil, but that car of his isn't exactly quiet and I couldn't sleep anyway. Are they in trouble again?"

"I shouldn't tell you this, but you'll guess it anyway. They haven't done anything, if that's what you mean. But the old talk is stirred up again. The fact that they went into that swamp and worked like troopers without their breakfasts, that they were with us when we found him and did all they could to help — all that doesn't seem to count at all. Marv talked to some of the men and they're ready to get real rough on the boys. The worst thing about it is that the boys know, or have a good idea as to the guilty parties. But they want to handle it themselves. We can't let them do that. We have to keep them under control until Uncle Dick can tell his own story. Then if it's a case for the law we'll call it in. The boys from the Hollow and the men from the town have to be made to wait!"

"Who are the men?"

"Mostly the ones whose stores were pilfered."

"What are they still griping about? They all got damages, didn't they? And probably they padded their claims."

"They're hostile anyway. Mr. Hunter is saying that the parents need punishment as well as the boys. Says if he had a kid like that he'd punish him in a way he'd never forget."

She shook her head as if the whole problem were too much for her. Noting her flushed cheeks and the tired droop of her shoulders he spoke sympathetically.

"Cheer up. The nurse will get in tonight, and Terry said his dad was having another doctor to consult with Dr. Anderson. Everything is going to be all right."

She answered almost angrily. "Everything can't be all right as long as folks stay as dumb as they are. You men! You can't see beyond your short noses! If there's an open accusation against those boys I'm going to speak up and split this town wide open!"

"*What* are you talking about?"

"Oh, you're the stupidest one of the bunch!"

With a movement so quick that she overturned the chair in which she had been sitting she jerked away from his detaining hand and fled up the stairs. He heard her door slam and shook his head in bewilderment. He mounted the stairs slowly. Maybe even if he *were* the dumbest of the dumb he might be able to help Mrs. Harding a bit.

"I'm so glad to see you!" she greeted him at the door. "Uncle Dick is getting restless, and occasionally he calls for you. He isn't completely conscious, but he seems worried about something. Perhaps you can reassure him, and you might be able to understand some of the things he says."

"Glad to stay. Who's to sit with him tonight?"

"Dr. Anderson called from Mendon an hour ago. He's at the hospital and will probably be there all night. He says if we can get along tonight he'll bring a nurse back with him in the morning. If we have any trouble we're to call his wife again. She'll come, though she needs her sleep. She was with him on another case last night."

"I'm staying until someone else comes. May I see him now?"

He was somewhat relieved at his first sight of Uncle Dick. The flush on his face, even though it might come from a high temperature, was more reassuring than the blue lips and chalky color of the morning. He was sleeping, but Mrs. Harding said that he might become restless again at any time.

"He's worried about something. Look. Even in his sleep he seems distressed. If you're going to stay I'll go down to my children awhile. Maybe he will waken and talk to you.

175

If you need me just call on that little phone. Harry Rossiter had it installed this afternoon. It rings in the kitchen and saves me a lot of steps. Lissa is here and one of us will come at once.

"Did Mr. Rossiter go back to the lodge?"

"He's asleep in the little room you had. He was completely worn out. The doctor gave him a sedative and he ought to sleep until morning. If the nurse doesn't get here Harry will help me tomorrow. He's as good as a woman at a bedside."

The thought of the owner and publisher of the *Ledger* serving as attendant in the sickroom would have been amusing to his associates in the city, but Neil, having seen the display of affection between the two men, accepted it with understanding. Taking the chair that had been drawn close to the bed, he watched for any sign of waking. But as the sleeper lay quietly his thoughts went back to the talk in the cabin the night before. There was something about that conversation that he could not understand, reminding him of other remarks, too vague to be noticed when taken one at a time, but adding up to much. Why were the boys so determined to "take care" of the culprits themselves? Did they have any real evidence against anyone, and if so why had they never been willing to tell it, even when they were being unjustly accused of the various misdemeanors? It did not seem possible that there was another element in the community, one who resented the presence of the "mountaineers" and purposely tried to make them appear lawless and troublesome. Yet Bill's words, coupled with Lissa's repeated references to the blindness of the adults in not seeing what was happening, convinced him that, improbable as it might seem, it must be true. Did the Bushwhackers know who these persons were, and were they carrying on a counter warfare in which they wanted no interference from their elders? If this were the case something must be done before greater trouble erupted.

He wondered as he looked at Uncle Dick if perhaps he knew more of all this than he had ever spoken of to anyone. Was that the reason he had spent hundreds of dollars in the rehabilitation of the old schoolhouse? Did he love this village in the hills so much that he would spend from his own small savings to insure its peace and the welfare of its youth? If all these speculations were correct, if such a condition could exist in a placid little town like this, no wonder the authorities had difficulties with the youth of the cities. Something was wrong someplace. The longer he thought of it the more sure he became that he was beginning to see a bit of light in the situation. For the good of Appleboro the rival faction must be revealed and peace made between them and the Bushwhackers.

How could one go about getting the information that was necessary? He knew Bill well enough to be sure that further persuasion would avail nothing. And the rest, under Bill's orders, would be just as uncooperative. Mentally he called the roll of the town boys whom he knew. From his position on the paper he had become familiar with most of them. They seemed ordinary American boys, such as could be found in any middle class community in the nation. Some were dull, some showed evidence of leadership, some had high scholastic averages, others were poor students. Most of them were somewhat regular in attendance at church. Could the Sunday school class which the Bushwhackers had refused to join be the core around which another gang had formed? That was too fantastic to merit thought. With a sigh he gave up the problem for the present. He was too tired to think of such a complicated matter. Tomorrow would be another day. An easier one, he hoped!

25

SITTING BY THE bed where his old friend lay sleeping, Neil concentrated on trying to stay awake. He was losing the battle, however, and was nodding over a magazine when Uncle Dick's voice brought him to full wakefulness. Leaning closer he caught his own name and answered.

"I'm here, sir. Do you want to tell me something?"

"Get the stuff from the Courthouse. I can't get there this afternoon."

"I'll take care of it all. Is there anything else you want?"

"I want Neil. If he were here he would get me out. Harry said Neil would take care of me."

"I will. You are out now. You are at home in bed. I will be right here all night if you want me."

"You're a good man. God sent you."

He became quiet again for a half hour, then the troubled ramblings began again. This time he was pleading with someone.

"I know you have promised each other never to tell. But there's no sense to that. You're doing more harm that way. Let me tell folks how it happened."

178

Then a silence as if he listened to another's argument, and again the weak voice. "Don't try to handle it yourselves. You'll all get into trouble then. Tell Neil. He'll take care of it."

After a time when Neil thought he had finally found a sound sleep, he started up saying with a tone of desperation, "If I could talk to Bill I could make him see it! But he won't talk to me. He knows what I'd say and he won't listen. There mustn't be a fight!"

Mrs. Harding was passing through the hall and came in with a quieting medicine. The rest it gave was broken, however, and neither the invalid nor the watchers had much rest. Through all the delirium ran the persistent plea for Bill's presence, and when dawn began to show through the windows, Mrs. Harding asked if it would be possible to reach Bill at that hour.

"Yes, I can call the Hawkins house and one of the boys will take the message. Bill will come, I'm sure. But what he will do after he gets here, I can't say."

As they waited they tried to quiet Uncle Dick by assuring him that Bill was on the way. As his tired and confused brain tried to grasp the meaning of their words, he smiled and reached for Neil's hand.

"You are a good man, John Harding, one of the best. One mistake in a man's life can only draw him closer to God. Don't underrate His forgiveness. It is full and final."

Mrs. Harding turned away with a half sob, but did not leave the room even when the rambling continued.

"No, the time for you to have anything to say is past, Nita Winchester. Lissa is *not* your daughter. She belongs to Grace Harding. Leave her alone. I say, leave our little girl alone!"

Mrs. Harding had gone to stand at the window, and Neil talked soothingly to Uncle Dick, hoping that he could be quieted before Bill came. This was certainly not a thing Bill should hear! The low tone and soothing touch brought quietness at last, and a light but untroubled sleep. When Lissa came to the door with Bill, Neil motioned to the boy to wait until called. It was almost an hour later that Neil heard the weak question,

"Is Bill here?" and the frightened, self-conscious youth came to stand by his side.

"Bill is here, Uncle Dick. Did you want to say something to him?"

"I can't see him."

"Here he is. That's his hand on yours. Do you want me to go away?"

"No, don't leave me! Harry said you'd help me. Is this Bill?"

"It's me, Uncle Dick." Bill's cracked adolescent voice showed the nervousness he felt in these strange circumstances.

"Bill, I'm tired. You've got to help me. Wake me up if I go to sleep. Bill, you've got to forget it all. You tell the other boys. You mustn't do it, Bill. You tell them!"

Although the watchers did not know the reason for Uncle Dick's distress or the meaning of his words there seemed to be no doubt in Bill's mind. But he gave no answer. The thing being asked of him seemed too much for him to grant. He shook his head in silent refusal, and Uncle Dick's weak eyes caught the gesture.

"You have to stop the boys, Bill. You can't do anything that would cause more trouble. Don't do it, Bill. Don't do it!"

Still Bill stood silent, and Neil wondered what thing it was that meant so much to him that he could refuse the pleadings of the old man who might, even now, be slipping away from life. As the silence grew longer, Uncle Dick struggled to a half-sitting position and clung with both hands to the boy's arm. His voice was shrill and desperate.

"Bill, you *have* to. You can't take punishment into your own hands. That belongs to God. You *have* to forgive them, Bill. They didn't know what they were doing!"

Bill covered the shaking hands with his own big one and gulped, "All right, Uncle Dick. I give my word."

The old man fell back on the pillow and Bill rushed from the room. Mrs. Harding reached for the wasted wrist and spoke sharply to Lissa who hovered in the doorway.

"Call Dr. Anderson. We're going to need him in a hurry."

While Lissa ran for the telephone Neil ran downstairs. There was nothing he could do for Uncle Dick now, but Bill Banning needed a friend. He found the boy on the porch just outside the front door. He was leaning against the wall and his head was on his folded arms. When he felt Neil's arm come across his shoulder he broke into sobs, while Neil found his own eyes wet with sympathetic tears. He felt he could not bear to see Bill cry!

"Let's go to my cabin again. I want to talk to you, and I'm sure you don't want to go home for awhile."

In the cabin he talked casually as he prepared some coffee and put some bread in the toaster. "It's handy to have these things here if I don't want to take time for a regular breakfast. Do you want coffee, or would you rather have milk?"

"I don't drink coffee much, but it might make me feel better now."

"Do you want to tell me about it, Bill?"

"I guess I'd better. We all said we wouldn't tell anybody, but a fellow just can't stand up against something like that!"

"I agree. Uncle Dick gets under a fellow's skin, doesn't he? May I guess what it was that he wanted you to promise?"

"Do you know?"

"I think I do, though how Uncle Dick guessed it I'll never be able to tell. There's another gang here, isn't there? They've been trying to get you fellows in bad with folks and you had decided to punish them in your own way. Isn't that it, Bill?"

Bill nodded. It was evident that he still did not like to give up a cherished plan.

"Yeh, that was it. And we could have done it, too. We'd have made those fellows so sorry that they'd wish they'd stayed at home with their kiddy cars and blocks. We'd a dealt with them good!"

"But you've given that up now. Don't forget your promise."

"I'm not forgetting. I gave my word and I'll keep it. But I don't want to at all. Not at all! But how could a fellow help himself with Uncle Dick askin'? I couldn't say no to him. When he asked me to forgive them because they didn't know what they were doin', it sounded just like Jesus in that story you told the other night. I couldn't say no to Him, could I?"

Neil's throat tightened as he tried to say the words he knew he must. If he failed to use this opportunity he would have proved himself a complete failure in his Master's service.

"No, you couldn't say no to Jesus. But have you ever said yes to Him, Bill?"

"Whadda you mean?"

"I think you know. You heard and remembered the story of Jesus' death on the cross. You heard what Mr. Horne said when he talked to us a week ago. You know how Christ died for you. You know how He asked for forgiveness for His enemies. He wants forgiveness for us all. But He can't force it on any of us. You know the way, Bill. Are you ready to take it? He died for you as well as for me. He bought your pardon from God. But it isn't yours until you take it."

"What do I do?"

"The Bible says that whoever calls upon Him shall be saved. Here, let me show it to you. It's in the tenth chapter of Romans. 'Whosoever shall call upon the name of the Lord shall be saved.' That's all. If you realize that you're a sinner that wants God's forgiveness, and understand that Jesus bought it for you on the cross — well, then you must tell Him so and ask Him to save you. If you believe in your heart that He died for you, that He rose again, that He is living now to be your Lord and Master, just tell Him so, Bill. He will hear you and you will be His."

"When did you get to be His?"

"When I was twelve. But I didn't grow as a Christian

should. I'm still a pretty weak child of God, but I *am* His child, and I'm growing."

"Will I be His child if I just say yes?"

"If you mean it."

Very simply the boy bowed his head and in his uncertain voice whispered, "I want to be God's child. Jesus, I say yes."

Neil's arms went around him in a rough but happy clasp.

"Now we're brothers, Bill."

"Whadda I do, now?" The careful enunciation and careful use of language which had been one of the things that marked him as unusual for one with his environment, was forgotten. He had reverted to the speech of his mountaineer parents, but neither of them noticed.

"We do it together. Just try to live the new life He has given, in a way that will please Him. We'll help each other."

Outside, as Bill prepared to leave, they noticed the doctor's car in the Harding drive.

"I hope he brought a nurse," said Neil. "Those women can't carry on alone."

"Do you think I made him worse?"

"I think you have helped him. The excitement may have caused a bit of trouble, but the doctor can take care of it. After Uncle Dick has had more rest he will remember what you promised and that will be a big help to him. Don't worry. You did the right thing."

He gave a reassuring pat to Bill's shoulder, that said more than words could, and with a relieved smile the boy slid behind the wheel of his car. He started the engine, shifted with a clash of gears, then, as he released the brakes, said gruffly,

"You've a right to know, 'cause somebody has to do something. It's Howie and Ernie. There's no real gang. Just them two. They haven't a bit of sense. They did it all. I guess Uncle Dick is right. They just didn't know what they was doin'."

He was off, scattering gravel as he swung into the road, while Neil looked at him in complete astonishment. It couldn't be true, he thought. It didn't merit consideration. Yet, with another part of his mind he was already accepting it. If it *were* true, it would explain many things. But *why* choose Uncle Dick as a victim? He was tired, too tired to think or worry over such problems. He must find out how Uncle Dick was, then sleep for the entire day. Even then he would not be entirely rested, he felt. Yet with all the weariness he felt strangely lifted up. For the first time in his life he had led a soul to the Lord!

He went to the back door of the house, and found Lissa in the kitchen. She greeted him, looking weary after a sleepless night, and answered his question about Uncle Dick.

"I don't know yet how he is. The doctor came awhile ago and brought a nurse. If Uncle Dick can be left with her I'm going to give Mother a good breakfast and send her to bed for the whole day."

"Good for you. And I think you should follow her. Should I go up, do you think?"

"Yes. The doctor asked about you."

"Where is Mr. Rossiter?"

"With them. He heard the doctor come and got up to meet him. Maybe you and I had better wait outside."

It was a sober group of people who awaited the doctor's verdict. Several times he shook his head as he went back again and again to his careful examination of the chest and its too-slow breathing. An occasional low word to the nurse was the only sound as he gave close study to the blue-veined hands and the cold fingertips, then returned again to listen to the heart beat. After what seemed an hour to the anxious watchers he hung the stethoscope on his neck and turned away, drawing a long breath of weariness.

"Well, he's not any worse. I'm leaving enough of the medication to last until tomorrow. I'll give you some prescriptions then. The cut on his head will give him a headache for a few days, but it's clean and will do all right. It looks as if he fell against something. If we can keep him quiet he should have no serious trouble. I wish I had him at the hospital, but I'd be afraid to try the trip. He is dangerously weak, and in a state of semi-shock. Miss Morton here will be on the job and she knows what to do. I'll come if I'm called, but just now I'm going home to bed. I make it a rule to get one night's sleep a week — whenever possible!''

They had breakfast together in the dining room while Ruthie got breakfast for the children in the kitchen and Bud and Pug did the chores. It was a leisurely meal, for it was the first time of real relaxation they had had since the discovery of Uncle Dick's absence.

"We're a bunch of sad looking sacks," said Mr. Rossiter. "If I look as bad as the rest of you do I'm going up to the lodge and crawl into the first bed I meet and sleep it off. It was mighty kind of Grace to send me to her hospital last night, but I heard Dick's babbling all night. I couldn't sleep, so I just lay there and prayed. What was that boy doing here?''

Neil did not answer so Mrs. Harding told the story of Bill's trip through the cool dawn to reassure Uncle Dick and give him the promise that seemed to be of such vital importance to him.

"We haven't the least idea what it was all about," she said. "But apparently the boy knew and gave a promise that was very difficult for him. I hope Uncle Dick will remember it and stop worrying about it.''

"Maybe Neil could tell us what it was about," volunteered Lissa. "Bill went home with him and something big happened. Neil's 'got a glory' in spite of that sleepy and unshaven look he wears.''

They all looked inquiringly at him and he was quick to respond. How Lissa had known about the glory he couldn't guess, but he wanted to share it. He told the story of the talk in the cabin, and when he had finished with it and they all knew of the lad who couldn't say no to Uncle Dick because he saw Jesus Christ on the cross in the old man, their eyes were wet. Bill's own decision to say yes to that Christ brought joy to them all. Mrs. Harding squeezed his hand, Lissa smiled shakily, and Mr. Rossiter gazed at Neil in astonishment, then rose to put his hand on the young man's shoulder.

"And all for the want of a horseshoe nail," he said.

Neil and Lissa looked at each other, then at Mrs. Harding who laughed at their bewilderment, even while wiping the tears from her eyes.

"You don't know what he meant, do you? Well, the old readers your grandparents used to study taught how great things can come from small incidents, by telling in rhyme how a kingdom was lost because a blacksmith left one nail out of a horse's shoe."

"And in this advanced age, we use cameras instead of horseshoes to bring about cataclysmic events. Like the rise and fall of gangs, and the breaking down of a boy's stubborn pride," said Mr. Rossiter as he left the room.

"Meaning what?" Neil asked, realizing that he was so sleepy that he had not followed the remarks at all. "I guess I'm missing on most of my cylinders."

"He means that maybe there was a cause, or at least a good effect, for your missing that train last winter. Do you get it now, or are you still asleep?"

"I've been snoring for half an hour."

"Can you stand one more question?" asked Mrs. Harding. "Did Bill say anything that would clear up the mystery of how Uncle Dick got locked in that shed?"

"He didn't tell the *how* of it. But he told *who* it was, the same pair that have caused the troubles all summer, the ones who broke into the stores."

"He told you that?"

"Yes, and the information is so explosive that I don't know what to do with it. Maybe you can help me. It's Howie Winchester and Ernie Hunter."

Mrs. Harding stared at him as if unable to comprehend his statement, but Lissa had turned away and gave no sign that she had heard the astounding remark. The mother looked first at Neil, then at the girl and spoke gently.

"Did you know this, honey?"

"I've known it for weeks."

"How did you — no, I'm not going to start asking questions. We're all too tired. Let's not talk about this at all until we have had time to think and pray and perhaps consult with someone else. Just now our duty lies in getting some rest. When we've done that, we may be able to think more clearly.''

As Lissa left to help Ruth fix René for Sunday school, Mrs. Harding followed Neil into the hall. She seemed embarrassed, and he waited for her to speak, wondering what further disclosure might be made.

"Did you hear all that Uncle Dick said last night?"

"I think I did. I couldn't help it, really. I'm sorry."

"I'm not. I suspect that you already know much of my story. Lissa has been troubled about it this summer and may have made a confidant of you. She needs someone, and it's a subject that she doesn't talk about freely to me. I'd like to explain it all to both of you when we have the opportunity. You know enough that you should know more. After you have rested could you come back for supper? We eat at five o'clock on Sundays, and I can tell my story before time for you to leave for church. I won't go. Mr. Horne and the Lord understand, I am sure."

"I'll be here. I don't want you to think you have to tell me anything, but I'm flattered that you want to. I think you're the finest woman I know."

"Thank you," she said soberly. "I have a wonderful Lord."

26

THE TALK DID not come off as planned, however. Uncle Dick was worse, and there was thought of nothing else in the house that night. Mr. Rossiter came back with another nurse, that Mrs. Harding might have none of the care of watching. One of the young wives from the Hollow came in every morning to help in the kitchen, for the addition of three more persons to the already large household made a greater burden than Mrs. Harding could carry. Mr. Rossiter had settled himself and his belongings in the hall bedroom, and his presence was a relief and comfort. Lissa had moved into her mother's room and the nurses kept her room occupied by shifts.

There were two anxious weeks when even the doctor seemed baffled by the weakness and lethargy of the patient. On some days the heart seemed to be at last responding to the medicine, and they were encouraged. But most of the days were spent in slumber that did not bring renewed strength but rather a lessening of the meager vitality. When he was awake he was conscious of his surroundings. Since the second night there had been no delirium. Neither was there worry about anything, for there was no interest in anything. He ate when he was fed, obediently swallowed the medicines given him, and required so little attention that the nurses found time heavy on their hands.

A day came, however, when the doctor smiled as he looked at his patient. "You're going to get well, you rascal! This is the third day that the chart has been good. Another week and you'll be cross as a little boy getting over the measles."

Uncle Dick smiled at the words, and said weakly. "I have to get well. Both the *Ledger* and the *Advocate* are going to the dogs. Somebody has to get busy." He smiled weakly as he saw the emotional working of Mr. Rossiter's face. "You big baby," he said weakly.

In another week the house had settled down to a more orderly routine. Only Miss Morton was left to care for the invalid, Mr. Rossiter had gone back to the city, promising to return each weekend until Uncle Dick was back at his desk. The cards and letters continued to pour in to both office and home, and gave the invalid entertainment for the long hours he must spend alone.

It had been agreed that Mr. Horne should be told of the statement Bill had made, and, to the relief of the others, he agreed that he should be the one to interview the parents of the two boys and try to work out the problem of why they had committed the misdemeanors and how they were to be punished for them. As pastor he had a contact with them that gave his counsel weight. A few discreet words spoken here and there had quieted the gossip, and even the most belligerent had agreed that it was best to wait for Uncle Dick's story before action was taken. The lull was welcome both at home and the office, and Neil found himself wondering again about his own future.

On a chilly November afternoon when a cold rain and a northwest wind made one appreciate the warmth of a good furnace, Mrs. Harding called at the office and suggested that Lissa bring Neil home for supper.

"It's pea soup, pear pickles, hot rolls, with pumpkin pie for dessert. And you don't have to come if you don't want to!'' said Lissa when she delivered the invitation.

"Well, thanks! But I do want to and I'll be there. So swallow your disappointment and be a nice hostess.''

She gave him a smile and began to clear her desk. Smiling was easy for her these days. For some reason the pressures from the Winchester house which had made her summer miserable had been lifted of late and she had shown herself the happy young lady Uncle Dick had described. Perhaps some inkling of the cause of the accident had trickled into that home, bringing with it the thought that it might be better to urge no action until that matter be straightened out. Neil did not know this, but he knew that Lissa was happy and therefore the office was a place of peace.

Uncle Dick was not yet able to come down to his meals, so his nurse, who was also the daughter of one of his old friends, had set up a table by his bedside and often they ate together. That mealtime fellowship brightened his day and gave the Hardings privacy they had missed for many weeks. Tonight when Neil and Lissa entered the hall the warmth wrapped them about like a blanket, and the spicy odors of pumpkin pie tantalized. It was a hilarious meal, for it was Friday and a neighbor had invited all the children over to see the pictures of a trip taken to Alaska — an evening of entertainment complete with refreshments and games.

When they were gone and the kitchen cleared for the night, Mrs. Harding, who had been somewhat more quiet than usual in the midst of the clamor, said, "Let's go in the living room. Bud built a fire in the old Ben Franklin stove for me. I want to tell you the story I promised, and it will be easier without the lamplight.''

She sat in the easy chair on one side of the stove, while Neil sat across from her. Lissa took a pillow from the davenport and sat on the floor with her head against her mother's knee. In the dim light she looked more than ever like a little girl, and Neil knew that this was a position they had taken many times in the past.

Lissa, as if sensing that it was hard for her mother to

break the silence, said, "Mother, Neil and I have been arguing for over a year. Don't look so startled, Neil. We *have*. It all started that time I was visiting Sara last year. We got in an argument then and we just can't get out. Neil can't — or won't — admit that all things do work for the good of a Christian. Now I admit it but I don't live it. I don't *like* some of the things that I know are working for my good. So my arguments don't weigh much with him. Can't you convince him?"

"That's a large order. Are there any special events that are troubling him? Can you tell me about them?" she turned to Neil.

"Well, I'm almost ashamed to tell you. I didn't know Lissa was going to call you in as an ally. We were discussing it at our church group that night, and I couldn't accept it literally. Then when I got stranded up here I couldn't see any good in it at all. But Lissa insists that it *is* for my good whether I admit it or not. There was another big disappointment at that time and I've had a hard time adjusting to it. It was all caused because I forgot my camera and went back after it. That's the story. It sounds pretty silly, but it has changed my life. I thought I was all set for a career in the city. Now I don't know when, if ever, I can get back to it. And a forgotten camera caused it all."

"Just like a pebble in the stream?" said Lissa impishly.

"It could be like that," agreed her mother. "And I can see how it could be for the better, for the 'good,' if you please. First of all there's Uncle Dick and the *Advocate*. They might have hired someone else to come in here. Harry Rossiter might have picked one that seemed to him to fit nicely, and it might have proved disastrous. You've done a remarkable work of carrying on as Uncle Dick would have."

"In spite of all your griping," said Lissa.

"Then there's your work with the boys at the Hollow. You've made friends with them when no one else could. You've won their confidence as no one, even their parents, had done. Mr. Marsh says there is beginning to be a spirit of cooperation that had not been before. There's much more that I could say. For some reason you have a heart full of sympathy for the underprivileged, the misunderstood, the ones whom others pass without noticing.

"You spent money and time to help the women in the Hollow help themselves and children. You went to the defense of the Bushwhackers when almost everyone else was condemning them. You proved them not guilty because you were able to see and understand their side of the case. Now I'm sure you are worrying about Howie Winchester and Ernie Hunter, because you think that they are underprivileged!"

Lissa laughed at that idea, but Neil spoke defensively, "They *are* underprivileged! I don't care if their folks *are* wealthy or even that Mr. Winchester is a power in state politics. That doesn't mean a thing to a couple of boys who aren't allowed to play baseball for fear of getting hit by a ball, or football lest they break a bone in scrimmage. Don't you see how such things make them feel? They see all the other kids in town playing, and *they* have to sit on the sidelines and pretend they don't want to play. It's no wonder they broke loose. They had to prove that they were just as big and just as tough as they come."

"But why pick on the Bushwhackers? It wasn't their fault about ball playing."

"Ball playing isn't all of it by any means. That's just what we know about. There were, and are probably prohibitions every time they turn around. All the resentment building up in them had to burst out against someone, and they didn't dare show it at home. Then who is the logical target? Why, the kids that have everything, the Bushwhackers whose parents let them pursue their own happy course with little interference unless real wrong is involved. Also, the boys from the Hollow had entered high school in town with a chip on the shoulder over having to come. Add that to the natural mountaineer's independence, and you can see that they had done their share of building the wall between themselves and the town boys. So it was a natural for two such groups to war with each other. I've talked to the Bush-whackers about it and they're beginning to see that some of the fault lies at their door. That doesn't excuse Howie and Ernie, though, and when Uncle Dick is well enough to tell what happened to him, they'll have to face the music. In the meantime Mr. Horne and I are trying to get our toes in the door so we can get to the heart of it all. He's working on the parents and I'm trying to make friends with the boys. They don't trust me completely because of my connection with the Bushwhackers, but I'll get them yet. I don't want them sent away, as Mrs. Winchester is advocating. I'd like to see them stay and face the music when the town learns about it."

"How did the parents learn? Did Mr. Horne tell them?"

"Yes, and I think he had quite a scene in both homes. Mr. Hunter wouldn't believe it until Ernie spoke up and said it was true. Mr. Winchester already suspected about the burglary. It was he who sent the money to pay for it. I think Lissa tipped him off to it. I don't know what they told about Uncle Dick's accident. Mr. Horne doesn't want to talk about that until Uncle Dick can. It's all a sorry mess, and I feel sorry for those boys. They shouldn't be sent away to school. They'd never feel at home here again. Let them stay and face it. They're pretty fine fellows underneath the hurt pride and childish desire to show off. I'd like to help them live it down."

"I think you can do it," said Mrs. Harding.

"I'm sure he can. And when he does he will still keep insisting that God doesn't direct our lives, or that His leading might be operated through the medium of a forgotten camera."

Neil shook his head in baffled resignation at Lissa's retort. "She just worries that theme like Shep playing with René's old doll. Can't we get her onto some other subject? Didn't we come in here to listen to Mrs. Harding? Let's not talk about me."

27

MRS. HARDING'S FACE in the firelight looked sober. It was evident that the telling of this story would not be easy, but was a thing to be done regardless of the pain it caused.

"This is a story I have never told anyone since the day my husband and I stood before his mother and gave it to her. Uncle Dick and Harry Rossiter stumbled onto so much of the truth once when searching through old records in the courthouse, that we admitted other details rather than have them drawing false conclusions. This is a story of two girls, and a boy that both wanted, and of two women and a girl they both wanted. It isn't a pretty story, but it is full of God's care and provision for His own, and when I am through telling it I think Neil will admit that all things *can* work together for good to those who put them into His hands. I'm telling Lissa because I want her to know the full story of how she became my daughter. She has learned much of it, and must now learn it all. I'm telling Neil because he heard what Uncle Dick said in his delirium and must draw no false conclusions. He has proved himself a true friend, and I'm trusting him with this confidence because I know he will not abuse it.

"I was the youngest child of a poor family who lived

back in the hills about twenty miles from here. My brothers and sisters were grown before I was born and I must have been a very unwelcome member of the family. To make my situation even less happy I was born with both hips dislocated. My mother, who might have had more love in her heart for me than the others did, died before I could remember her. My father followed her before I was six. My brothers and sisters married or found jobs in another locality, and none of them wanted a little crippled girl to burden them. I was put in a home for handicapped children.

"Living here in Appleboro at that time was a family whose name I will call Farrell. They were wealthy as Appleboro counts wealth. Mrs. Farrell was on the board of that home, and on a visit of inspection saw me, and my plight touched her heart. She had heard of a doctor in New York who had successfully operated on several cases such as mine. She was determined to give me my chance at normal living, so left her own small daughter in the care of a relative and spent six long months in New York with me. She must also have spent many thousands of dollars. I can only remember two things about that experience. Pain there must have been, but I have forgotten it. It was blotted out, I am sure, by the wonder of the day I took my first steps and realized that I would be like other children. The other thing I can never forget was the surge of love I felt for Mrs. Farrell who had done this wonderful thing for me. No one else in the world had ever been kind to me except as a matter of duty. Mrs. Farrell who had no duty to discharge toward me, had given me life as other little girls knew it. Over and over I thanked her and vowed I'd always love her and work for her.

"When we could leave the hospital she took me home with her. For ten years I was treated as another daughter. Her own little girl was a year younger than I, but because of my illness we were in the same grade at school. Mr. Farrell had been dead several years and Mrs. Farrell's life was given to the care of her daughter and myself, and to the charities she loved. I'll call the daughter Mary, as I do not want to tell the real name unless, when I am finished, Lissa desires it. Mary and I had the same friends, the same kind of clothes, bicycles just alike, and equal treatment in everything. There was no resemblance in looks. I was large for my age, and not noticeably pretty. Mary was small, dainty, and the loveliest girl I ever saw. She had a charm I could never attain, and a personality that made her a leader everywhere. There was another difference, too. My heart was so full of love and gratitude toward Mrs. Farrell that I could never give enough in the way of service. Probably because I gave so much Mary developed the habit of giving little. The tasks that were supposed to be done by both were left for me alone, and by the time we were entering high school Mary had become a very selfish and spoiled girl. She was not unkind to me. She just coveted all the attention she could get, and she didn't want me to have anything that in any way outclassed her own. Once in our junior year we had to write original themes. We read them to each other and both realized mine was by far the better of the two. She had written hers too hurriedly after putting it off until the last day. I won't tell you of the arguments that she used to persuade me that if I loved her mother I should trade themes with her, but I did trade and saw her take home a note of special commendation from the teacher, while I was required to rewrite the carelessly done theme.

"I'm not telling you this to put another person in a bad light. I'm just telling you the truth so that you will understand the compulsions that worked in the final outcome of the friendship. I know now that she was jealous. Her mother, all that she had as a family, had given an equal share of herself to another child and it did not seem right. In some way she felt she must prove herself always superior.

"The year we were seniors at high school John Harding began to pay attention to me. I don't know why that should have bothered her. John was a quiet country boy, too bashful to take leadership in any class activities and never having as much money to spend as the other boys with whom she was popular. But his choice of me for a friend aroused her desire to have him for her own. All her wiles were turned on John. A young boy who has never been popular was sure to be flattered by the attentions of the prettiest and most wealthy girl in school and poor John was completely bewitched. I used to feel sorry for him because he evaded me as if he were ashamed but could not help himself. I knew she did not care for him and I thought him too good and kind to be hurt. I had hoped that he would ask me to go to the Washington's Birthday party with him, but he asked her and I stayed at home using Mrs. Farrell's illness as an excuse. I didn't want to go unescorted and see him with her.

"After that party she seemed to turn against him, and petulantly declared that she hated him. She had come in very late and her mother had been cross with her, and I thought that the cause of her mood. I would have been glad to be friends with John, but he avoided me more than ever, and as soon as school was over he got a job in the north woods and apparently forgot all about us.

"I wish I didn't have to tell the rest to you. It isn't easy even after more than twenty-five years. I won't go into detail. I couldn't, if I wanted to, tell of the heartbreak and hysteria in the Farrell household when it was discovered that the flirtation that had been indulged in to prove that Mary could take my friend as well as my theme, had ended tragically. A foolish girl had deliberately aroused passions that she could not control, and had let her desire for conquest go beyond the point of no return. In the mother's mind there was no question of marriage. Mary was only seventeen and a fine education with social advantages had been planned for her. She seemed to have little realization of her plight, the mother and I being the ones to grieve and plan what should be done. It was known that Mrs. Farrell was ill, so the explanation that she was going away for a rest and treatment was accepted. It was natural, of course, that the daughters should go with her.

"We left almost at once and went to a small town in the west, as far from Appleboro as we could get, and so out of the way that there was no danger of meeting friends. The three of us lived alone in a big house at the edge of the town. A

197

woman came in daily to help, but I carried the responsibility of the home, for Mrs. Farrell was so broken by the thing that had happened that she was unable to face even the light cares of our transient home. We did not make friends and I alone went out to market. Mary pouted in her room, and refused to help in planning for her baby's birth. We had brought books, there were magazines, and I was fairly happy. My heart ached for Mrs. Farrell who was both ill and sad, and I was terribly sorry for Mary. She was paying a very high price for proving that she could take John from me. Mrs. Farrell had promised that I should enter business school next year and I saw a bright future before me.

"Mrs. Farrell had promised her sister in the east that she would bring Mary there for the season, and she asked me if I would remain in some home here and care for the baby until their return in the spring, when she would arrange for its adoption. She wanted to be sure that it had the best home she could find, and wanted to do nothing hurriedly. I did not like the idea of assuming the care of a small baby, but I had such a deep sense of obligation to Mrs. Farrell that I could not refuse any request. She deposited enough money in a local bank to care for us amply and assured me there would always be more if an emergency arose. The morning she left with Mary to go to the hospital she kissed me and said, with tears in her eyes,

"God bless you, Gracie. If I've ever wronged you, forgive me, and try to understand. You are very dear to me.'

"A week after they came home with the baby girl I moved to the home of a dear Christian woman who proved almost a mother to me in the love and tenderness with which she taught me the things I needed to know about caring for a baby. In all my life until the day the baby was brought home from the hospital I had never held an infant in my arms. I had never lived in a home that had a baby in it. I had never seen one being dressed. I knew only the things that had been taught me in that too short week, and without Mrs. Butner I would have made some disastrous blunders.

"It wasn't a sad time, however. I had my books for the

hours when I was not busy with the baby. Mrs. Butner was taking a correspondence course of Bible study and I studied with her. I had always gone to church with Mrs. Farrell and I *thought* I was a Christian. In that study, however, I found that being a Christian meant a great deal more than I had ever understood. I asked questions, Mrs. Butner answered them and led me along in the way of knowledge, until one night, alone in my room, I found the Lord. For that reason the memory of that waiting time has always been a blessed one. I never forgot, though, that it was just a waiting time, and in the spring Mrs. Farrell would be coming back to get the baby, and I could go on with my schooling.

"Before spring came, however, other news came that brought all my dreams crashing to the ground. Mrs. Farrell had been much sicker than she had let anyone know, and in early February she passed away at her sister's home in New York. I received the word through the lawyer, but there was no message from Mary. I wrote her a letter of sympathy and told of my own deep sorrow, but never did receive a reply.

"In a couple of weeks there came another letter from the lawyer, containing several legal documents and the baby's birth certificate. I looked at the certificate first, for the others looked too long to be read hastily. After I had read the certificate, it was many hours before I could read the others. I had a problem that had to be faced, one that I could not share with even my dear Mrs. Butner. God alone must be the one to hear my cries and tell me what to do. For that birth certificate stated that the child born on that November day in the hospital of that western town was the child of John Harding and Grace Lennon. Without my knowledge Mrs. Farrell had registered Mary in my name. It could only have been done with Mary's knowledge, of course, and for many sleepless and tortured hours I wept in grief and frustration as I realized the trap in which I had been caught. No wonder that we had had no contacts with anyone during those months. I could not think of a person I could call upon to prove that I, and not the blonde, lovely girl who had borne the baby, was Grace Lennon. I have realized since that there were many things I could have done, but a girl of eighteen who has been shielded to an unusual degree, doesn't know about such things. Then there was another deterrent from any action to clear my name. If I proved the truth the baby might be taken from me, and more than anything in the world I wanted that baby girl. Now she was mine, and I determined to keep her no matter what the cost to me. I had no idea how I would support her, but I knew I would do it somehow.

"When I had reached that decision I was able to read the other papers. One of them was a letter from Mrs. Farrell to be delivered to me only if she passed away before she had time to return and arrange the adoption. It was a pitiful plea for forgiveness for doing such a thing, and I have always felt that it was written when her mind had begun to cloud from the pain she bore. She could not bear, she said, to trust a child of her own flesh to the uncertain mercies of the courts when she could not be present to assure its well being. Mary, she knew, had only abhorrence of it. I was the only one she had to turn to. Her sister, who would care for Mary, must never know about the child. For the sake of the love I had often avowed, and in return for the health she had given me, would I accept the baby on those terms and forgive the wrong done me by a frantic mother? Already I was forgiving her. The strong body she had given me was a gift I could not despise. The other gift, the adorable baby girl, had become already the most precious possession I could ever own. Not a trace of bitterness was left in my heart after I had read that letter.

"The other paper was a copy of Mrs. Farrell's will, and it ended any worries I had about my ability to care for the baby. She had divided her estate equally between Mary and me, and I knew I need never be concerned about money. The lawyer assured me that it was invested in solid, conservative bonds and stocks that would insure a comfortable living to me for the rest of my life.

"It was only two weeks after this that John Harding came asking for me. He had heard of Mrs. Farrell's death and that Mary was with an aunt, but had been unable to find where I was until Uncle Dick persuaded the lawyer to give him the address. John had come almost two thousand miles to assure himself of my well being. He had no thought of marriage, for he had condemned himself so bitterly for the events of that February night that he thought himself unworthy of me. I can't tell you of his shock and anger when he saw the baby of whose existence he was not aware, and when I showed him the birth certificate. He made no excuses, offered no alibis. I learned later that two of the boys, thinking it a great joke, had 'spiked' the fruit punch at the party, and that there were many things about that evening of which the parents would not have approved.

"He wanted, then, to marry me at once. We would go to a new community he said, and no one could ever think shamefully of me. We decided to consult a lawyer about the situation and find how we could be sure the baby would never be taken from us. When we gave him the facts and papers in the case he was sure he could accomplish it, so we were married and John found work so that we need not be dependent on my legacy. We did use it for the court and lawyer's fees for we could never have financed them otherwise. It was two years before the tangle was made straight and we received adoption papers for our baby.

"I had been given the privilege of naming her, but it was only when John came that we decided to call her Alicia. When she was just eight months old, and just when the lawyer had a good start on the case John's father died and his mother wrote him to come home and help with the farm. He did not want to go because of the shame which I would be sure to bear undeservedly. He wanted to tell the whole story here in Appleboro and let Mary bear the blame. But to do so would blacken Mrs. Farrell's name, for her part in the deception would have to come out. I could not permit that. There was nothing for us to do but come home with Alicia and let the town say what it would. We did tell John's mother, and while she grieved over John's mistake she never referred to it after that first day. We were happy here together and after a few years we did not let the gossip disturb us.

"By the time Lissa was a few years old it could not be

denied that she was a Harding, and the world accepted her as mine. And she *is* mine. She has been a constant joy to me, even more so now that he is gone and I see his dear face in hers. He was the best husband any woman could have, and his mother is still my dearest friend. I don't know how long Lissa has known that she is not my daughter, nor how she found it out. I think she has been troubled for weeks about it, and I believe that just recently she has resolved in her own mind the question of her parentage. I have not given you the real name of the mother who disclaimed her. If Lissa has guessed it, I hope it will not in any way disrupt her happiness. She is a woman now, and if a choice of any kind lies before her, she must do the choosing alone. I do not wish — "

"Mother, Mother!" Lissa interrupted with a shaky voice. "There will never be a choice to make. I've been pretty sure for several months who that other girl was, and I've never been tempted to accept anything that the Winchesters had to offer me! Why does she want me now, after you have had all the trouble of raising me? And the expense, too? I've been sitting here putting two and two together, and you can't tell me that you kept Mrs. Farrell's money. If you did, why did my father go without an overcoat the winter I got that nice red suit with coat to match? And why do you have to take in the children to raise? I know they're a joy to you and that you love them all, but you watch for the check from the state every month, all righty. Please tell me you didn't keep that money!"

"No, we decided we didn't want it."

"Hurrah for our side! Now tell me *why* she wants me at this point in the game."

"I think she is lonely."

"Lonely? With all the activity she gets as the wife of the party boss? With Howie there to shed sunshine all over the place? Why can't she leave us alone?"

"I think none of us has realized how much pressure has been put upon you. There have been things you didn't tell us, haven't there?"

"A lot of them. If she had told me the story and wanted

to claim me as her child I might have listened with more sympathy. But I'd not have left you, even then. You're my *mother,* the only one I ever had and the only one I'll ever claim. But she wanted no relationship to be known. I'm not even sure Mr. Winchester knows the facts. He just knows that she wants me as friend, secretary, companion, or what-have-you. And whatever she wants is just exactly the thing he wants. If ever I get married I'd like to think I had my husband tied in a double knot around my finger like that woman has. But that's off the subject. What I'm really wanting to find out is *why!* Why does she want me around her? Why doesn't she just leave me alone?"

"She is a wife and mother now. Twenty-five years are bound to give maturity. She is realizing that she missed something from her life when she turned her back on that baby long ago. When she held Howie in her arms she must often have been reminded of that other baby, and there would bound to be things that would make her think and wonder. She must have wanted a daughter — all women do. As the years went past and no daughter came — well, she let herself brood over it. When they came back here ten years ago she may have been startled by seeing you on the street and learning who you were, and the sight of you was a continual reminder that she did have a daughter."

"Oh, no, she didn't. She never did. There's no way she can prove that I'm not yours, is there?"

"Not a way in the world. Your father and I spent two years making sure of that, and in the courthouse in that little town in Montana there are papers which tell the whole story. She wouldn't want to make them public, I'm sure. She is just lonely, and has had a hard time with her conscience. My heart aches for her, for she is the loser in the sad story."

"That isn't any reason why *I* should cater to her whims, is it?"

The mother laid her hands on the tumbled head against her knee, and her voice was full of compassion. "Honey, no one is asking you to do anything. If you want to go to Mrs. Winchester and give her your friendship, go with my blessing. I know, and you know that you are now and always my own dear daughter. No one else has the slightest claim upon you. Some day if you come to me with a man whom you have decided prayerfully you want as your companion through life, I will gladly give you to him. Until then you are mine.''

Neil had been sitting with bent head as he listened to the story, parts of which he had guessed but the whole of which no one could have imagined. Lissa had risen and was standing by the window where her face was hidden by the shadow. When neither of them spoke Mrs. Harding rose to leave the room.

"That's the end of my story," she said wearily. "I would never have told it had Uncle Dick not spoken in his delirium. He found out about the will from the records in the courthouse at Mendon, and gradually guessed at other things. I hope you can both forget it and let things be as they were before. Lissa is the child that I could never have borne John Harding myself. Whatever wrongdoing there was on others' parts, to me she was God-sent. My Lord planned the way I have gone and it has been a way of blessing. I have had more than the average share of joy and love, and I have no regrets. Neil has shown himself a true friend, one whom we can trust, and I'm glad to have him know the facts about a situation that must have puzzled him. I must go to Uncle Dick now.''

Neil sprang to her side as she turned to the door. "I want to thank you for telling this to me. I'm not sure I can express what I feel, but it means more to me that just a story. I'm beginning to see some things I didn't before, about how God leads, and all that. You just have to go on and trust and, well, I can't say it right. I'd better get my thoughts in order before I try to express them. I'm going to say this though. I'm awfully proud to have you say I'm your friend!"

He hurried from the room for he had a sudden fear that he might start to cry, and from the glimpse he had of Lissa rushing past them and up the stairs, he thought no further emotion was needed on the scene.

28

BY EARLY DECEMBER Uncle Dick was well enough that the doctor gave his permission for him to join the family for his meals. Miss Morton had gone, Mr. Rossiter's visits were becoming less frequent, and as Lissa said, the hospital smells had been thoroughly banished. Dr. Anderson would not, however, permit any office visits by the old man, so he and Mrs. Harding were busily planning an office in what was called "the back parlor" and which was, in reality, the catch-all for the whole family.

"Half of the stuff that's there should have been burned long ago, and we will burn it now," said Mrs. Harding firmly. "Two thirds of the rest can go to the barn shed, and the rest can go where it belongs — in the closets of the family. And if anyone has any special treasures there he'd better put them in his own room or forever hold his peace!"

The three office workers bought a new file that could hold Uncle Dick's notes and papers in the order in which he delighted, and Mrs. Harding found an old-fashioned kitchen cupboard which had served in the basement as a repository for empty fruit jars. This Bud and Pub cleaned, sanded and varnished until one would not have recognized it. The girls, not to be outdone, made with Lissa's help a new cushion and slipcover for the easy chair that sat by the window of the new room. On the day that it was pronounced ready for occupancy a basket of flowers on the desk brought tears to the old editor's eyes.

"You shouldn't have done it," he whispered tremulously.

"Oh, we didn't," explained Lissa. "Read the names on that card and you'll see that the whole town did it. We only took in the money and wrote those names. Not one single person was allowed to give more than a dime, and no one wanted to give less. In fact, that money came from all over the country. Why, if we had let them they'd have bought a whole greenhouse!"

The others drifted out one by one, and Neil was left alone with Uncle Dick.

"You're not going to be so happy over this office that you will forget what the doctor said about being careful, are you?"

"Of course not. Don't act like a fussy grandparent, young fellow. Just you go along with the work downtown and I'll pull the wires from here. And when you come home next time bring my typewriter. You can get another and charge it to me. But I want that one. It and I were colts together!"

"Any other instructions?"

"Not about the office. But when are you going to open the Center? It's doing no one any good just sitting there idle."

"Why — why, whenever you say. We didn't want to open without you."

"Forget about me. I'm not going to be playing basketball there anyway. Get those fathers who are willing to oversee it evenings lined up and bring them up here for a talk. It's been dedicated since the day I bought it. Let's get busy now. Now tell me, how are the boys behaving?"

"Fine, as far as anyone can tell. Bill is keeping them to

his promise and everything seems quiet. Howie and Ernie seem as usual except a bit more quiet. Nothing has been done about any disciplinary measures. They're waiting until you can tell what happened."

"They won't have to wait any longer. I talked with Winchester and Hunter last night. They know it all just as it happened, and I think they are relieved. I told them I was sure the boys had no idea that it was anyone except some of the boys in that shed. They couldn't know that I'd fall and knock myself out so completely that I couldn't do anything except crawl into the car and try to die. A boy would have got out of there in no time at all. I told those men that."

"Did they take it in good faith?"

"Oh sure. They are two fine men. And in spite of what anyone else says, I say they have two fine boys. But one thing I told them they didn't like."

"Such as?"

"I told them to go home and take themselves to pieces and see what was the matter that would make their sons do such childish and mean little things as those boys pulled all summer. Shutting me in the shed was an accident. Those other tricks were malicious and something wrong in those homes is responsible for it."

"Whew! You really did say something! But I can't say that I blame you. Why haven't they known what their kids were up to?"

"Too busy. Left the boy raising to their wives. Nita Winchester is a neurotic, and Mabel Hunter takes her for a model. When Nita has nerves, then it's nerves for Mabel. Boys need a dad who can carry a big stick."

Neil smiled at the thought of the gentle Uncle Dick advocating the use of a big stick, but as he pondered on it the idea grew. Perhaps the lack in the lives of the two pampered boys had been just that. He imagined that the boys from the Hollow knew all about the disciplinary paddle.

"I think you may be right," he said with a smile. "You usually are. Some day when I get time I'm going to plan a new column for the *Advocate*. It will be called 'Sayings of the Appleboro Sage,' and will be made up of things I have gleaned in these last ten months.''

''You'll do nothing of the sort. Just now, help me up to bed and forget such nonsense. You're a great comfort to me, but don't let me ever catch you putting that sort of trash in my paper. I might use the big stick on you!''

One Friday evening when Neil had stayed late at his desk to work over some advertising copy that he wanted to submit to Uncle Dick when he next visited him, Mr. Rossiter tapped on the locked door.

''Can't lock me out of here, young man. Are you all alone?''

''Yes. Is there anything I can do for you?''

''I believe there is. Call Dick and tell him I got in on the train and want you to drive me to the lodge tonight. The weather is a bit too uncertain up here in December for me to make this drive alone in a car, and Terry is busy with some important paper he has to write. I don't want to talk to myself all evening and I do want to talk to you. Come up with me for supper.''

Over the supper which was served to them in front of the fire in the big family room of the lodge, he asked many questions about the *Advocate* and the affairs of the village in general, and was highly pleased that the Center had been opened even though the planned dedication could not be held.

''Dick is right. He planned it for the kids. Let them enjoy it. What plan have you worked out for supervision?''

''We're having Mrs. Banning put in charge of assignments. She has both boys and girls in her family and will be fair. Different parents will be responsible for supervision on different nights. Boys and girls can use it at the same time if there is no conflict of interest. Whenever any girls are there a woman must be on hand, and a man for the boys. It's all very simple. The kids can do as they please as long as they behave. Accidental damage will be accepted as inevitable, but anything that is damaged willfully must be paid for by the ones responsible.''

"Sounds good. Are you making any provision for the town kids to participate?"

"I don't think so. Uncle Dick hasn't mentioned it. Do you think we should?"

"I certainly do. No other thing will heal that old division like having them all play together. And wouldn't it be a fine thing for Mabel Hunter and Nita Winchester to come down and play monitor when the Bushwhackers are going strong? They'd learn something that might be good for them. They have thought their sons so 'different' from the ordinary boys that they can't even accept the truth now. Why, from what I've learned from gossip around the square, there has been a vendetta waged between those kids and the Bushwhackers ever since that Bill and those twin friends of his started into high school. And nobody guessed it!"

"I think most of the boys in town knew about it. Lissa caught on from chance remarks she heard from Bud and Pug. But she wouldn't tell. She was pretty upset about it. Some of the rest of us should have got wise to the situation."

"Poor Lissa! It was a hard spot for her to be on. Grace told me she was going to tell her story to you and Lissa so I'm free to speak of it here. Lissa, poor child, has somehow found out who she is, and she is angry and hurt for Grace's sake. Yet she could not quite bring herself to expose Howie, I guess. After all, he is her half brother, and she has a strong streak of family loyalty. I hope she will be happier now that the situation has been taken care of. If Nita Winchester has any sense at all, she'll leave her alone now and try to be a better mother to that boy. Alf and Howard will keep more of a rein on their sons and maybe you and Mr. Horne can eventually get the diverse elements to mix."

Neil did not answer. That last remark had seemed to take for granted the fact that he would remain in Appleboro. How he felt about that he was not sure. The old hope of achieving success on the *Ledger* staff was still with him and at times pushed every other consideration aside. On the other hand, he had formed more and stronger ties here than he had in the city. To leave them would be a real strain on his emotions. He had unfinished business here. Should he risk it for the questionable success he might achieve elsewhere? Was success worth such a price?

He had spent many hours struggling with that problem. After Mrs. Harding had told her story, his own trouble had appeared in a different light, and he had earnestly prayed that the Lord might lead in the decision. As yet he had felt no leading, and he waited for Mr. Rossiter to continue.

"I guess I know what you're thinking, Abbott, and I don't blame you for feeling let down. I didn't intend that things should take this turn. When you got caught here last winter by your own carelessness it seemed a good chance to kill two birds with one stone. You did deserve a bit of punishment, you know. Missing that train was a stunt worthy of an irresponsible teenager — or of one of my kids. I was ready to sentence you to Probate Court reporting for ten years. But when I got here and found how you had stepped into the situation and saved the day for Dick and the *Advocate,* I decided that I'd leave you here for a while. I never dreamed that it would be for more than a few weeks.

"I guess you wonder why the old paper means so much to me. Well, in the first place, I love it because it has been in the family so long and has meant so much to this valley. Until someone discovered what a delightful place this was for a vacationland, the valley had retained more of the clean, wholesome life that was the heritage of our fathers, than any place I knew. In spite of the influx of the customs and appliances of this day, the *Advocate* has kept its old stand-ards and the people have retained a love for their traditions and habits. Our youngsters up here dress and play and read the funnies and watch TV just as others do. But it doesn't seem strange to them, or a thing to be laughed at, that when a person dies Uncle Dick writes an obituary and says, among other things, that the deceased accepted Jesus Christ as Saviour in his early youth. Can you imagine a thing like that in the *Ledger?* I like to think that it makes it easier for the boys and girls that grow up here to take that same step themselves because they have accepted it as a natural one.

"I know it sounds silly, but the *Advocate* means more to me than the *Ledger* does. I know I'm more fitted for the busy life, and I've been tied to it so long I could never be happy away from it permanently, but I often envy Dick here. He has done just exactly the things he longed to do, and he has more real friends than any man I know. I can't think of a thing that has made me happier than to have found out that Terry wants to come up here when he's out of school. I owe you a lot for that tip you gave me, and he and I have been closer than we'd ever been before since I let him choose his own way. For that I thank you.

"But Terry isn't ready, and Uncle Dick will never be able to carry on alone again. When I came up here for that dedication in October I intended to take you back with me. Your work seemed done and your lessons learned. I was going to give you the Juvenile Court assignment and the work with Henderson Institute and other neighborhood houses. Now, humbly, I am asking you to stay until Terry can take over. He'll not be ready for eighteen months yet. It will be quite a term. If you say no, I'll not blame you. If you accept, I'll always thank you. The choice is yours."

Neil hesitated although he knew there was but one answer he could give. For one short moment he looked back to the tempting field he had left behind. It was pleasant, but it was not for him. In his cabin alone he had knelt the other night and asked for leading, promising his Lord that whatever that leading be, he would follow it with thanksgiving. This request he saw as another stone in the path of the stream, one that would influence its further course.

"I'll stay," he said simply. "I'll stay until Terry comes. What lies after that I can only wait to have revealed. Maybe Terry will give me a job on the Probate Court, or I may forget another camera someday. I'll wait and see."

Mr. Rossiter's voice was husky as he tried again to express his thanks, but Neil did not notice. All he could realize then was the sense of complete peace that swept over him.

29

IT WAS EARLY in the next week, after Mr. Rossiter had returned to the city and the whole town had learned that Neil Abbott was to stay on at the *Advocate* office, that Howie Winchester came to stand before Neil's desk with a request.

"My mother wants you to come to our house for dinner tonight," he said with considerable embarrassment. "My parents want to talk to you. May I tell them you will come?"

In spite of his complete surprise Neil thought quickly and answered heartily, trying not to see Lissa's amazed stare behind Howie's back. "I'll be glad to. What time shall I be there?"

"We'll eat at seven. But I wish you'd come as soon as you leave the office. I'll wait and ride out with you. I — I just want to visit with you before the folks are ready."

"That's a good idea. Be here at five forty-five."

When the door had closed behind him Neil turned to face Marv's grin and Lissa's bewilderment.

"Now what is that supposed to mean?" he asked.

"You tell us," said Marv. "I do hope you know which fork to use. And may I say with sincerity, I'm not jealous!"

"Neither am I!" Lissa's voice carried conviction. "But

we all wish you well and hope you return with no battle scars."

"It's not my scars I'm worrying about," was the sober answer. "It's the scars someone has left on that boy's thin skin. I don't think it would hurt a bit if my friends did some praying while I'm absent on this mission."

His friends did pray, Marv and his wife in their bungalow, Mrs. Harding, Lissa and Uncle Dick in the new office, and the Hornes at the parsonage. Having prayed, Lissa wandered through the house restlessly starting one task and abandoning it for another, until her mother rebuked her.

"Don't be so impatient, honey. Nothing very serious can happen. What are you afraid of?"

"I'm worried for fear they will demand something of him that he shouldn't give. He doesn't realize how demanding they can be!"

"Perhaps he knows more than you think. He isn't exactly a child. He has managed to care for himself for years and does a fairly good job of it. He has recently put himself in God's hands in a more complete way, I feel, and together they ought to be able to meet even the Winchesters."

"I know it. But that's just the way I behave about most things. I don't make myself do and be what my better self knows I should. I shouldn't worry, but I *do* worry. I don't want them to make him do something he doesn't want to do. What time do you think he will get home?"

"I have no idea. Not before eleven, probably. If dinner was at seven their talk could hardly begin before eight-thirty. And it might be a long one. You'll just have to wait until tomorrow to ask questions."

"I suppose so. But don't you think that if he saw the light on our porch he would know we were still up and wanted to hear about it?"

"Yes, I'm sure he would. But perhaps he won't want to talk about it."

"I'm going to wait and see. You don't think I'm too inquisitive, do you, Mother of mine? I'm just so terribly concerned."

"I think you are a darling, and I can understand your concern. You must stop thinking about Mrs. Winchester, too. If you don't I'll be sorry I told you that story."

"You didn't tell me anything I hadn't already suspected. Just filled in some details. I *will* try to put her out of my mind. If she bothers me again I'll just tell her it *has* to stop — that I know who she is, that I just want to be let alone, and that every time she tries to coax me away from you I am more determined to stay right here. I wish I didn't feel so bitter about her, but it's going to take a lot of praying to make it any different. I *can't* feel sorry for her. I just want to be rid of her."

"I have a feeling that you will be. This trouble with Howie may make her feel differently."

"I hope it does. That boy needs a mother with some sense. Oh, I wish Neil would come!"

"It's only eight o'clock. Let's get at those quilt patterns you were making for the women at the Hollow. It isn't easy to copy them from a newspaper and get them geometrically correct. Few of the women could make them I'm sure. They sew beautifully, though. I was out yesterday. The quilt Vida Rossiter ordered is almost done and is a thing of beauty."

They worked over the patterns with ruler, compass and divider, and became so interested in the task that when Neil's tap on the door came they were astonished to find it was after ten o'clock. At sight of his sober face they knew it had not been an evening of pleasure. Mrs. Harding urged him to go into the living room where the chairs were more comfortable, but he refused.

"I've been squirming around in a soft chair for two hours, and I want something solid to rest on. When Lissa gets here with that coffee I smell, I want to talk. I have to spill the story to someone before I try to sleep."

Lissa came with the coffee and some cookies which he took with a grateful sigh. "These look good! From the size of the meal that was set before me out there you'd think I couldn't be hungry so soon. But I'd realized something of what I was in for, before I ever sat down, and I guess I didn't have much appetite."

"Help yourself. And if that's not enough, there's always bread and peanut butter. We buy the latter by the gallon. Now begin; I've waited as long as I can. You went home with Howie before six. You had almost an hour alone with him. What could he say that would take away your appetite? He isn't planning more rebellion, is he?"

"No rebellion against the Bushwhackers, the law or any organized authority. Just rebellion against his mother."

"Oh, oh! That *could* be trouble." This from Mrs. Harding. "I know Nita, and she is still the Mary of my story, determined to have her way. I'm afraid she'll never recognize her responsibility in this affair. Howie's in for real trouble."

Neil allowed himself a half smile. "I think it is Mrs. Winchester who is in for trouble."

"What do you mean? Is he defiant of authority?"

"Of her authority, yes. I think that when his father speaks he comes to heel at once. In this case father and son agree."

"Against her?" gasped Lissa. "I never thought they would."

"I think she never thought so either. But let me tell it straight. I'll make it brief since the details are neither necessary nor pleasant. When we got to the house neither of the parents was in evidence. I believe now that Mr. Winchester had planned it that way. Howie took me up to his room and we had a real talk. Do you know that is the first time I had ever had any personal contact with Howie — just an impersonal word or two at various times. He and Ernie are in trouble now and they know it. Mrs. Hunter will do whatever Mrs. Winchester says, so the boys have been threatened with being sent east to a select, private academy. Very select and very, very private. The boys are frantic, and the fathers are helpless, or have been until this evening. Howie told me all about it up in his room and then sprang his solution on me. He wanted and needed my cooperation to make it work and when

I tell you what it was, you'll understand why I lost my appetite.

"We went down to dinner, and for a few minutes it was, at least outwardly, a peaceful meal. It was the first time I had had other than a business contact with any of them, and I found them gracious and charming. Mrs. Winchester, however, soon began to get on my nerves. I couldn't keep from looking at her, and my strongest impression was that she was the saddest woman I ever saw. The next was that she was on the verge of hysteria. Her hands were shaking so much that often she held them in her lap, just to quiet them, I thought. Howie was sullen and untalkative. Mr. Winchester kept looking at Howie as if to reassure him, and at his wife in a pitiful sort of way that didn't set well with him at all. I think now that he was trying silently to ask her forgiveness for what he intended to do.

"What he did was this. By the time the meal was over we were all thoroughly uncomfortable and as soon as we adjourned to the living room he dropped his bomb. He had decided that it was nonsense to send Howie away. It would do the lad good to stay right at home and face up to the things that were being said. After all, two months since Uncle Dick was injured had already passed. The worst was over. Everyone concerned had agreed not to bring in any complaints, so there was nothing the law could do. That was his ultimatum and he issued it as if he meant it. The mother stared as if she couldn't believe what was happening, but before she could say anything Howie threw in his little explosive. He was for his father's scheme one hundred per cent, but with one amendment of his own. He knew his father would be out of town a great deal and he didn't want to be under his mother's authority. He would cooperate only on condition that he be paroled to me!

"Don't look at me that way, Lissa. I know I'm a soft touch for any kid that comes along. But that boy is desperate. I *have* to help him. And when Mr. Winchester had swallowed his surprise and received the suggestion with apparent relief, there was nothing for me to do but agree. There was plenty for Mrs. Winchester to do, though — and say! At first she tried to reason, but she was too frantic to be logical at all. Then she tried cajolery, and I'm here to say she is mistress of it. It has probably worked for her all her life, but this time it failed. Her men stood pat. Next it was tears, and when they came Howie left the room. The poor boy had had all he could take. I was shamed for him. But his dad didn't weaken. I could see why he is a power in politics. When he makes a decision he knows how to stand.

"The next scene is one I'll never forget. The lady had cried until her eyes were swollen and she was exhausted. Mr. Winchester just sat there through it all. It probably was the first time he had ever refused her anything, and she could not understand. Then for a long time she sat with her head buried in her arms on the table by her chair. When she looked up she seemed a different woman. There were no tears, although the marks of them were still there. She was terribly calm. I had an eerie sort of feeling that she *was* another person. And when she spoke her voice was flat and dead.

" 'You're right, Howard,' she said. 'Howie has to face it or he will go through life carrying his cowardice in his heart and hating himself for it. Life has to be faced or it beats you down. I know.'

"Then she just went into a heap on the floor. I didn't think anyone could go down so softly. At first I thought it was a trick, but it wasn't. We carried her into her room and the maid came running. Mr. Winchester said not to call Howie, then asked me to get Dr. Anderson. I sat in the living room feeling like a fifth wheel and finally the maid came and said Mr. Winchester couldn't leave her but would see me in the morning. She gave me my hat and overcoat and here I am. That's all. And I am *bushed!*"

"You've had a very hard time," said Mrs. Harding gently. "We all put our problems and burdens into your hands. How do you bear with us?"

"I'm not big enough for it. Help me to grow up into it, won't you, dear friend?"

Lissa had not heard them. Her face was troubled and

now she spoke pleadingly to her mother, "I want to call and see how she is. You won't be sad if I do that, will you, Mother? I feel so sorry for her!"

Mrs. Harding's eyes filled with tears and her voice was broken as she said tenderly, "Bless your heart, honey. I've been praying for those words."

They waited while she talked. When she came back into the room she had her coat on and the car keys in her hand.

"Mr. Winchester answered me. He sounded *so* glad that I'd called. Dr. Anderson has just left but she is crying again and can't go to sleep. She has been asking him to send for me and he didn't want to do it. But I'm going! And I'm going because I want to! Do you know what that means? I can't hate her any more. I'm just so *terribly* sorry for her. Is it all right if I go, Mother?"

"It's the biggest thing you ever did."

"Do you think I should go, Neil?"

"Yes. As my foster mother used to say, 'Go with God.'"

"Then kiss me, Mother. I won't be long. I'll be back for sure."

She gave Neil a long look and he realized with a shock that he had never known this Lissa Harding before. She was not the hot tempered, hoydenish girl that he had worked and played with for a year, but a woman who was definitely not his sister.

At Mrs. Harding's request he went up to see that Uncle Dick had settled for the night, and found him asleep with a book in his hand. The reading lamp made a circle of light about the worn face, and Neil thought, as he took the book away and reached for the lamp switch, that if modern saints wore halos this man could qualify for a permanent one.

When he went down Mrs. Harding was sitting wearily by the table. "Why don't you go to bed? I can wait for Lissa. I'll send her up to you if you're still awake, and if she doesn't come by the time she should, I'll call again," he promised.

30

Left alone, Neil sought an easy chair in the living room. The hall light had been left on for Lissa and he found its light sufficient. He was very tired. The scene in the Winchester home had been emotion-packed and even as an onlooker he had felt the tension. He hoped Lissa would not get into such a situation. They hadn't the right to ask so much of her, he thought. He hoped she would be home soon, for that davenport looked very inviting, and he did not want to succumb to its temptation and be found asleep by her.

Then he remembered what had been asked of him and the promise he had made. What had he gotten into now? Had he been crazy when he made such a promise? How was he going to serve as parole officer when Howie's dad was away? How could he do that without completely antagonizing the mother? What could he do for a youth who had led such a protected life as Howie had? It had been different with the Bushwhackers. They had had little and were glad of the friendship he had to give. Could he ever make friends of Howie and Ernie? If they were receptive there was much that could be done to restore the confidence of the public in them and give them a place in the life of the school and town. It would not be too hard if the mothers did not interfere. He could only hope that Mrs. Winchester knew what she was saying in those last minutes before she fell. If she did, and if she remained in that mood there might be some chance that it could work out yet.

Maybe he could get the Bushwhackers to help him. They had known about the restrictions that the two mothers had put on the boys, and could surely be convinced that things could be different now. He had talked to his boys the week after Bill's big decision in the cabin, and had found them more responsive than ever before. He had tried to show them their own part in building the caste feeling between the two groups and had been pleased to note what he hoped was a change for the better. If he appealed to their sense of fairness and showed them how a better feeling would help not only themselves but the boys and girls who would come after them, they would surely respond. Maybe he could get Bill and the twins together with Howie and Ernie in his room some evening and give it to them all straight from the shoulder. If Bill gave the word, the Bushwhackers could do more than anyone else to make the town forget that the two boys were in disgrace, for it was the Bushwhackers that had been wronged most by them. It was a challenging task that he faced, but with prayer and patience and the help of the interested men in the community he believed it could be done.

He should turn up the light, he mused. But the darkness was restful and he felt too relaxed to move. He thought of the things that had happened in his life since that day a year ago when he sat in the apartment in the city and planned with B. Franklin the three-day holiday that had turned into a year's task. Who could have imagined that so small a happening could have so much influence on a life? What would Jane say to it all? He smiled as he answered his own question. She would just say that it was God's way of shaping his life. Perhaps she was right. During the last weeks he had come more and more to accept it all as His leading. He felt once again the longing that had been with him often before, a yearning for a sense of reality of the Presence of the Lord he loved.

"I wish I could have had just one glimpse of His face. It — it must have been a transcendent experience just to have seen Him. Not only the mountain top glory that Peter, James and John saw, but the everyday sight of Him that all men saw as He walked among them!"

Lost in this thought, he sat in silence. The ticking of the clock on the mantel was a monotonous sleep inducer, and he drifted into half-slumber that brought with it hazy thoughts and pictures. He saw again Lissa's face full of tender compassion as she hurried to meet the woman she had despised. He saw Mrs. Harding as he had seen her often looking up at the stars or the moon over the distant hills and wearing a look of peace that was beyond his understanding. He saw Uncle Dick's haggard features and heard the weak voice pleading,

"You have to forgive them, Bill. They didn't know what they were doing!"

He sat up with a start, realizing that he had dozed. He was wide awake now, but the pictures had been so real that they stayed with him. And in that moment he knew the reality of the Presence. Jesus Christ was not just One who had revealed Himself to men almost two thousand years ago. He was alive now, and was revealing Himself wherever He could find a willing channel for the sight. It was the indwelling Christ who had shown Himself in Uncle Dick's cry, "Forgive them!" It was Christ revealed in the life of Grace Harding as she had borne the shame of another's sin. Only that same Christ could have softened with tears the face of a rebellious, resentful girl and sent her to comfort the one she had despised.

"Why, I *have* seen Him! He's walked along with me all this way. And I didn't recognize Him. I've been like the disciples on the Emmaus road. Just how dumb can a Christian be?"

As he sat glorying in the experience, he found himself humming a tune he had sung just last Sunday and never given a second thought until tonight when it came alive to him.

I have seen Him, I have known Him,
For He deigns to walk with me;
And the glory of His presence shall be
mine eternally.

A half hour later when he heard the car outside he waited Lissa's coming with anticipation. Would the glow he had seen be with her still? Had this been a night of victory for her, or would her problems remain? She came through the door wearily as if the evening had taken strength from her, but when she lifted her face to the stairway he drew a breath of relief. Her face was drawn with strain from her ordeal, but her eyes were still shining. She did not see him, but hurried up to her mother who had called from above. He waited, knowing she would be back, and holding the picture in his mind. It had not been a rebellious girl who had passed the door, but a woman who had taken that girl's place and had grown in stature toward the fullness of Christ.

She came running down the stairs and paused a moment in the door to locate him in the half light. Then, after a long, incredulous look at his face, she walked into his outstretched arms.

"Does this mean what I think it does?" she asked shakily.

"I hope you realize all that it means. I'm not used to acting like this, and it means a lot to me. It means that I've just found out that I'm so much in love with you that I'm feeling shaky. Can we sit down and let it soak in a while before we start to talk?"

"Let's do. Kiss me again, Neil. I've been wanting that kind of kiss from you for such a long time!"

They turned up the light and talked until long after midnight. He had to hear the story of the evening's visit. Lissa had gone to Mrs. Winchester with no reproaches but with words of assurance. She had learned that the reason for the desire to have her close had been a defensive one, the fear that sometime the girl might feel resentful and disclose to someone the relationship.

"We talked quietly but quite frankly. And we found a place of agreement. I am never to tell what I know — I wouldn't anyway — and she is to leave me alone except as we meet casually as neighbors. I think that when she's feeling better she may even want me as a friend some day. That will be all right with me. She understands that I am Lissa Harding, the child of Grace and John Harding, and that is a closed subject. Then when we had talked awhile I bathed her head and sat by her until she went to sleep. She will probably be weak and sore from emotion in the morning, but I think she will go along with the plans for Howie now and try to pretend that she likes it. Maybe in time she *will* like it. But don't expect her to go to football games and see Howie tackled and tumbled in the dirt. She's not made of that kind of stuff."

"Does she accept the scheme of having me monitor her son?"

"Yes, apparently. After she quit crying she decided that was the best way. And I want to tell you how much I like it. I think it will be the making of the boys, and I do want them to face the music and come out on top. After all, Howie is my brother although he will never know it."

"Now let's talk of something vital. Can we get married right away?"

"Ask my mother."

"I'll ask her the first thing tomorrow. I'm going to ask Mr. Rossiter if we can have the lodge for a couple of weeks. I'd have to come in for work, and I guess you would, too. But we could have that quiet place to go back to."

"It sounds wonderful. But do you realize what time it is now? If you don't get going, Mother will be down after me."

"Okay, okay, but do you know what I'm going to do tomorrow?"

"I couldn't guess."

"I'm going to call my Janie and have a chat."

She stiffened in his arms and drew back to look in astonishment into his eyes. "Jane? Mrs. Greg Lowrey? Whatever for?"

"For to thank her." He drew her back into his arms. "I have a lot to thank her for and I believe Jane is big enough to appreciate it."

"I think so, too. And tell her a big, big 'thank you' from me."

She lifted her face for his good-night kiss, then watched as he ran down the steps and across the road. He was whistling and, recognizing the tune, she hummed it with him.

> I have seen Him, I have known Him,
> For He deigns to walk with me;
> And the glory of His presence shall be
>   mine eternally.